Guilt and Ginataan

“A good bet for fireside reading on a fall night.”

—*Publishers Weekly*

“The plot has satisfying twists to go along with the mouthwatering food.”

—*Booklist*

“This exhilarating, cozy mystery beautifully weaves themes of friendship, loyalty, and the indomitable spirit of small-town life amid the thrill of a chilling whodunit.”

—*The Seattle Times*

“A fast-paced mystery with lots of humorous interplay between the characters, crimes to solve, and recipes to try as well.”

—New York Journal of Books

“This highly entertaining cozy mystery weaves into its tightly coiled plot depictions of Filipino American heritage, the importance of a close family, and the family one chooses.”

—Shelf Awareness

“Mia P. Manansala is a true master of the cozy mystery genre. . . . *Guilt and Ginataan* is a deftly crafted and unfailingly fun read from first page to last. Clever, original, and unreservedly recommended.”

—Midwest Book Review

PRAISE FOR THE TITA ROSIE'S KITCHEN MYSTERIES

"I love to read a well-written and quirky cozy mystery. Manansala has created just that . . . a tale full of eccentric characters, humorous situations, and an oh-so-tricky mystery. Check [*Homicide and Halo-Halo*] out for the poetic prose and the mouthwatering recipes that are integral to the plot." —*The Washington Post*

"This book hits the exact right spot. . . . Mia P. Manansala manages to create a murder mystery where nothing is too horrifying and you know everything will be okay in the end. . . . I've heard it described as a 'cozy mystery' and that's exactly what it is: a perfectly cozy puzzle to solve."

—Taylor Jenkins Reid, *New York Times* bestselling author of *Carrie Soto Is Back*

"The perfect cozy and lighthearted mystery."

—*The Washington Post*

"Hands down the tastiest whodunit you'll consume this year."

—*Kirkus Reviews*

TITLES BY MIA P. MANANSALA

BERKLEY

Arsenic and Adobo

Homicide and Halo-Halo

Blackmail and Bibingka

Murder and Mamon

Guilt and Ginataan

Death and Dinuguan

YOUNG ADULT

Death in the Cards

Death *and* Dinuguan

Mia P. Manansala

BERKLEY PRIME CRIME
NEW YORK

BERKLEY PRIME CRIME
Published by Berkley
An imprint of Penguin Random House LLC
1745 Broadway, New York, NY 10019
penguinrandomhouse.com

Book design by Kristin del Rosario

Library of Congress Cataloging-in-Publication Data

Names: Manansala, Mia P., author.
Title: Death and dinuguan / Mia P. Manansala.
Description: First edition. | New York: Berkley Prime Crime, 2025. |
Series: Tita Rosie's kitchen mysteries
Identifiers: LCCN 2025009585 (print) | LCCN 2025009586 (ebook) |
ISBN 9780593549209 (trade paperback) | ISBN 9780593549216 (ebook)
Subjects: LCGFT: Detective and mystery fiction. | Novels.
Classification: LCC PS3613.A5268 D43 2025 (print) | LCC PS3613.A5268
(ebook) | DDC 813/.6—dc23/eng/20250325
LC record available at https://lccn.loc.gov/2025009585
LC ebook record available at https://lccn.loc.gov/2025009586

First Edition: November 2025

Printed in the United States of America
1st Printing

The authorized representative in the EU for product safety and compliance is
Penguin Random House Ireland, Morrison Chambers, 32 Nassau Street,
Dublin D02 YH68, Ireland, https://eu-contact.penguin.ie.

To you, the reader.

And to everyone who's been with Lila since the very beginning.
Thank you all so much for going on this journey with me. ❤

Author's Note

Thank you so much for picking up *Death and Dinuguan*! As this is the last book in the series (and, you know, a murder mystery), this story touches on some rather emotional and potentially triggering topics.

If you want to avoid possible spoilers, skip this section. If you'd like to know the content warnings for this book, see below.

Stalking, child illness, misogyny, sexual harassment, physical violence, mentions of past emotional abuse, and death of spouse (happened in the past; death is not on the page).

Glossary and Pronunciation Guide

HONORIFICS/FAMILY
(THE "O" USUALLY HAS A SHORT, SOFT SOUND)

Anak (ah-nahk)—Offspring/son/daughter

Ate (ah-teh)—Older sister/female cousin/girl of the same generation as you

Kuya (koo-yah)—Older brother/male cousin/boy of the same generation as you

Lola (loh-lah)/Lolo (loh-loh)—Grandmother/Grandfather

Ninang (nee-nahng)/Ninong (nee-nohng)—Godmother/Godfather

Tita (tee-tah)/Tito (tee-toh)—Aunt/Uncle

FOOD

Adobo (uh-doh-boh)—Considered the Philippines' national dish, it's any food cooked with soy sauce, vinegar, garlic, and black peppercorns (although there are many regional and personal variations)

Arroz caldo (ah-rohz cahl-doh)—A savory rice porridge made with chicken, ginger, and other aromatics

Biscocho (bihs-coh-cho)—Similar to Italian biscotti, this is a twice-baked bread, often coated with butter and sugar and baked low and slow; often used to repurpose stale bread

Champorado (chahm-puh-rah-doh)—A sweet chocolate rice porridge

Dinuguan (dih-noo-goo-ahn)—A savory Filipino stew of pork and pork offal simmered in a rich, lightly spicy gravy of pork blood, chiles, garlic, vinegar, and other spices

Ginataan (gih-nah-tah-ahn)—Any dish cooked with coconut milk; can be sweet or savory

Lumpia (loom-pyah)—Filipino spring rolls (many variations)

Mamon (mah-mohn)—A Filipino chiffon cake, made in individual molds as opposed to a large, shared cake

Pandan (pahn-dahn)—A tropical plant whose fragrant leaves are commonly used as a flavoring in Southeast Asia; often described as a grassy vanilla flavor with a hint of coconut

Patis (pah-tees)—Fish sauce

Salabat (sah-lah-baht)—Filipino ginger tea

Ube (oo-beh)—A purple yam

OTHER

Bruha (broo-ha)—Witch (from the Spanish "bruja")

Diba (dih-bah)—Isn't it? or Right?; short for "hindi ba"; also written as "di ba"

Macapagal (mah-cah-pah-gahl)—A Filipino surname

Oh my gulay—This is Taglish (Tagalog-English) slang, used when people don't want to say the "God" part of OMG; "gulay" (goo-lie) literally means "vegetable," so this phrase shouldn't be translated

Chapter One

"This might be the most delicious thing I've ever eaten."

Adeena Awan, my best friend and business partner, stared down at the pistachio rose white chocolate bar she'd just bitten into. The creamy white chocolate was studded with whole pistachios, dried rose petals, and flecks of cardamom, creating a feast for the eyes as well as the tongue. She glanced at Elena Torres, her girlfriend and my other partner at the Brew-ha Cafe, who was sampling the Mexican hot chocolate bar. The bittersweet chocolate was flavored with cinnamon and chiles plus cacao nibs for texture and vanilla bean for richness.

Elena's eyes were closed to fully experience the complex flavors, so she didn't see her girlfriend move to swipe the chocolate bar out of her hand. "Hey! You could've just asked, you know. I would've been happy to share."

Adeena broke off a large piece before handing back the

chocolate with a grin. "I know, but it's so much more delicious when I steal it from you."

The two of them bantered back and forth while our guests chuckled over their drinks.

"I'm sorry you have to deal with our ridiculousness so early in the morning," I said to the two chocolatiers, who sat watching us in amusement while they sipped their spiced mocha and white chocolate chai. "I appreciate you developing these specialty chocolates for us when you already have so much on your plates."

"No worries. After these past few months, I'd be disappointed if you didn't help us start our day with some fun and banter. Plus, these drinks are amazing, so no complaints from me. What do you think of the ube truffles?"

Hana Lee was not only the newest arrival to my hometown of Shady Palms, Illinois (two hours outside of Chicago), she was also my boyfriend's cousin. I'd been wanting to meet her for a while since I knew she was a big-sister figure to my boyfriend, but she'd always been too busy to visit. However, her husband's sudden passing gave her the need for a fresh start, so she moved to Shady Palms at the end of last year to work at Choco Noir, the new chocolate shop that her friend Blake Langrehr (who had moved here shortly before Hana) had just opened in town.

Choco Noir offered the most amazing confections, from Blake's simple, good-quality bean-to-bar chocolates to Hana's inventive creations. With Valentine's Day just a month away, the two of them were hard at work prepping for the big day and were also kind enough to collaborate with my business to create chocolates for us to sell as a cross-promotion for their new shop.

The pistachio rose white chocolate bar was meant to represent

Adeena's Pakistani background while the Mexican hot chocolate bar was for Elena's Mexican heritage (shocker). I wanted something simple and decadent for my Filipino chocolate representation, so Hana created white chocolate and milk chocolate versions of ube truffles. The subtle earthy vanilla tones of the purple yam paired well with both types of chocolate, and the beautiful violet color drew your eyes to the small spheres. Everything Hana and Blake presented to us was an absolute winner, and my partners and I quickly signed off on the collaboration.

"I almost forgot, but I also made this ube white chocolate bar for you, Lila," Blake said, handing over a small lilac-colored bar. "The ube truffles were cuter, so they fit you better, but I want to sell these in the shop, too. I was playing around with coconut milk to make a vegan chocolate bar, and this is what I came up with. It's simple, but that's what I like about it. What do you think?"

"Oh my gulay, it's fantastic!" I said, after letting a large chunk melt on my tongue. "You're right, it's simple and subtle but that's its charm. How are you so good at this?"

Blake winked at me. "You were my muse. It was tough nailing that light ube flavor, but I'm so happy with it."

"Aww, why does Lila get two fancy chocolates? I want more fancy chocolates," Adeena whined.

I stuck my tongue out at her. "Didn't you hear Blake? I'm her muse. Be more goddess-like, and maybe she'll get inspired by you, too."

"Yes, sticking your tongue out is so goddess-like." Adeena rolled her eyes. "I guess I'll have to create a special Blake drink to put on the menu. Then she'll have to supply me with more of the good stuff."

"Ladies, ladies, there's no need to fight over me," Blake said, holding her hands out jokingly. "I promise to supply you all with plenty of delicious chocolates from now on."

Adeena and I fake-swooned, and Elena laughed. "Be careful what you promise. These two will definitely take advantage of that."

After figuring out the logistics of our chocolate order, we spent some time chatting while savoring our drinks and sweets.

"I'm sorry my cousin couldn't make it to this meeting. Now that they've got the event space fixed up, he and Izzy have been spending all their time getting ready for the big Valentine's Day event they're hosting," I said. "It's their first time doing it, so they want everything to be just right."

My cousin Ronnie and his girlfriend, Izzy, ran the Shady Palms Winery and were also supposed to be part of this collaboration. Chocolates and wine—what could be a more perfect pairing for Valentine's Day? Throw in my desserts, Adeena's coffees, and Elena's teas, and that was my idea of a fantastic fête.

"We were able to secure a meeting at the event space later today while the florist is there. It makes more sense for us all to meet there anyway to make sure our contributions all vibe together," Blake said. "From what I heard, the florist has a genius touch, so I'm looking forward to meeting them."

"You won't be disappointed," Elena said, puffing with pride.

The florist for the big event was one of Elena's fifty million cousins, and she was right to be proud of her. Rita had taken over the old flower shop after the owner retired last year and had quickly made a name for herself for her beautiful blooms, inventive bouquets, and extensive plant knowledge. It helped that much of what she sold was grown in Elena's mom's greenhouse since Shady Palms citizens loved supporting local businesses. Which wasn't all that hard, honestly, considering how few chains made their way here, and those that did often didn't last long. I wasn't sure if it was by design or just bad luck for Big Business, but Shady Palms kept its unique small-town charm by investing in its local entrepreneurs. It made for a thriving, although rather contentious, chamber of commerce.

Especially lately, considering the number of burglaries that had hit several Shady Palms shops this past month. All the businesses affected were woman-owned, but so far, the police weren't sure if women entrepreneurs were purposely being targeted or if it just skewed that way since most of the successful businesses in town happened to be run by women. A fact that quite a few misogynistic members of the chamber of commerce had been grumbling about for a while.

"Adeena, this white chocolate chai is amazing," Blake said. "Do you think the drink mixes will be ready in time to launch for the event?"

Adeena was the cafe's barista and mixologist, and Blake had been after her to create packaged mixes for the chocolate-based drinks we offered. She wanted to sell the mixes as well as some prepared drinks at Choco Noir as more cross-promotion. Something about synergy. I didn't really get it when she was making her pitch, but Elena, our strongest salesperson and marketer, latched on to the idea.

In response, Adeena got up and plucked a few bags from the counter. "Test it out later and let me know what you think. I wrote the instructions on the bag, but I don't know if I'm one hundred percent happy with the chocolate-to-spice ratio. Of course, what type of liquid you use also changes the flavor, so I can't account for all the variables."

"I'll keep that in mind." Blake's phone alarm went off, signaling the end of our meeting. "The security system people will be at the shop soon, so we need to head out."

"Did you go with the company Detective Park suggested?" I asked.

Private detective Jonathan Park was not only my boyfriend's much older brother (there was a fifteen-year gap between the two), but he was also dating my aunt, Tita Rosie. He used to be a detective with the Shady Palms Police Department, but for various reasons he had left the force and opened his own private investigation agency. He had quite a few connections in the security world as well, and with the rash of burglaries lately, he'd advised us all to upgrade our security systems. I hadn't been sure it was worth the expense (we were a cafe; it's not like we were making the big bucks anyway. And what were they going to steal? Our artisanal flavored syrups?), but when my boyfriend, Jae, pointed out that our espresso machine cost almost ten thousand dollars, Adeena had screamed and ran to hug it.

"No one's taking Mr. Peppy! Lila, quit being cheap and get that security system installed."

That was all the push I needed, and we'd quickly contracted Detective Park's friends at Safe & Secure Solutions to update our system.

"My cousin promised that his buddy's company was the best one in the area, so we went with them. They're a bit pricey, but I like that they offer regular maintenance checks and have a team assigned to us in case of emergencies. Especially since we're a new business and the last thing we need to deal with is a smash-and-grab. Besides, better safe than sorry, right?" Hana said, gathering her notes from our tasting.

"It's a cliché, but it's a cliché for a reason," I said. "Definitely better safe than sorry."

Especially in this town.

Chapter Two

"Ronnie, when you told me to close the cafe early for an urgent meeting, this isn't exactly what I had in mind."

About two hours before closing time, I got a call from my cousin saying he needed me, Adeena, and Elena to come over to the Shady Palms Winery event space ASAP. Considering how ridiculous my life has been the past couple of years, I thought we'd get there and find him standing over a dead body. Instead, the three of us rushed into the event space only to see Ronnie, Izzy, Hana, Blake, and Rita standing around drinking wine and nibbling on chocolates.

My cousin's girlfriend and business partner, Isabel "Izzy" Ramos-Garcia, held up a bottle of wine. "Don't be too mad at him; there really is an emergency. We're just testing this new chocolate wine to try to make the best of a crappy situation."

While she poured each of us a glass, Elena made her way over to Rita. "You OK, prima?"

Rita sat hunched over next to the tasting table, staring into her half-full glass. At her cousin's voice, Rita set down her drink and jumped up to wrap her arms around Elena. "I'm so glad you're here!"

Elena squeezed the younger woman in a tight hug and then stepped back, her hands on Rita's shoulders. "You're shaking. What happened?"

"Someone broke into Mundo Floral last night."

Adeena gasped and started to say something, but Elena waved her hand to get Rita to continue.

"I went in this morning to open up and there was a huge mess. All my cash is gone and the place was ransacked, like they were looking for more valuable stuff. I doubt they found anything, but the police want me to do an inventory to see if anything else was taken."

"Was there any physical damage to the shop? Broken windows, torn-up plants, anything like that?" I asked.

My aunt's restaurant and my godmothers' laundromat had been the victims of vandals, not burglars, but the memories of both events were traumatic enough that I worried about the state of Rita's shop and was already creating a mental checklist of what needed to be done.

Rita shook her head. "Some of the plants were knocked over and one of the vases was broken, but it looked more like an accident that happened when the burglar was looking for something and not deliberate damage."

"Well, that's something at least," Elena muttered. "You said the police wanted you to log the inventory? So you already filed a police report?"

Rita nodded. "I called them as soon as I saw the shop was messed up and waited outside because I wasn't sure if the burglar was still there or not. They had me do the report and take pictures for insurance. I don't know what else I need to do after that."

"I'll put you in touch with my brother," Adeena said. "He can advise you since the law firm he works at has him handling all those break-in cases."

Rita thanked her before taking a large gulp of her wine and sighing. "I haven't told the rest of the family yet, but I don't know how much longer I can put it off."

"What? Why no—" Elena cut herself off. "Never mind, I get it. Want me to put it in the cousins group chat and have my mom handle all the tíos and tías?"

Rita let out a deep sigh, and her shoulders sagged as Elena took the metaphorical weight off them. "I'll tell my parents 'cause I'll never hear the end of it if they have to find out from Tía Carmen. But I'll leave the rest to you. Thanks, prima."

Elena once told me that her mom was the second oldest of seven kids, and all the siblings had children, most of them multiple children (Elena and one other cousin were the odd ones out as only children), so family gatherings and gossip could often be . . . a lot. Wonderful when you needed help since everyone was all too willing to jump in and do their part (like when Elena's mom took over her younger brother's restaurant, El Gato Negro, due to some unpleasantness) but also overwhelming because they did not know how to let things go or leave you alone. Like me and Adeena, Elena was both blessed and cursed with a family that loved hard and didn't know how to mind their own business.

Once the two of them had delivered the news and dealt with their family's responses, I made a suggestion. "Why don't you all come over to my aunt's restaurant for dinner? Detective Park will be there since he's always there, and we can invite Amir, too. That way you can ask him questions about next steps and also talk to Detective Park about that security company his friend owns."

"Oh, that's perfect. I wanted to stop by El Gato Negro and drown my sorrows in tamales, but I didn't want to have to deal with my family just yet," Rita said.

"Can't top good food and free legal advice," Adeena said. "I'll call my brother. Elena, you ride with Rita since she shouldn't be alone right now. We'll meet you there."

"Wish we could join you, but we have to talk to our contractor about some issues we're having," Ronnie said. "Tell my mom and Lola Flor that I said hi and that we'll be over for lunch tomorrow. Rita, let us know if there's anything we can do to help."

"Hana, Blake, are you two free?" I asked. The two women had been hanging out awkwardly in the background, and I could tell they didn't feel comfortable inserting themselves into the conversation. "No worries if you're busy. I just want to give my aunt a heads-up on how many people to expect."

"I don't want to intrude," Blake said, glancing over at Rita. "It's a sensitive time right now and—"

"No, please, join us. I wouldn't want you to miss out on a good meal on my account," Rita said, managing a weak smile. "I'd appreciate having more people around, actually."

Blake returned her smile. "Then count us in."

Plans made, we headed over to Tita Rosie's Kitchen.

• • •

I'm sorry to hear that, Rita. You've got great timing though. Ben runs Safe & Secure Solutions, and he's one of the best guys I've ever worked with," Detective Park said, clapping his hand on the shoulder of the man next to him.

Ben Smith was a tall white man in his early fifties with tanned, weathered skin, hands that felt like sandpaper when you shook them, and possibly the kindest eyes I've ever seen. Rather than the head of a security company, he fit the image of a friendly gardener who offered you clippings from his plants and a basket with way too many zucchinis in the summer. When he visited the Brew-ha Cafe to inspect the place after we told him we were interested in a security update, his calm presence immediately put the three of us at ease and we knew our cafe was in good hands.

"Appreciate you putting in a good word for me, Jonathan. We've been busier than ever thanks to you talking us up," Ben said, gesturing to the two employees who were with him. "Hector's been with the company since the very beginning, but poor Vinny here's been thrown in the deep end with all the work we've been getting."

Vinny Bianchi, who was the younger of the two employees and looked like he was barely out of high school, nodded, quickly chewing and swallowing the huge spoonful of rice he'd shoved into his mouth. "I'm not complaining. Between word of mouth and all these burglaries lately, business has been great!"

Ben frowned. "Don't talk like that. It makes it seem like you're happy about the burglaries."

Vinny flushed. "I didn't mean it like that, boss. I was just happy that people are starting to see our value."

Hector Diaz, who was probably around Detective Park's age, said, "It would be nice to live in a world where our services aren't needed, but as long as they are, we'll be here to provide them."

Ben smiled and nodded. "That's right. Now, Rita, if you're worried about the cost, we could always . . ." and the two of them started talking about flex plans that would fit Rita's needs.

With those two occupied, I turned my attention to Vinny, who was refilling his plate. "You're really enjoying that dinuguan, huh? Have you ever tried it before?"

He shook his head. "Your aunt called it 'chocolate meat,' so I thought it would be like mole, but it's not. I can't really describe the taste, but there's something familiar about it. It's really good, even if the texture is a little . . . you know."

Hana agreed. "I can't put my finger on it either. Maybe a Korean dish my mom makes?"

I laughed. "'Chocolate meat' is a euphemism some older Filipinos use since Westerners can be kind of squeamish about our food. If it reminds you of a Korean dish, you're probably thinking of soondae."

"Blood sausage?"

I nodded.

Understanding dawned in Hana's eyes. "Oh, now I get it. The stew is thickened with blood, isn't it? There's a Korean hangover soup that my mom likes to make sometimes. It has cakes of blood in it, so that also reminds me of this."

Vinny set his spoon down. "You all got me eating blood? That's kinda . . ."

He glanced down at his plate, and the expression on his face made me think he was debating if he should continue eating it to be polite or push it away.

Hector didn't seem to have that problem, considering the way he steadily plowed through the giant mound of food on his plate. "I get what you're saying, but isn't morcilla one of your favorite foods? How is blood sausage any different from this?"

"Well, one, you didn't tell me what it was when you first served it to me. And two, no one really thinks about what's in a sausage, right? It's like, better off not knowing. But here . . ." He eyed the dish for a moment before picking up his utensils again. "You know what? It tastes good and that's all that matters. I'm gonna stop running my mouth and just eat."

Tita Rosie, who wasn't eating with us since the restaurant was still open but had come to check on our table, smiled at him. "I appreciate you being open-minded about my food. I'm sorry if it seemed like I was hiding something from you, but 'chocolate meat' is such a common way to refer to dinuguan, I didn't really think about it."

The young security guy grinned at my aunt. "Don't worry about it. Every time Jonathan brings us here, he introduces us to something new and delicious. As long as you're the one cooking, you'll hear no complaints from me."

That brought a huge smile to my aunt's face, and I decided Vinny was a decent guy if he could make Tita Rosie react like that. Surprisingly open-minded too, considering I was way less cool about it when I found out what was really in dinuguan as a kid. She thanked him for the compliment and left to check on her other customers.

Blake, who didn't eat pork, had passed on the dinuguan and was slurping down a large bowl of shrimp sinigang along with Adeena and Elena, who were (mostly) vegetarians. She was in conversation with Amir, Adeena's older brother and a local lawyer, who was chowing down on his favorite chicken adobo.

"Have you figured out what to get Sana for Valentine's Day yet?" Blake asked.

Sana Williams was Amir's girlfriend and the owner of the town's fitness studio, and she also did business coaching for women of color entrepreneurs on the side. I'd introduced Hana and Blake to Sana back when they first moved to Shady Palms, and they'd quickly become part of our group. Blake was worried that she didn't belong as one of Sana's clients since she was white, but Sana said that because Blake's business partner was Korean, it was important that she understood some of the difficulties that Choco Noir would face. Not just as a woman-owned business, which Blake was used to, but also because of the unique challenges that many women business owners deal with based solely on their skin color or ethnic background.

Amir shook his head. "I forgot about Valentine's Day last year, and even though she said she doesn't care since it's a manufactured holiday, I still feel bad. I want to do something nice for her this time. Something special, but not over-the-top. That's not really her style."

"She's elegant but not fancy, if that makes sense," Blake mused. "I think something one of a kind but not expensive or flashy would suit her best."

Amir smiled. "Exactly. But what would that be? Custom jewelry? A nice piece of art for the house? Ever since we moved in together, she's been talking about wanting to redecorate."

"We're all meeting up tomorrow for Sana's Sangria Sunday, so we could do a little detective work for you," I said. "See if there's anything she really wants."

"That would be great," Amir said, the relief evident on his face.

"And hey, if worse comes to worst, you can't go wrong with chocolate." Blake winked at him, and we laughed.

As dinner drew to a close, the conversation turned back to the burglaries that have been plaguing the town lately.

"Happy to be working with you, Rita. Sorry about your shop, though," Vinny said. "The paper said only established businesses have been hit so far. I thought you'd be safe since you just opened."

Rita mustered a smile. "Maybe because I took over an older store, the burglar added me to their list. I'm just glad they didn't take much. Did you hear about the photography studio last week? I heard the owner lost thousands of dollars' worth of equipment. I feel so bad for her."

Detective Park frowned. "With a haul that big, you'd think the SPPD would be closer to finding who's behind all this. There's no way they can offload that much equipment without raising some kind of notice."

Ben laughed without humor. "I bet you said that to them and they told you to mind your business again."

"As always."

Detective Park had left the SPPD for many reasons, but his sense of justice was as strong as ever. That was why he had opened his own detective agency. He wasn't trying to show up the department. In fact, he was constantly offering his assistance. But whether it was the sheriff's incompetence, the new detective's pride, or the lingering resentment from his former colleagues (or all of the above), they never took him up on it.

Ben clapped him on the shoulder. "Hey, just means more business for us. Too bad the people of Shady Palms have to suffer for their egos. Anyway, let's just count ourselves lucky that nobody's gotten hurt and there hasn't been permanent damage."

"That's true. Even with the big losses at the photo studio, I heard that insurance is covering most of it. Everyone affected should be back on their feet soon," Hector said as Tita Rosie arrived to box up the leftovers.

"Thank heaven for small blessings, ah?"

I loved my aunt's optimism, but it felt like we were setting the bar kind of low to be thankful about something like that. Then again, considering the alternative, I'd take what I could get.

Small blessings indeed.

Chapter Three

"Izzy, I didn't know what to expect when you said you were bringing chocolate wine, but you and Ronnie have outdone yourselves."

Sana took another sip of the deep red liquid in her glass and sighed in appreciation. "I don't usually go for sweet wines, but this has enough body to match well with both red meat and desserts. It's so delicious and nuanced."

Izzy clinked her glass against Sana's. "I should have you write our wine descriptions. And thanks for the compliment."

Yuki Sato, who ran the restaurant Sushi-ya with her husband and younger daughter and was part of our WOC entrepreneur group, nodded in agreement. "I don't have Sana's palate, but I get what she's saying. To be honest, I was worried you were going to serve us a sugary liqueur like Baileys or Kahlúa."

Adeena, the sugar hound, said, "What's wrong with that? They're so tasty in coffee and White Russians and stuff."

Yuki laughed. "I don't have your sweet tooth and I'm not in college anymore, so anytime I drink sugary alcohol, I always feel it the next day."

Adeena looked mystified. "What does college have to do with it?"

Sana and Yuki smiled knowingly at each other before Sana answered her. "You're still in your twenties, so you don't get it. Come talk to us when you get your first hangover in your thirties. Then you'll understand."

"And then again when you all reach forty like me," Yuki said. "Hangovers don't even wait until you wake up. You'll be drinking cheap champagne at brunch and suddenly have the worst headache at like eight o'clock. So much fun."

Hana and Blake laughed and groaned at that. Because of Jae, I knew that Hana was five years older than him and figured Blake was around the same age, putting them in the same age range as Yuki and Sana. Yuki's statement must've hit home for both of them.

"Your new wine pairs perfectly with our chocolates," Blake said. "I can't wait for the event next month."

"Same! I'm looking forward to unveiling all my new creations. You all will just die when you see them," Hana said. "I couldn't go too wild since it's not in our budget, but I've come up with some of my favorite flavor combinations thanks to this group. And Blake's even letting me make a small chocolate sculpture."

"I wouldn't call an almost two-foot chocolate sculpture 'small,'" Blake said, rolling her eyes affectionately at her business partner.

"Well, that creativity is why I asked you to open Choco Noir with me, after all. You bring all the razzle-dazzle to our team."

"I'm the Magic Johnson while Blake's the Larry Bird. Super solid, with the absolute best fundamentals in the game. You want chocolate done *right,* you pick up one of Blake's chocolate bars." As if to prove her point, Hana broke up a slab of Blake's bean-to-bar 60 percent dark milk chocolate and passed it out. "Even people who claim to hate dark chocolate love this."

"If I didn't already know you and Jae were related, I definitely do now. That was a basketball reference, right?" I said, popping the piece she just handed me into my mouth. It was smoother and creamier and a touch sweeter than pure dark chocolate, but it still had all the complexity and richness. With offerings like this, Hana and Blake were both wonderful and dangerous to know.

Hana grinned at me. "You know it! Basketball is big in our family. Jae's been spending his spare time teaching my daughter how to play. Bought her a child's hoop and everything."

"How old is your daughter again?" Yuki asked. She was the only member of our friend group who was married and had a kid, and she lit up when Hana mentioned her daughter. Maybe she thought she had finally found a parent friend since I knew she didn't care for most of the people in our local PTA (with good reason).

"She's turning four soon. I thought about enrolling her in pre-K so she could make some friends, but I don't really have the funds or bandwidth for that right now," Hana admitted.

"I can't blame you," Yuki said. "Even in a town like this, childcare can be so expensive! My daughter, Naoko, turns sixteen this year and wants more work outside the restaurant, so if you ever need a babysitter, let me know."

"Luckily, my imo volunteered to take care of her while I'm at work. Jae's mom," Hana clarified. "She's my mom's younger sister and my favorite aunt, so I'm happy to leave Aria with her. It would be good for her to have an older girl to look up to though, so I might take you up on that sometime."

"Naoko's great," I assured her. "She designs all the Brew-ha Cafe merch and is really sweet and responsible. Great artist too, if your daughter's into art."

"Jae told me that the Shady Palms community was welcoming and supportive, and he wasn't kidding. I'm so glad I moved here," Hana said, her eyes suddenly teary. "Things are still pretty tough for me, but it's all thanks to Blake and Jae that Aria and I are doing so well now."

Blake wrapped her arms around her. "I'm glad you decided to take on this new adventure with me. You know I've always got your back."

"Hate to burst this beautiful bubble, but not everyone in Shady Palms is welcoming and supportive," Adeena said. "I mean, we're awesome, but there are definitely people you need to watch out for."

"Oh, don't worry, I wasn't including the chamber of commerce when I was talking about the community," Hana said. "We've only been to a few meetings, and we're already weighing the benefits of networking versus having to associate with those people. Some members have been great about showing us the ropes and filling us in on things, but there's a weird vibe I can't explain there."

"Misogyny," Blake said. "And pettiness. Those are the vibes you're thinking of."

"As someone who's also new to the chamber of commerce, I'm glad I'm not the only one who feels that way," Rita said.

She hadn't wanted to come because she was still in shock from the previous day's burglary, but Elena coaxed her out of the house by pointing out that staying at home meant having to deal with her family hovering around her all day. She wasn't talking much, but she was a quiet person in general. She seemed happy enough sipping on wine and sampling the various goodies Elena kept piling on her plate.

"Beth mentioned things have been pretty tense, especially with all the burglaries going on," I said, picking up a white chocolate chai blondie. "I know she and Valerie are working on it, so don't give up yet."

Beth Thompson and her ex-sister-in-law Valerie Thompson were the heads of the Shady Palms Chamber of Commerce. They'd taken over early last year when the previous head stepped down and had been doing their best to make it less of an old boys' club.

Adeena said, "I wouldn't be surprised if the burglar or burglars turned out to be part of the chamber of commerce. For the last few years, when the top ten most successful businesses in town were announced, they've all been woman-owned. Makes some of the old guard big mad."

Rita visibly paled at the mention of the burglaries, and Elena turned to glare at me and Adeena. We both apologized, and an awkward silence filled the room before Sana got up and changed the topic.

"It's Sangria Sunday, so why don't I try making a pitcher with this new chocolate wine Izzy brought us?"

"I'll help you," Izzy said, getting up, too. "The cheese I brought is probably at the right temperature now, so I'll also prep more snacks. Anyone need anything while I'm up?"

The rest of us shook our heads, and after they left, we split into smaller conversations, with Elena speaking softly to Rita, Adeena and Blake chatting it up, and me trying to get to know Hana better. We'd become friends during her visits the past few months before she became a permanent Shady Palms resident, but I still felt there was so much about her I didn't know. She was Jae's favorite cousin, but his stories about their childhood, while sweet, didn't form a complete picture of the woman in front of me.

Her husband passed away last year, and I knew she was still grieving his loss. Maybe that was why I'd sometimes felt there was a wall between us, like she was afraid to get close to anyone new. She'd moved to Shady Palms for a fresh start for her and Aria, and I figured her daughter was a good topic to start a conversation around.

"How's Aria adjusting to the move?"

Hana gave me a little half smile. "Better and faster than me, that's for sure. I was worried that I was being selfish, moving her away from my parents and our old home, but she loves it here. Jae and my imo are spoiling her rotten, which is exactly what she needs right now."

I studied Hana. As happy as I was to hear that Aria was thriving, I hadn't missed the first part that she said. From what I'd seen of her, she wasn't the type to wear a lot of makeup, mostly relying on her beautiful asymmetrical-cut blue hair to provide color and style. The lack of makeup drew attention to her dark undereye circles, and I couldn't help but notice how exhausted she looked.

"Glad to hear Aria's adjusting well. I don't think I've ever seen Jae so happy as when he's talking about you and your daughter."

That drew a genuine smile out of her, but then I said, "But what about you? I know you don't know me that well yet, but you can talk to me if something's bothering you."

She tucked her hair behind her ear and forced a laugh. "Just the usual. I appreciate it though. Jae said—"

But I never found out what Jae had said because she got a text at that moment, and when she looked down at her phone, the blood drained from her face.

"Hana? Are you OK?"

My voice must've risen in my panic because the others crowded around us to check on Hana. Blake grabbed Hana's phone and made a disgusted noise when she saw the name on the screen.

"Him again? I thought you told him to stop contacting you."

"I told him that he could only message me if it was about work."

Blake rolled her eyes. "Yes, I'm sure his texts are always super professional. What does this one say?"

Hana unlocked her phone and read the text out loud. "'The truffles are a huge hit with our clients and we're thinking of stocking the chocolate bars, too. Can I come over and try some samples? We can grab dinner together after if you're free.'"

"You're not responding to him, right?" When Hana didn't answer, Blake narrowed her eyes and repeated the question.

Hana didn't meet her partner's eyes. "I can't ignore him, he's our best customer. You know it's hard enough getting people to pay attention to us since everyone in this area is loyal to The Chocolate Shoppe in Shelbyville. We can't afford to alienate someone who brings in so much business."

"I don't care about—"

"Who is this guy anyway?" Adeena, either trying to prevent an argument or just indulging in her nosiness, cut into the conversation.

Hana sighed. "His name is Shawn Ford. He works for a fancy hotel in Shelbyville and comes to the shop all the time for business. But he's always asking me out, too. I told him I wasn't interested, but that hasn't stopped him."

"Why does he have your number?" I asked.

"There was an issue with one of the orders, so I called him from my phone to work things out. Guess he saved it since he's been texting me the past couple of weeks."

"Hana doesn't want to risk losing his business. She tells him no and tries to set boundaries, but since she's not firm, he thinks he can wear her down. I know his type," Blake said. "I handle his orders now, but he still tries to pull stuff like this. Just ignore him and let me take care of it."

"But—"

"I am not just your friend, I'm also the boss, so this is my responsibility. Block his number and let me take care of it. OK?"

Hana sighed but complied. "You're the best."

"Damn right I am. Now enough of this. We've got wine to drink and gossip to discuss. Right, ladies?" Blake held up her glass. "Who needs a refill?"

The rest of the night was filled with much lighter conversation and laughter, and as I joked around with my friends, I did my best to push down the feeling in my gut that trouble was coming.

Chapter Four

"And here she is trying to dunk. Isn't she the cutest?"

My boyfriend, Jae, held up his phone to show me the fifty-millionth video he'd taken of Hana's daughter, Aria, who he considered his niece. She was playing with the mini basketball hoop he got her and showing off her dunking skills. It was really quite adorable.

Dr. Jae Park, dentist extraordinaire, basketball nerd, and all-around geek, had shown a new side of himself ever since his cousin and niece had moved to Shady Palms: doting uncle and the beginnings of what I was sure would become a total Girl Dad.

As his girlfriend, who was nearing thirty yet nowhere near ready to start thinking about kids, it was a little worrying. As a woman who loved and respected softness and vulnerability in men, it was both heartwarming and reassuring. And just as a person with, you know, a heart, it was super cute.

Other than Ronnie, who I'd had issues with growing up (to put it mildly), I didn't have any blood relatives around my age. Tita Rosie was Ronnie's mother and my dad's only sibling. My mom came from a big family, but they were really poor, and she was the only one to come to the U.S. From what Tita Rosie told me, all of my mom's other siblings either stayed behind in the Philippines or were OFWs (overseas foreign workers) employed as domestic help in countries like Singapore, Hong Kong, and the UAE. My mom had been good about writing and calling and sending money when I was a kid, but after both of my parents died in a car accident when I was eight years old, I lost contact with that side of the family.

It's not like I was totally isolated as a kid, since I had all my play cousins: Bernadette, the daughter of Ninang June, one of my godmothers and my mother's best frenemy, plus Marcus and Joseph, the sons of Ninang Mae, another one of my godmothers. So it's not like I was a complete loner. But when I'd observed the easy affection between Hana and Jae, listening to their shared stories of family vacations and how they loved to prank the too-serious-since-birth Detective Park, it made me realize how lonely I was as a child.

As I mentioned before, Ronnie and I had issues growing up. Bernadette was my rival—not by choice, but due to our mothers' weird, competitive friendship. Joseph and I had nothing in common, although he was a decent guy. And Marcus was four years younger than me. Not a big deal now, and we'd become actual friends since then, but that's a huge gap when you're a kid. On top of that, I never felt like I fit in with the other kids at school. Part of that was my, ahem, snobbishness (as Bernadette likes to put it) that took me a very long time to outgrow (Bernadette would say I'm still a snob, but she doesn't know everything, does she?) and part of it was that I was surprisingly introverted as a child. It was easier for me to escape into books and my future dreams of getting away from Shady Palms than deal with everything else. Like the fact that my mom and dad were gone.

I shook my wistfulness away.

"She's super cute." I indulged Jae with a grin as I watched the screen. "Oh, is that your dad playing ball with her? How's he doing?"

The Park family patriarch had been battling health issues for the past year. After a scare last year that led to a quadruple bypass, Tita Rosie started working with Jae and Detective Park's mom to come up with tasty, heart-healthy recipes for the family while the brothers developed a fitness regimen that kept him moving but wouldn't tax his heart.

Jae and Detective Park had been taking turns helping out, whether it be shuttling their parents around to doctors' appointments, going grocery shopping, or fixing things around the house. Sometimes one brother would stay home with their dad to hang out and watch TV while the other would take their much more outgoing mother to see friends, go dancing, or hit up the local state park to get some hiking in. As excited as Jae was to see Hana and Aria again, he was worried that a young child would be too much for his dad to handle. After all, Jae himself was a later-in-life "surprise" and his dad had had his hands full as an older man trying to raise a son who was so different from himself. How would he fare around a little girl?

Luckily, all those worries were for nothing. Aria's arrival breathed new life into Papa Park, and he showed levels of energy, curiosity, and, above all, patience that the rest of the family hadn't seem from him in . . . maybe ever? I'd always been a little afraid of

Papa Park—he and Mama Park very much embodied the-grump-and-the-sunshine dynamic, and his grumpy side only grew the worse his health became. He was never rude or cold or anything like that (unlike my ex-fiancé's parents). I just didn't know how to act around him or what to talk about.

I guess since my paternal grandfather passed away before I was born, I'd never met my maternal grandfather (who I think was still alive in the Philippines), my Tito Jeff (Tita Rosie's estranged husband and Ronnie's terrible father) ran out when I was young, and my own father passed away when I was a kid, I'd never really spent a lot of time around older men or father-figure types.

Even with godparents, I only ever spent time with my godmothers: Ninang April, Ninang Mae, and Ninang June. My godfathers were Ninang Mae's husband, who left Shady Palms after they divorced and we never heard from again; Ninang June's husband, who passed away from an illness; and Ninong Rick, my dad's best friend from work. But even he left Shady Palms eventually, and the most I'd hear from him was the occasional birthday card with a check for the dollar amount of however old I was turning that year. I guess it was Ninong Rick's way of proving that he didn't forget me and knew exactly how old I was (although I couldn't help feeling like it was kind of ridiculous to have to deposit a check for twenty-seven dollars).

Maybe all that was why I'd had such bad taste in men before Jae—but I digress.

"My dad's doing so much better lately. He's looking forward to the spring when he can take Aria down by the Riverwalk and is already talking about getting her her first bike for her birthday."

He was still smiling down at his phone, but something a little more complicated crept into his tone.

I put my hand on his and squeezed before turning my attention back to my plate of green chile chilaquiles. Today's late dinner date was at El Gato Negro, the Mexican restaurant that used to be run by Elena's mom, Carmen, but had recently been turned back over to Elena's aunt and uncle. The restaurant had been theirs previously, but they'd left town due to some nonsense caused by my (now-deceased) ex-boyfriend. Long story short, they were back in town and heading up the restaurant so Carmen could go back to focusing on her art career, which had really taken off recently.

Jae put his phone away and dove into his steak quesadilla. "Anyway, the important thing is that my dad's health is better, Aria is settling in, and Hana seems happier than I've seen her in a long time. Coming here has been good for them."

"Glad to hear it. And I'm particularly happy that Shady Palms gets to enjoy the amazing chocolate they're churning out at Choco Noir. Your cousin is so, so talented."

"She's always been the creative one in the family. Her parents tried to get her to do graphic design since they consider that a stable career in the arts, but she wouldn't budge. The number of fights they had over her going to school to 'make overpriced candy bars,'" he said, shaking his head. "I get that the school was expensive, but it hurt to see them making so little of her dream."

"At least she seems to be doing well now," I said. "I mean, I know she's still dealing with a lot, considering it's only been a year since her husband passed away. But I'm sure seeing how well Aria's adapted to life here in Shady Palms and getting her chocolate shop up and running has been a huge help."

"That's all thanks to Blake. Hana never would have thought of moving here on her own if Blake hadn't reached out to her about opening up a shop together." Jae wiped his mouth and took a sip of his horchata. "Blake was all set to open a solo business, but when she saw how badly Hana was struggling, she offered Hana part ownership. I think she knew that Hana needed to get away and start a new life for her and Aria."

"But you're the reason she chose to open the store in Shady Palms, right?"

He shrugged. "Blake told her that she wanted to open a cute, cozy chocolate shop and that she didn't care where as long as the place had small-town vibes and thriving local business and was somewhere in the Midwest so she wouldn't be too far from her family in Minneapolis. Shady Palms checked all those boxes and put Hana close to my family, so it was the natural choice."

"Well, whatever the reasons, I'm glad she's here. And that she has you, your family, and Blake. A strong support system can get you through most anything."

Jae absolutely inhaled his steak quesadilla and hailed the waiter to ask for another one. As soon as it arrived, he tore into it. "Mmm, I'm absolutely starving. Sorry to postpone dinner for so late, but we had an emergency dental appointment, and then my parents needed help fixing the sink, and time just got away from me."

"No worries. I'm just glad we didn't have to cancel," I said.

It was already after nine p.m., and he'd called earlier to let me know he'd be running late, so I'd at least had a snack to tide me over. That being said, I was still pretty hungry and definitely in the mood for something sweet. I held up my hand to flag down our waiter for the seasonal dessert menu. But before I could put in an order, Jae's phone rang, Bernadette's name flashing across the screen.

"That's weird. I wonder why she's calling me," he said as he picked up. "Hey Bernadette, what's—"

His eyes widened and his grip on the phone tightened as he listened to what she had to say. "Oh my God, is she OK? Can I—" He paused to listen again. "We'll be right there."

He hung up and looked at me with an expression I'd never seen on him before, as if he was fighting back tears. "Hana's in the hospital. She was attacked."

"We're here to see Hana Lee! What room is she in? Can you tell me her condition?"

Jae ran through the doors of the Shady Palms Hospital's emergency department and up to the front desk as I struggled to keep up with him. After he got the call from Bernadette, I had the server put the meal on our tab and drove us to the hospital while Jae called his family to pass on the information.

"Jae, over here!" Bernadette waved to get our attention. Detective Park and Mama Park were already with her.

I grabbed Jae's arm before he could dash over and made him slow to a walk rather than a sprint. I understood his worries, but in his frame of mind, he was likely to cause an accident and get us kicked out.

"I was just telling your mom and brother about Hana's condition." Bernadette glanced around the relatively empty room and motioned for all of us to follow her to some seats far enough away from the front desk that people wouldn't overhear her. "First of all, I'm sorry to be the bearer of bad news. I—"

"She's not . . . You don't mean—" Jae kept getting choked up as he tried to ask about his cousin's condition.

Bernadette grabbed his hands and gave them a squeeze. "She's alive, Jae."

"Oh, thank God." Jae's shoulders slumped down in relief, and his mom slid her arm through his to pull him close. "When can we see her?"

Bernadette and Detective Park exchanged worried glances. What was going on? If Hana was alive, why was everyone acting like the worst had happened?

I guess Detective Park decided he'd be the one to break the news since he was family, and he had the most experience with this kind of thing. "Jae, she's in a coma."

"Wha—"

Detective Park held up his hand before Jae could interrupt him again. "We think Choco Noir was the latest victim in the string of burglaries. Usually, the culprit strikes after the store is closed and all the employees are gone, but Hana and Blake were still there. Detective Nowak was the one who called me."

He sighed deeply, wiping a hand down his face. That's when I realized that his eyes were red-rimmed and watery, as if he was holding back tears. "They think Hana and Blake showed up unexpectedly mid-burglary and the burglar or burglars panicked and attacked them. Hana suffered blunt force trauma to the head and has yet to wake up. Blake is dead."

I grabbed his sleeve, clinging to it as if I'd fall over without his solid presence. "I'm sorry. Blake is . . . ?"

Detective Park wrapped his hand around mine, the warmth and solidity bringing me comfort. "I'm sorry. Detective Nowak didn't go into detail. It was a courtesy call since Hana is family and I was his mentor. I plan on going to the Shady Palms Police Department after this. He's going to be tight-lipped since I'm not officially on this case, but I've got my ways."

"I'm going, too," Jae said. "After I check on Hana. I know she's not awake, but it'll make me feel better to see her, to confirm that she's still alive."

"I'm not sure it's going to make you feel all that much better, honestly. Seeing her like that was tough. Even for me." Detective Park looked into his little brother's determined eyes and must've known nothing he could say would change Jae's mind. He clapped his hand on Jae's shoulder. "But you're right. Go check on her while I drop Umma at home. I'll meet you at the station."

"Do you want me there too, or should I hang back? I can wait outside," I asked Jae as Bernadette led us to Hana's room.

"I need you there. Please."

"Of course." I intertwined my fingers with his and squeezed. Before I could remind him that I'd always be there for him, Bernadette stopped in front of the room and turned to us.

"I just want to prepare you for this. It's going to look bad because she's all wired up and is currently intubated."

Jae's eyes widened. "It's that bad? She can't breathe on her own?"

"When she was first brought in, there was some obstruction in her airway making it difficult for her to breathe. We're hoping in a few days she can be taken off the ventilator, but it's too soon to say anything concrete." Bernadette paused. "Are you ready?"

Jae glanced at me before nodding. "I'm ready."

We weren't ready.

But to be fair, was anyone ever prepared to see their loved one like this? In a condition that made it clear they were straddling the line between life and death? With all of my previous cases, I saw some terrible things, but when I got involved in an investigation, the victims were already past the point of saving. There was a finality to it.

Even with my parents, they had died at the scene of their car accident. There were no hospital visits, no lingering hope. Just one day they had left to run some routine errands and then suddenly they were gone.

But with Hana, it was different. There was still hope. But it was a hope tinged with despair because we had no idea if she would get better. The uncertainty made it worse.

Also, and I know how horrible this sounds, I didn't know most of the victims from my past cases very well. There was my ex-boyfriend, the start of all of this nonsense, but he was my ex for a reason. And the death of Ninang April's niece, Divina, was tragic, but I hadn't gotten the chance to get to know her. Her investigation was one born of duty and justice—it wasn't personal. I only ever got involved in cases because I or someone close to me was accused of false charges. Yes, justice was important to me, but my concern was clearing our names and preventing more tragedy. It was the cops' and lawyers' jobs to find justice for the victims.

But Blake was my friend. We'd spent hours and hours together, planning the collaboration between our shops, hanging out with our WOC entrepreneur group, and bonding over what it meant to not only start a new business but also a whole new life. There was still so much I wanted to talk about with her, to learn from her, and now I'd never get that chance. Someone had taken that away.

And Hana? She was more than a friend to me. Her connection to Jae made her family. And I didn't let anyone mess with my family.

As Jae openly wept next to me, I made a silent promise to Hana: *I'm going to find the person who did this to you and Blake.*

Clichés be damned, but this time, it was personal.

Chapter Five

"With all due respect, you are no longer a member of the Shady Palms Police Department. You know I can't discuss an ongoing investigation with you. However, I do have a few questions for—"

"I don't give a damn about your questions! You know I'm the person best equipped to help this useless department. Stop being so stubborn, Feliks."

When Jae and I arrived at the police department, Detective Feliks Nowak was trying to calm down a raging Detective Park, to poor effect. I'd never seen Detective Park like this. He was usually so careful not to let his feelings show, keeping up his detective poker face even in his everyday life. And as much as he disapproved of certain members of the town's police department, he'd always made sure not to bad-mouth the SPPD since he respected the ones trying to make a difference, like Detective Nowak. But he looked ready to deck his former mentee, and Jae rushed forward to make sure his brother didn't do something he'd regret.

"Hyung! You're not helping Hana. Go cool off for a minute." Jae waited until his brother stormed outside before turning to Detective Nowak. "I'll answer whatever questions you need. But what can you tell us about my cousin's case?"

Detective Nowak sighed and rubbed his temples. "Nothing that I haven't already told your brother. About an hour ago, we received a call from a customer who'd gone to Choco Noir to pick up a special order. When they arrived, the lights were off, which they thought was strange since the owners told them they'd be at the store at that time. They called the owners but didn't get a response. They then tried the doors and found them unlocked. When they entered, they saw two bodies on the floor and immediately called 911."

"Who's the customer who called this in?" I asked.

Detective Nowak shook his head. "I'm sorry, but I can't share that information. Rest assured, we are doing everything we can to find whoever is behind these attacks."

"Do you think this is connected to the recent burglaries?"

"I also cannot speak on that at the moment, Ms. Macapagal. Now, I have some questions regarding Ms. Hana Lee. Jae, would you and your brother please join me in my office?"

"And Lila, too?" Jae asked.

Detective Nowak hesitated. "Family only, I'm afraid."

"Don't worry about it, Jae," I said, putting my hand on his arm. I knew he'd tell me everything later anyway. "I have no problem waiting for you out here. Let me grab your brother."

When I stepped outside, Detective Park was resting his

forearms on top of the low wall in front of the station, tapping an unopened box of cigarettes on it.

"I didn't know you smoked," I said, leaning my hip against the wall.

"I don't. Or at least, not anymore." He exhaled loudly, a puff of smokelike vapor curling in the cold air. "I promised your aunt I wouldn't start again. But I still keep them on me for moments like this."

I waited for him to elaborate, but when he didn't, I decided not to push it. "Detective Nowak wants to talk to you and Jae in his office."

He sighed, straightening up and tucking the box inside an inner pocket of his winter coat. "Can you do me a favor? Update Rosie on what's going on. I was at your house when I got the call, so she has an idea of what happened, but she's probably out of her mind with worry."

He could've done that while he was out here brooding, but I didn't point that out. He had enough on his mind.

"Of course. Is it OK if I let the rest of the group know, too?"

"Might as well. If this really is related to the burglary ring, you and your friends perfectly fit the target criteria. Staying informed and aware is probably the best way to keep you all safe," he said, before disappearing into the police station.

Despite the freezing temperature, I stayed outside while texting my aunt and my WOC group chat to let them know what was going on. The cold air bit against my exposed cheeks and fingers, but it also helped clear my head.

I couldn't believe Blake was gone. I may not have known her as well as Hana, but I still considered her a friend. Smart, passionate, loyal. She had such high hopes for Choco Noir, and more than one Sangria Sunday was spent with her and Hana regaling us with their plans to become one of the premier chocolate shops in the Midwest. If Hana woke up . . . No, I couldn't think like that. *When* Hana woke up, she was going to be devastated. She already suffered so much loss after her husband passed; what was she going to do when she found out her best friend and business partner was gone, too?

A shiver ran through me, one I couldn't blame entirely on the cold, but I figured that was my sign to head back inside. By the time I'd plopped down in one of the uncomfortable plastic seats in the waiting area, my group chat was blowing up.

WOC ENTREPRENEUR CHAT

ADEENA: **WTF**

SANA: **That's absolutely awful! Is it OK if I tell Amir? He might be able to help in some way**

ELENA: **Are you OK? Do you need us to wait w/ you?**

BETH: **I'm sorry to hear that. Do the police think it's connected to the burglaries?**

YUKI: **I can't believe it. Let us know how we can help. How's Hana's daughter doing?**

Oh my gulay, I totally forgot about Aria. Not only did she lose her father last year, but now her mother was in a coma. At almost four years old, she was probably too young to really grasp what that meant, but she was still old enough to know something was wrong. My heart broke for her.

My phone buzzed again, this time with a text from Izzy.

IZZY: Does Blake have family in the area? We should take up a collection to help w/ funeral costs and hospital fees

ME: Good idea. I think Blake's family is all in Minneapolis. I'll have to ask Detective Nowak

I put my phone away and closed my eyes for a moment. I had no idea how long I dozed, but the next thing I knew, Tita Rosie and Lola Flor were shaking me awake.

"What're you two doing here?" I asked, wiping my mouth.

"I want to be here for Jonathan. Neither of you were answering your phones, so I figured you were still at the station," Tita Rosie said, casting an anxious glance toward the back where the offices and interrogation rooms were.

Lola Flor pulled a packet of tissues from her purse and wiped down a couple of seats before sitting beside me. Next, she unearthed a large thermos from her bag and poured me a small cup of tsokolate. The thick hot chocolate was still steaming, and at my grandmother's urging, I took a long drink. The bittersweet beverage coursed down my throat and warmed my stomach; as I inhaled the familiar, chocolatey scent, I could feel my tense muscles loosening little by little.

"Thanks, Lola Flor."

She nodded at me. "Tough times lie ahead. Best to recharge when you can."

She was right. As I sipped my drink, I could feel my mind clearing and the last bit of sleepiness falling away.

My grandmother stopped my aunt's pacing and made her sit with us. Tita Rosie's butt had barely hit the seat before she was back on her feet at the sound of a door opening. Jae and Detective Park came out from the back, accompanied by Detective Nowak. Detective Park seemed to have calmed down, but he still didn't look too pleased with his former mentee.

"Jonathan!" My aunt launched herself forward. Tita Rosie was not big on physical affection—I could probably count on my hands the number of times she'd hugged me—especially not publicly, but she must've sensed that Detective Park needed her because she immediately wrapped her arms around him.

The hard look on Detective Park's face melted away as he returned the hug, and the two of them held each other for a moment before Tita Rosie pulled away to gaze into his face.

"Are you OK? Do you need something to eat? I packed your family's favorites."

Detective Park smiled at my aunt's familiar brand of kindness. "I'm good for now, but I'm sure my mom will appreciate not having to cook tomorrow. I wish we could spend more time together, but we need to head to my parents' house. I have to let them know what's going on."

I approached Jae, who was drinking the hot chocolate Lola Flor had shoved into his hands. "Will you be joining us for breakfast tomorrow? I want to hear all the details, but I know you're in a hurry."

Jae flashed me a weary smile. "Yeah, sorry. Aria is over at my parents' house and has no idea what's going on. I want to be the one to break it to her. I'm not sure how much she'll understand, but she deserves to know."

I intertwined my fingers with his and gave them a squeeze. "Let me know if you need anything."

"Can you round up the troops tomorrow? There's not much to share, but it's always easier to have everyone together at once."

"Of course. I already let everyone know what happened in the group chat, and we're talking about starting funds for Blake and Hana, to help with any costs."

Jae's eyes watered, and he took a deep breath before fixing another smile on his face. "Appreciate it. We're still paying off the bills from my dad's surgery last year, and Hana sunk her savings into Choco Noir. Every little bit helps."

I put my hand on his cheek, and he leaned into it. "We're all here for you. Now go with your brother to handle everything and get some rest. And maybe you should take tomorrow off."

He started to argue with me, and I held up a hand to stop him. "Do you want me to call Millie?"

Millie Barnes was his receptionist, and she was extremely protective of him. Whenever Millie and I teamed up, Jae didn't stand a chance.

He winced. "Don't do that! I'll call her in the morning and see how many of my appointments Dr. Wheeling can take on and which can be moved to another day."

"Good. Don't forget I work a few doors down and can easily check that you did that."

"You know I'd never lie to you."

"Because I'd figure it out right away and make you pay?"

He finally laughed. "Exactly."

"Jae! Are you ready to head out?" Detective Park waited at the door with a cup of hot chocolate that my grandmother must've forced on him, considering he didn't have much of a sweet tooth.

Jae gave me a quick kiss. "See you at breakfast."

My aunt, grandmother, and I followed them out and watched in silence as they got into Detective Park's car. Once they pulled out of the lot, Tita Rosie turned to me.

"I'll let your ninangs know what's going on. And I'll make everyone's favorites for breakfast."

"Perfect. Adeena and Elena will be there, and possibly Amir, too."

"Might as well call Ronnie, too," Lola Flor said. "He's useless, but his girlfriend is sharp. The more people we have gathering information, the better."

My aunt winced at her own mother calling her son useless but didn't comment. We were both used to picking our battles when it came to Lola Flor, and she must've figured this wasn't the time. I usually wasn't one to go to bat for my cousin (to be honest, our negative opinion of Ronnie used to be one of the few things Lola Flor and I had in common), but he'd changed since returning to Shady Palms. Over the last year or so, he'd been working on rebuilding the relationships he'd destroyed in the past and had proven himself to be a valuable ally. And a somewhat trusted member of the family. I said as much to Lola Flor, who snorted but didn't say anything else.

Tita Rosie shot me a grateful look before she and my grandmother climbed into Tita Rosie's car while I got into mine and followed them home. After taking care of my nighttime routine, I snuggled into bed with Longganisa, holding her close as I shed quiet tears. I didn't go to church anymore, but I said a quick prayer for Blake and Hana anyway. Then I popped a few melatonin and waited for sleep to take me, hoping that a good night's rest would give me the strength I needed to get through the next day.

Chapter Six

"This is all so awful, I just can't believe it. Please let us know how we can help."

Detective Park had just finished recounting everything that had happened yesterday to our breakfast crew, and everyone was so horrified they didn't know what to say. Even Tita Rosie, Lola Flor, and I, who were at the station last night and already knew the information he'd just shared, were at a loss for words after hearing everything laid out again so bluntly.

Izzy was the first to recover and added, "Isaiah will be with us this coming weekend, so if your mom needs a break from babysitting, you can bring Aria over for a play date."

Isaiah was my cousin Ronnie's son from a previous relationship—with his current girlfriend's cousin, I should add, since my cousin used to be an absolute F-boi. Ronnie and his ex, Penny, were on good terms (they realized they were better as friends), but her parents absolutely HATED Ronnie. As such, he was only able to see his son one weekend a month, and he had to make the trek to Wisconsin since they wouldn't allow him to take their grandchild out of state. Penny and Izzy had been advocating for him though, so Ronnie had finally been able to bring his son to Shady Palms for visits for the past few months and was hoping to work out longer visitation rights during the summer. Isaiah and Aria were around the same age and would make perfect playmates.

Jae perked up at Izzy's offer. "That's a great idea! Aria hasn't had a chance to be around other kids since moving here, and I'm sure my mom would appreciate a break. Thanks, Izzy."

"And we'll help with meals, of course," my aunt said. "Do you know if that girl Blake has family in the area? If so, we should reach out to them as well."

Detective Park swallowed a giant mouthful of beef tapa. "According to Detective Nowak, Blake's parents, siblings, and ex-husband all live in the Twin Cities of Minnesota. He's already contacted the parents, and I believe they're arranging to come to Shady Palms so they can talk to him in person."

He helped himself to another serving of beef tapa, as well as some pork tocino. Tita Rosie had been carefully lessening her red meat breakfast offerings after Papa Park's health scare, but she must've figured an occasional indulgence during such a trying time was OK because she'd made the Park brothers' favorite breakfast items. Detective Park seemed to be taking full advantage of the rare occasion.

"Do the police think this attack is related to the burglaries? Was anything stolen from the chocolate shop?" Ninang June asked.

My godmothers—Ninang April, Ninang Mae, and Ninang June, aka the Calendar Crew—were invited to this breakfast because they were the nosiest women in the county (and possibly the entire Midwest) and as such, they knew just about everything about everyone. Even when they weren't directly involved in an investigation, they liked to be updated as to what was going on, if only because they thrived on tsismis. We indulged them because behind their curiosity was a genuine desire to help. We just had to put up with their rather unconventional methods and unnecessary side comments, that's all.

"We're not sure, which is one of the reasons I'm going to need everyone's help on this. Detective Nowak is being even more tight-lipped than usual, and considering they've made zero progress on the burglaries, I'm not going to trust them to handle Blake and Hana's case. Can I count on all of you?"

Tita Rosie broke into a gentle smile. "You know I'll do whatever it takes to support you. Just let me know how I can help."

I echoed my aunt's sentiments. "Blake and Hana are my friends. There's no way I'd just sit this out."

Adeena and Elena agreed.

Elena added, "And if this really is connected to those robberies, we need to solve this before anyone else gets hurt. My cousin Rita's store was already hit, although luckily she's safe. But who knows where they'll strike next?"

Detective Park nodded. "That's my concern as well. If it's the same person or group that's been going after local businesses, it's not in their MO to hurt people. They've always struck when no one is around. I don't know how this most recent attack is going to affect their operations. Either it'll spook them, since they never meant to go that far, convincing them to stop entirely. Or . . ."

"Do you think maybe they'll escalate?" Jae asked. "Like, in for a penny, in for a pound?"

"You don't really think it'll come to that, do you?" my aunt asked worriedly. "They killed someone on accident. Why would they take a chance and risk doing it again?"

"Sadly, we don't know that it was an accident," Detective Park said. "Remember, it's just speculation that Blake and Hana's attack is connected to the burglaries."

"In your professional opinion, do you think it's the same person or group?" Ninang April asked.

Detective Park pressed his lips together as he thought it over. "It's hard to dismiss the possibility. It's a known fact that every establishment that's been targeted is woman-owned. And according to Detective Nowak, the cash register was emptied and there were signs of the place being ransacked. However, Choco Noir was a brand-new store. They can't have been making enough money to catch the eye of a thief. So why them?"

Everyone sat quietly, likely turning over that information in their head, wondering the same thing. Why them?

Amir broke the silence. Adeena's older brother was the town's best lawyer and had assisted everyone at the table numerous times. "From what I understand, there were signs that they were victims of burglary, but the facts don't really add up in your mind?"

Detective Park nodded. "Exactly. That makes it difficult to direct the investigation since I can't discount that it was a botched burglary, which means focusing on not just the past break-ins but also anticipating where they'll strike next. But I also don't want to ignore my gut, which says there's a possibility the scene was staged to look like a botched burglary and that Blake, Hana, or both, were always the intended victims of this violence."

Jae reeled back. "But they just got here! Who'd want to hurt them?"

"Don't forget, people can hold grudges for any number of reasons and for any length of time," Ninang April said. "Even if we think there's no way our loved one could be a target, even if we'd like to believe they would do nothing to invoke such ire . . . we can't know what's in people's hearts. We can only ever see what they choose to show us."

My godmother was sitting directly across from me, and I reached out to place my hand over hers. I knew she was thinking of her own loss last year, and the secrets that were unearthed during that investigation.

Ninang April gave my hand a quick squeeze before pulling away. "Considering there are so many potential avenues for this investigation, it's extra important that we all do our part. What are our assignments?"

"I'd like your group to use your connections to find out as much as possible about Blake, Hana, and Choco Noir. If anyone had a bone to pick with them, even if it's something minor, I want to know about it."

"Got it," Ninang Mae said. "I already have an idea of where to start."

Detective Park thanked her before addressing Ronnie and Izzy. "I'd like you two to handle the chamber of commerce. Out of everyone here who's currently a member, you two are the most neutral."

Ronnie laughed. "They don't exactly like me, but I get you. Izzy can charm them, and the old guard is more comfortable talking to me, so I can pretend I'm indulging in guy talk."

"Amir, I'd like to hire you to represent my family. The SPPD is not going to be very forthcoming with me, but as someone who is officially and legally involved in the case, you're better placed to receive updates, request documents, and do anything else you think will be helpful."

Amir bowed slightly. "Of course. Happy to do my part."

"What about us?" I asked. "The Brew-ha Cafe fits the profile of the type of businesses that've been hit. Should we talk to the previous victims?"

"Absolutely not," Jae interjected. "The burglaries are the most dangerous investigation avenue. Even if the burglar or burglars aren't involved in the attack, we have no idea how they'll react if they find out you're asking questions and getting close to uncovering their operation."

Before I could point out that this was the fastest and clearest line of investigation, Detective Park backed up his younger brother. "Lila, he's right. You know that Jae and I want to find whoever hurt our cousin and killed Blake more than anything, but not at your expense."

Jae echoed his brother's statement, and I sighed. Not like I could argue with something like that. Not when I knew they were right.

"Then what would you like us to do?"

Detective Park looked relieved that I wasn't going to push back on his decision. "We don't know who or what the intended target was, so the more we understand everyone involved, the better. I want you to also learn all that you can about Blake, Hana, and

Choco Noir. Your godmothers have a very different network than you, Adeena, and Elena. Between your two groups, you should be able to sniff out anything worth knowing."

"Works for me. But Hana is your cousin. Shouldn't you or Jae be in charge of learning more about her?" I asked. "Blake and Hana are my friends, but it's not like we were close enough for them to divulge any deep, dark secrets."

"We'll be looking into what Hana was up to before she moved here, of course. But that'll mainly be through the family and her connections in Minnesota. Your part of the investigation will be local, looking into Hana as Blake's business partner and everything surrounding Choco Noir. Does that make sense?"

After I nodded, he paused, his eyes flicking over toward the Calendar Crew before returning to mine. "Although you and your godmothers will be looking into the same people, I'd prefer that you, Adeena, and Elena be the ones to reach out to Blake's family once they arrive. You all were friends with their daughter and would have a, um, softer approach, I believe."

What a diplomatic way to say he didn't trust the Calendar Crew to not run their mouths in front of Blake's bereaved loved ones.

"We'd like to help, too," Tita Rosie said, volunteering herself and Lola Flor.

Detective Park's eyes softened when he looked at her. "I don't want you doing too much. Just as usual, keep an ear out when people are talking in the restaurant and at church, and let me know if you hear anything interesting. And my mom is going to need extra help with meals and childcare, if you don't mind."

Tita Rosie agreed, and Lola Flor added, "And our house is open to everyone as well. I'm sure we'll need to get together like this out of the public eye, so we should aim to have dinner at our home at least once a week."

Lola Flor waved her hand at Detective Park's thanks and told everyone to wait a moment before leaving. She disappeared into the kitchen and came back with takeout bags for everyone.

"Mocha mamon. One of our regulars requested champorado and asked me to bake something using chocolate. Mocha is close enough, but I've never made mocha mamon before. Take these with you and let me know what you think later."

Lola Flor . . . asking for feedback? Actually caring about the opinions of others?

Tita Rosie and I looked at each other, our eyes wide, and she shook her head slightly, as if warning me not to draw attention to it. I tried to wipe the shock off my face and rearrange my expression to something more neutral, but wow. I guess people can change after all.

Adeena, either because she sensed how momentous this was and that I had no idea how to respond or because mamon was her favorite Filipino baked good, reached for the bag. "Thanks so much, Grandma Flor! I can't wait to try it."

As if to prove her point, she stuck her hand into the bag and helped herself to an individual chiffon cake right then and there. "Mmm . . . that subtle mocha flavor is such a perfect match for that light, fluffy texture. I might like these even more than the plain butter ones . . ."

Adeena wasn't one to mince words, especially when it came to her beloved sweets, so Lola Flor likely knew my bestie was being sincere. She smiled at my friend (smiled! My grandmother!), which caused me and my cousin Ronnie to be the ones exchanging bewildered glances this time. Was my grandmother softening up now that she was older? Was she going to become one of those white TV grandmas, smiling and baking brownies and being, I don't know, nice?

As those thoughts were running through my head, my grandmother clapped her hands together loudly. "Hoy! Why are you still sitting here? I gave you those goodie bags, now it's time for you to leave. We all have work, diba? Stop wasting my time!"

As my grandmother's sharp words chased us all out of Tita Rosie's Kitchen, I heaved a sigh of relief. Lola Flor was still Lola Flor. With all that had changed over the last day, I wasn't sure I was ready for such a seismic shift.

Chapter Seven

"Now that we have our assignments, how do you all want to handle this?"

Adeena, Elena, and I had all hurried next door to our cafe after Lola Flor basically kicked us out and were now handling the last-minute duties before opening. As the baker, the majority of my tasks were done in the morning, with an afternoon replenishing of our snack shelves and whatever admin work needed completing. My schedule made me best suited to leaving the cafe for our investigations, an arrangement that I'd taken for granted until I got called out for it by Elena last fall. I learned from my mistakes, and this time I wanted to be sure we were all on the same page before jumping into investigation mode.

Elena smiled appreciatively at me. "I'm going to have my hands full supporting Rita, so feel free to handle any leads that take you away from the cafe. I'll talk to Chuy and my other cousins about the situation and also keep an eye out here."

Adeena added, "With Elena and Leslie watching the shop, I can join you for any trips that Jae is too busy to take."

Leslie was our only other full-time employee, and their mother, Helen, was our part-time delivery person. Our staff was quite small, so we usually couldn't afford to have more than one person out at a time.

Still, the three of us were all partners in this business, and if they said that Adeena and I were free to investigate off-site, there was no reason for me to argue.

"I'd appreciate that. I know Jae wants to join me as much as possible, but his schedule is way less flexible. Although I'm pretty sure he took time off this week. If he didn't, I'll make sure to talk to Millie and try to rearrange his schedule."

Jae owned a dental clinic that was in the same plaza as the Brew-ha Cafe and Tita Rosie's Kitchen. It was a popular clinic (well, as popular as you could be for a dentist's office), but his staff was even smaller than mine, consisting of his receptionist, Millie; a part-time assistant; and a newer full-time dentist who Jae had hired last summer.

Adeena grimaced. "I'm OK playing backup. With Hana being his cousin and all, he'll want to be even more involved than usual. And with the cafe being a target for future burglaries, he's gotta be more on edge than usual having you involved in a case."

Oof, I didn't even think of that. Maybe it would be best for me and him to take point on the investigation, just to keep him busy so his mind didn't start running wild. I made a note to prepare his favorite peach mango crumble cookies and maybe schedule a game night to help take his mind off things. I glanced at the clock and moved to the front door to unlock it. Time to get my head in the game.

The morning passed quickly, and I spent most of the time refilling the pastry cases, greeting customers, and parading Longganisa, my adorable dachshund and the cafe's unofficial mascot, around the shop to get some face time with her many admirers. Today, she and I wore matching hand-crocheted black cardigans patterned with pink and white hearts—while dealing with yet another investigation last fall, Adeena had immersed herself in her crochet hobby and her creative output had greatly padded the closets of just about everyone she knew.

Some of our customers had already heard what happened to Blake and Hana, courtesy of the *Shady Palms News*. I'd been so busy this morning fulfilling my cafe duties before the breakfast report at Tita Rosie's Kitchen that I forgot to check the paper. There was no love lost between me and the *Shady Palms News* team, but my family still had a subscription for the local paper since forewarned is forearmed, after all. I made a note to read it during my next break to see if they'd uncovered any new information that could help.

A text from Valerie Thompson at half past ten had me scurrying back to the kitchen to unmold the chocolate mochi muffins I'd prepared for her. She was one of my best customers, and thanks to her requests, I'd developed a good number of gluten-free dessert options to serve at the Brew-ha Cafe. She'd asked for something chocolaty and simple to serve as part of a light luncheon she was hosting as co-owner of the Thompson Family Company.

These mochi muffins, made with glutinous rice flour, fit the bill.

They were dense, chewy, and ever so slightly sweet, yet full of chocolaty goodness. They were still a touch warm, so I left them to finish cooling while I packed the rest of her order—white chocolate chai blondies, longganisa rolls, and ube scones, none of which were gluten-free but were popular brunch selections at her company. A final check of the chocolate mochi muffins let me know they were cool enough to handle, so I just gave them a quick dusting of powdered sugar and they were good to go.

Normally, our part-time delivery person, Helen Kowalski, would drop off this catering order, but I wanted to talk to Valerie and Beth. Even though Ronnie and Izzy were supposed to be handling the chamber of commerce side of the investigation, Valerie and Beth were good acquaintances—although I hesitate to call them friends—and I figured they'd be a good place to start my questioning.

I texted Jae to see if he could join me for the delivery.

> **Are you working today? Need to drop an order at the Thompson Family Co. Wanna come with?**

He responded: **Be there in 10. Need to finish some paperwork**

Perfect. That gave me enough time to pack some snacks and drinks for us.

I left the kitchen and made my way behind the counter. Leslie was assisting someone at the register, and Elena was chatting with a customer in her corner of the store, so I went up to Adeena.

"Jae's coming with me for the Thompson Family Company

delivery. Can you prepare our drinks while I fill the to-go boxes for Valerie's order? You know what we like."

"But of course. The new Dr. Jae for everyone's favorite dentist and a Mexican mocha for you. It's gonna be a long day, so you could use the extra caffeine and sugar."

Adeena, Elena, and I all had signature drinks at the Brew-ha Cafe, and Jae did as well. However, his old drink was too similar to mine, so he'd worked with Adeena to come up with something new and worthy to add to the signature line.

Right on cue, the bells above the front door tinkled, letting me know my boyfriend had entered the cafe. He strode toward us and gave me a quick kiss before leaning against the counter and groaning.

"So. Much. Paperwork. I know it's the least I can do since I'm taking an emergency week off, but my eyes are killing me."

"Oh, is that why you're wearing your glasses? I just noticed," I said.

Jae usually wore contacts because it was more comfortable when he had to don safety goggles for work, and this morning at breakfast was no different.

"Yeah, I had to take my contacts out. I didn't get much sleep last night, and with the extra strain of all that paperwork, my eyes couldn't take it."

He'd finally replaced the cheap, ugly frames he'd been wearing for years, and the stylish plastic frames he was rocking looked amazing. Geek chic was such a good look on him.

While I was busy ogling my boyfriend and filling the coffee and tea to-go boxes for delivery, Adeena had been preparing our drinks.

"I've got a Mexican mocha for Lila, and here's the Dr. Jae, made extra hot, just the way you like it."

Jae grabbed the cup and took a swig (how he didn't burn the heck out of his mouth, I have no idea) before sighing appreciatively. "You're the best, Adeena. I really needed that."

She smiled at him. "You know I got you. I'm just glad I finally nailed this drink. It's been super popular."

Jae's signature beverage was a honey butter latte—Adeena based the flavor profile on his favorite brand of Korean snacks and tweaked it until the honey butter syrup perfectly complemented her hand-roasted coffee. The honey came from Elena's uncle's apiary, and high-quality butter was something we always had in stock, so it was the perfect addition to our menu.

The Mexican mocha took our special Mexican hot chocolate blend and added a triple shot of espresso. If I wasn't awake before, I certainly was now. Bittersweet and perfectly spiced with a heat that lingered on your tongue just so . . . exactly what I needed.

Leslie arrived as Jae was helping me load the goods in my ancient SUV, and after giving them brief instructions to look after Longganisa, I hopped in my car and headed to the Thompson Family Company in the heart of Shady Palms. The building was huge, and I had to wait for security to wave me through before pulling into the lot designated for deliveries. I texted Beth and Valerie about my arrival before pulling a folding trolley from my trunk. Jae set it up while I grabbed the box of treats, containers of beverages, and the other assorted goods that came with the delivery. Together, we wheeled the delivery up the ramp and toward the elevator, following the instructions that Beth had just messaged me.

Considering it was the largest building in town and provided employment for a good percent of the Shady Palms population, I expected people to be rushing around, too busy and self-important to pay any mind to me and Jae. But the energy in the place was warm and inviting, and even though I could see that everyone was hard at work, it wasn't at the frantic, anxiety-filled pace that I was used to. Before I landed my internship back in college, I'd worked a part-time office job in Chicago to help pay tuition and it was one of the most miserable experiences of my life. Beth and Valerie obviously provided a very different working environment than my previous boss did.

We finally pulled up in front of the meeting room where they were hosting the brunch, and I knocked on the open door before wheeling the trolley inside.

Beth Thompson was deep in conversation with someone when we entered, so it was Valerie who greeted us. Leaning lightly on her mobility device, she crossed the room to shake our hands and direct us on where to lay out the goods.

"Thank you for being so accommodating, Lila. I know you usually like a bit more notice for a catering gig."

Ordinarily, I would turn down such a large catering order if it wasn't put in at least a week in advance, but Valerie was so frantic and the Thompsons were such good customers that I couldn't say no.

I told her as much, and added, "And don't feel too bad. You know how Elena is. She made sure to charge extra for the rush job."

The lines on Valerie's face smoothed out as she burst into laughter. "Oh, I like that girl. And Beth has your check, but she should be done soon." Valerie leaned forward, her voice pitched so only Jae and I could hear her. "She's talking to one of our board members who's rather dissatisfied with how Beth and I are running the place. He's been trying to stir up trouble lately, but luckily many on the board are pleased with our results. This brunch is an emergency effort to smooth things over while also rewarding those who've helped us the past few years."

I wasn't surprised that there were still people unhappy with the current administration—the previous head of the company was Valerie's younger brother, Rob, the golden boy of the town who was the absolute definition of "charisma." Unfortunately, he had a rather messy past that led to his untimely death a few years ago. After he passed, Valerie partnered with Beth, her now widowed sister-in-law, to head up the company.

Valerie had the brains to run the family enterprise, but she lacked the confidence and charisma necessary to get people to follow her. Beth had beauty, brains, and ambition and was happy to be the face of the company while Valerie provided the name and backing. For two people who cared little for each other while Rob was alive, they made a heck of team with him gone.

"Lila! Jae! Lovely to see you both."

Beth beelined toward us and greeted Jae with a kiss on the cheek and a quick hug for me. She looked stunning as usual, her tall, trim figure highlighted to full effect in an exquisitely tailored pale pink suit. The color popped against her dark brown skin, and I admired how her makeup and nail color coordinated with her outfit. Her hair was freshly pressed, and her accessories were simple but effective. As much as I loved fashion, I could never hope to reach Beth's level of perfection.

"Always good to see you, especially when Elena can squeeze you for all you're worth," I teased. "Jae and I were hoping to chat with you and Valerie for a bit, but I'm guessing now's not a good time?"

My eyes flicked toward the disgruntled board member she'd just been talking with, who was now eyeing us with open distrust.

"Unfortunately, it's not. But we can schedule you in after the brunch."

I glanced at my watch. "I should probably be getting back. I'll text you to—"

"Wait, Lila. You're supposed to stay and help serve, remember?" Valerie joined us as the brunch guests started filing into the room. "We need you to explain the various items and mix up the lattes. Didn't I mention that on the order form?"

I pulled up the form and showed her the note section where customers could write special requests. It was blank.

Valerie groaned and rumpled her hair as if she wanted to yank it out in frustration. "I put the order together all slapdash so I must've forgotten. Could you please stay until the brunch is over? We will of course compensate you appropriately."

"Let me call the cafe and see if they need me. Jae, could you finish setting up?"

I put in the call, and Elena picked up. "Valerie made a mistake on the order form and forgot to mention that she needs me to stay and serve during the event. Is that OK, or do you need me to come back?"

"You work the event and find out what information you can about the burglaries and the attack on Blake and Hana. Adeena, Leslie, and I will hold down the fort. Just let Beth and Valerie know that I'll be calling them later to work out the new price."

I laughed. "No mercy, huh?"

"Not when they push two outrageous orders in a row on us during one of our busiest times. Besides, they can afford it."

"Got it. I'll let you know when we're done."

I hung up and relayed what Elena said to Beth and Valerie. They both shuddered, and I knew they were up for some tough negotiations. I made my way over to Jae, who'd set out all the food, with the signs explaining what they were and what potential allergens they contained, and helped him lay out the drinks station. In addition to several boxes of Adeena's house blend and decaf coffees, there was also chai, plain black tea, and Elena's special herbal blend of mint, ginger, and cinnamon. The cafe's platinum drink package included all these beverages as well as various milk and milk alternatives plus sweeteners and flavored syrups.

For the first half hour or so, Jae and I explained the different offerings, mixed drinks, served pastries, and answered any questions the guests had. Once everyone was more comfortable, they were free to help themselves to whatever they wanted and Jae and I only stepped in when needed. We circulated the room to clean up, occasionally chatting with the guests and picking up various bits of information. Nobody seemed to be talking about anything related to the case, although we overheard this very telling conversation between two men who didn't seem to care that Jae and I were standing right next to them:

"Did you see the news this morning? Another burglary and this time a murder? What is this town coming to?"

"Another woman-owned business got hit? Maybe this'll finally put them all in their place."

"Shh! That's a terrible thing to say." The smaller man looked around nervously. "You never know who's listening."

The pompous man helped himself to a pastry on my tray, not bothering to look at or thank me. "I've got nothing to hide. Beth and Valerie have been so smug, but they'll soon see this can't last. Hell, I bet they've been fudging the numbers and lying about the top businesses in town—"

"Come now, you'll have to do better than that." The board member Beth had been talking to earlier sauntered over to the duo, interrupting the man's hateful remarks. "I'm still not entirely convinced about all the new plans they've implemented, but the Thompson women's business acumen far exceeds your own."

The pompous man spluttered and stomped off, and his companion apologized to the board member before hurrying off. "Sorry about that, Mr. Whitmore."

Mr. Whitmore, looking completely unbothered, helped himself to a longganisa roll from my tray.

"These are wonderful," he said before giving me a courteous nod and wandering off.

Neither of those men—or anyone else at the brunch—seemed to be involved with the burglaries or attacks, but at least there was one good thing about me being there: My pastries were a huge hit. They were so popular, I had to put in a call to Tita Rosie's Kitchen as well as to the Brew-ha Cafe to have Helen drop off chicken adobo empanadas—a collaboration between me and Tita Rosie—plus some sweet corn and cheese muffins and the tray of chocolate mochi muffins that I'd set aside for the cafe.

Once everything was gone and I'd shoved all the business cards

I had on me into the hands of the departing guests, Jae and I helped the Thompson Family Company staff who'd come in afterward to clean up. Beth and Valerie had both collapsed into chairs near the drinks station, with Beth nursing a giant mocha and Valerie alternating between sipping her herbal tea and sighing loudly.

"Are those sighs of satisfaction or exhaustion?" I asked as I tossed the last of the dirty cups into the trash.

"A little of both, honestly. But Elena's special herbal blend is working its magic. Give her and Adeena my thanks. I'll make sure to drop by the cafe later this week to sort out the extra charge for your services."

Beth set down her travel mug and reached for her purse. "That reminds me, here's the check for the actual catering order. That board member, Walter Whitmore, was still a total grump, but he was at least an agreeable grump by the end of brunch, so you more than earned this. Thanks again. Especially you, Jae. I'm assuming it's your day off. And also . . ."

Here Beth trailed off and looked away, seemingly at a loss for words. Something that rarely ever happened.

Jae guessed what she wanted to say. "You heard about Hana? And Blake?"

Beth nodded. "I'm so sorry. I know you and your cousin are close. And to lose Blake, too. It's all so awful."

"Do you know yet if it's connected to the recent burglaries?" Valerie asked. "As the heads of the chamber of commerce, Beth and I have been working with the police to try to narrow down suspects and potential targets, but it's going nowhere. Every place that's been hit is owned by a woman who's part of the local chamber of commerce, yet the SPPD can't seem to find any leads."

"Valerie and I feel a certain duty to protect our members, but we honestly have no idea what to do." Beth drummed her fingers on the tabletop. "It is frustrating and terrifying. We have no clue who's next. At the very least, we'd comforted ourselves saying that the burglar only struck when no one was around. And now this tragedy with Blake and Hana. What are we supposed to do?"

Jae's shoulders slumped. "I have no idea. The only solution we've been able to come up with is to do what we usually do when something like this happens."

"You're investigating?" Beth asked. "Is that what you wanted to talk about earlier, Lila?"

I nodded. "You know all the people who've been affected by the burglaries, and you and Valerie are the ones who deal with all the chamber's complaints as well. I thought you might be able to point us in the right direction. Maybe someone who stands to gain from these burglaries or has been particularly vocal. Or anything you can share about Blake or Hana."

"I would think the two of you know them better than we do," Valerie said. "For my part, we only ever talked business."

"Did they ever mention any issues they were having at their shop? Customers, other businesses, money . . . anything like that?"

"Now that you mention it, Blake asked about a man who worked at the Lancaster Hotel in Shelbyville." Beth pulled her planner out of her purse and paged through it. "Ah, here it is. She wanted to know how to deal with a man named Shawn Ford. He's currently Choco Noir's best customer, thanks to the hotel account; however, he's been behaving unprofessionally toward Hana, and Blake wanted to nip it in the bud. Hana didn't want to lose his business, so they consulted me to see if I could offer some sort of compromise."

She scanned the page briefly before looking up. "I always document instances of harassment in case evidence is needed later. The most recent complaint was exactly a week ago."

"Blake and Hana told us about him a couple days ago," I said. "He texted Hana while we were all hanging out, so that's an even more recent instance of harassment. This guy is definitely moving to the top of the list."

Jae's hands were resting on the table, and I noticed one clench into a fist when I mentioned the text. I put my hand on top of his and squeezed.

His hand convulsed before relaxing and intertwining his fingers with mine. "I know, I know. You don't have to say anything. I'll keep my cool around this guy."

"I don't know if it's a good idea for you or your brother to approach him just yet. I know his type, and he's more likely to let his guard down around women. Especially pretty women," Beth added.

"That's even more reason for me to—"

"Babe, you know she's right. Besides, what reason would you have to talk to a hotel liaison? You're a dentist. Adeena, Elena, and I can try to chat him up like we're hoping the hotel will carry our products or maybe hire us to cater their events."

Valerie put in her two cents. "They're right, Jae. Besides, Lila's idea works as a cover story and could also be good business for the Brew-ha Cafe. The Lancaster Hotel holds a lot of special events like bridal showers, afternoon teas, things like that. The guests who put on those kinds of events at the hotel all have money to burn. The Thompson Family Company has hosted several collaborations there, and I think it would benefit Lila to make those kinds of connections."

Jae sighed. "I get it, you don't have to keep trying to convince me. But I do think either me or my brother should be in the general area in case you need backup."

"Works for me. So our next move is to get in good with that hotel and talk to Shawn Ford. Is there anything else you can think of?"

Valerie looked thoughtful. "This isn't something they mentioned, but I'd heard rumblings about it even before Choco Noir opened. Do you know The Chocolate Shoppe in Shelbyville?"

"Yeah, they're the only artisanal chocolate place in the county. Or they were before Choco Noir opened. Are they salty now that they have competition?" I asked.

Valerie nodded. "That store has been around for three or four generations and is known as the go-to place for quality chocolate. They're popular with locals and tourists alike and used to be the main provider for the Lancaster Hotel's gift shop. From what I hear, the current owners aren't happy having people who aren't even from the area nosing in on their business."

Beth rolled her eyes. "If they can't handle a little competition, maybe their product isn't as good as they think it is. Choco Noir isn't even in the same town."

Valerie shrugged. "Just passing on what I heard. Could be nothing but malicious gossip."

"I appreciate it. At this early stage, any and all information is welcome. It gives us a place to start, at least. We'll make sure to add a visit to The Chocolate Shoppe to our itinerary when we go to Shelbyville to talk to Shawn Ford." I stood up, and Jae followed suit.

"We've taken up enough of your time, and Adeena is probably cursing my name, considering how long I've been out. I really need to be getting back to the cafe."

"Thanks for always going above and beyond what we ask you," Beth said. "Let Elena know we'll be in later this week. She doesn't have to hunt us down."

I grinned. "Will do."

Chapter Eight

As soon as Jae and I arrived at the Brew-ha Cafe, we got roped into helping. The place was jumping, and not only were Adeena, Elena, and Leslie scrambling behind the counter to fill orders, but my godmothers were also on the floor.

"Ninang Mae, what are you all doing here?" I asked, snagging her as she passed by me to drop a white chocolate chai blondie at a nearby table.

"We came here for meryenda, but it was so busy we couldn't let your partners handle everything alone. Elena promised us some freebies, so don't worry."

"Salamat po, ninangs!" I called out to her, Ninang April, and Ninang June as I rushed to the kitchen to wash my hands and bake more goodies to fill the near-empty shelves. I needed to be extra polite when thanking them for something as thoughtful as this. Jae followed me, washing his hands and pulling my premade cookie dough out of the fridge as directed.

We needed to restock a bunch of our ingredients, so other than the cookie and scone dough that I kept on hand in case of emergencies, I didn't know what else I could make.

"Hey, what's that?" Jae reached past me and pulled a tub of honey butter out of the fridge.

"When Adeena was coming up with your drink, I was also playing around with how I could incorporate it into one of my bakes," I said. "It's great on the scones and with the corn and cheese muffins, but I haven't been successful with any of my experiments yet."

Jae glanced around the kitchen before grabbing a box of puffed rice cereal, several bags of marshmallows, and a container of mini mochi that I'd ordered but not used yet. I planned on incorporating them in a new dessert for Yuki's restaurant but hadn't had time to play around with them.

"What about honey butter mochi Rice Krispies Treats? My mom likes to dip fresh ddeok in honey, so I know it'll go well with the mini mochi since they're basically the same thing. But do you think it'll be too sweet with the marshmallows?"

"If I brown the butter and add a good pinch of salt, that should balance everything out," I said, picturing the flavor combinations in my head. "Or maybe some shiro miso for extra umami? This should be fun! Can you make the version you came up with? I'll make mine as well, and we can do special taste tests for our customers."

We both got to work and soon had our creations cooling in their pans. Good thing Rice Krispies Treats were fast and easy to make. I cut thin slices for both of us.

"First one up is your version," I said, biting into my sliver. Jae's treats were delicious—his instincts were spot on in combining these flavors and textures, but he could've browned the honey butter just a touch more to really bring out that special nuttiness.

I told him so, and he agreed. "I also went too light on the salt. I think it needs a stronger contrast. Still good though."

We helped ourselves to samples from my pan, and Jae legit moaned as he took a bite. "THIS. This is exactly what I envisioned when I suggested this flavor combination. I don't think we need a taste test; you absolutely killed it."

I grinned. "Thanks. But knowing my customers, they'd still want to participate, if only for the free samples. Could you cut these up into small two-by-two squares and arrange them on two platters while I handle the other baked goods? Oh, and label them A and B so people can vote anonymously."

"You got it, boss."

"Ooh, I like that. Feel free to continue calling me that from now on."

He raised an eyebrow. "That's what you're into?"

I flushed at the implication. "Never mind. Get back to work!"

He laughed and we continued working in tandem, sometimes in the kitchen, sometimes helping out on the floor. At the end of the day, we'd completely sold out of all of our desserts and the results of the taste test were in.

"It was actually pretty close," Ninang June said. "I appreciated the depth and complexity of B, but a lot of people liked the simplicity of A. That one was more popular with the younger crowd."

"Makes sense," I said. "That flavor would be more familiar to people. Jae, I know you said you liked my version better, but I think yours is the one that needs to go on the menu. Is that OK with you? You'll get the credit, of course."

Jae said, "I'm just happy I could contribute in some way. And now with my special drink and these treats, I get to have ALL the honey butter things. All that's left is for you to make something crunchy but not as sweet as the Rice Krispies Treats, and I'll be in heaven."

Adeena grinned at him. "Remember when you used to get on our cases about eating too much sugar because it was bad for our teeth? Whatever happened to that Dr. Jae?"

"You've corrupted me with your sugary ways, and there's no going back. Plus, there's such a thing as moderation."

"Not that she knows the word when it comes to sugar," Elena said. "And the more cafe items that use honey, the more business that means for my tío's apiary, so thanks, Jae! And the recipe is simple enough that even Adeena can make it if we're running behind like today."

I ignored their banter because my mind was still stuck on what Jae said about creating something crunchy but not too sweet with the honey butter. We didn't do deep-frying at the Brew-ha Cafe, so that was out. I could maybe incorporate our honey butter into a biscotti, but that didn't really excite me. Unless . . .

"Biscocho!"

"Is that like a Filipino version of eureka? You look like you've had some kind of revelation," Adeena said.

"I mean, I did have a lightbulb moment, but biscocho isn't some exclamation. It's like a budget Filipino version of biscotti, using day-old pandesal. Jae gave me the idea of trying to make a honey butter version."

Jae's eyes were practically sparkling. "Crunchy honey butter snacks?"

I laughed. "If it turns out well, then yes, we'll be able to serve crunchy honey butter snacks. I just need to talk to Tita Rosie about supplying us with old pandesal."

"If you need taste testers, I volunteer as tribute," Jae said.

"Ooh, me, too!"

My godmothers and Elena all echoed Adeena's enthusiastic addition.

"I'll stop by Tita Rosie's once I'm done cleaning up here. If she has any pandesal left over, I can get started on the recipe tomorrow morning and share it at breakfast."

Ninang June said, "Should we wait to reveal what we learned until breakfast then?"

"Unless it's something we need to act on immediately and you won't forget, might as well wait," I said. "It's better to do it when we're all together. The restaurant is reserved for a party later tonight, so we can't do our usual dinner."

Ninang April held up a small notebook. "Don't worry, I took notes to make sure we had our information straight. It'll keep until tomorrow."

I'd planned on giving my godmothers the leftover baked goods as a gift, but we were cleaned out. "Will you be at the laundromat tomorrow? I'll make a special delivery of whatever sweet you want as thanks."

"The peach mango crumble cookies!" Ninang April immediately ordered. "And we all have paperwork and cleaning to do, so we should be at the laundromat until three."

"Bring those honey butter mochi Rice Krispies Treats as well," Ninang June said. "The ones with the white miso."

Ninang April said, "They really were excellent. Maybe you can serve Jae's version at the cafe, and your version at Sushi-ya. The miso and mochi make it kind of like Japanese fusion, diba?"

Ninang Mae said, "If everyone's putting in requests, I also want something with chocolate. Feel free to surprise me."

The peach mango crumble cookies were the Park brothers' favorite, so I'd planned on making them anyway to keep their spirits up. And the honey butter mochi Rice Krispies Treats were a snap and likely to go on constant rotation, so that wasn't a problem. Ninang April's suggestion to pitch the miso version to Yuki as an addition to Sushi-ya's dessert menu was also inspired. But Ninang Mae's request made me pause. I'd already come up with a bunch of chocolate desserts due to next month's collaboration for the Valentine's Day event. I could easily make one of the chocolate desserts I'd served in the past. But the honey butter success had unlocked a well of creativity, and I was hit by the desire to experiment with something new. A mental review of the cafe's inventory reminded me that I needed to stock up on pretty much everything, and as I wrote out my list, Leslie popped into the kitchen to say they'd cleaned the front but didn't have time to walk Longganisa. That clinched it—I knew exactly where I needed to go.

I turned to Adeena and Elena. "Wanna go shopping?"

The Olive Oil Emporium in Shelbyville was run by Gladys Stokes, an older Black woman who looked like she could've been anywhere between the ages of fifty and seventy and owned one of the longest-running businesses in town. She was the perfect stop on my supplies shopping trip because 1) her artisanal olive oils, vinegars, preserves, and other fantastic items were used in plenty of Brew-ha Cafe offerings (she even sourced special peach-mango preserves for me that made my crumble cookies extra easy to pull together), 2) as a long-time Shelbyville entrepreneur, she knew many people in town and might have the scoop on Shawn Ford and The Chocolate Shoppe owners (a big reach, but worth a shot), and 3) she had a senior dachshund named Cleopatra Louise, who had become Longganisa's close friend, and the two were due for a playdate.

I had already filled my basket with every jar of peach-mango preserves in the shop when I heard Gladys's joyful voice call out, "Hello, my dears! So lovely to see you all again."

Gladys strode across the store, a baby blanket–wrapped Cleo in her arms. Seeing her old friend, Longganisa wriggled in her carrier strapped across my chest.

"Hey Gladys! Great to see you, too. Do you mind stepping outside for a minute? I want to set Longganisa down so she can say hi properly."

I left Adeena and Elena with my basket and followed the older woman out of the shop. Once outside, I unclipped Longganisa and lowered her to the freshly shoveled ground. She zipped over to Cleo, and the two sniffed and circled each other enthusiastically.

Gladys smiled down at the dogs before turning her attention to me. "Not that it's not a pleasure to see you, but are you here on a shopping trip or a fact-finding mission?"

Damn, she was good. I couldn't help but laugh.

"Both? We need to replenish our stock, and yours is just one of the stores we need to hit up. But I did want to ask you about something."

"Does it have to do with the latest robbery in your town? I heard one of the victims is related to your boyfriend. And the other one is . . ."

The warmth and empathy in her voice and gaze, while welcome and appreciated, were too much for me to deal with at the moment, so I ducked down to pet Cleo and hide the sudden moisture that threatened to spill from my eyes. "Jae's cousin, Hana, is in a coma. Her friend and business partner, Blake, died in the attack. We're not sure if it's connected to the burglaries that've been going around Shady Palms, or if Blake and Hana were specifically targeted."

"I'm so sorry to hear that. I'll keep all of you in my thoughts." Gladys touched a hand to her chest and ducked her head down for a moment before continuing the conversation. "Neither of those girls were from around here, were they?"

I shook my head. "They were both from Minnesota. But I want to chase down every lead possible. I heard something about a guy named Shawn Ford who works at the Lancaster Hotel. And also about the current owners of The Chocolate Shoppe."

"And you thought you'd check in with me because I know everybody?" Gladys raised an eyebrow. "Well, you're right, I do. That Ford guy is sleaze personified. I'm acquainted with several people at the Lancaster Hotel since they stock my products in the gift shop, and I've heard quite a few stories."

"Like what?"

"Probably best that you get it straight from the source. Tell you what, when you get a chance, go to the Lancaster Hotel and ask for Zoey Hong. Say that I sent you. She's one of the buyers for the hotel, along with Shawn Ford, so you can pitch your goods and get the dirt at the same time."

I made a note of that. "What about the people at The Chocolate Shoppe?"

"The Carters and I go way back. We were among the earliest Black business owners in Shelbyville, so we stuck together, supported each other. The shop's previous owners, and the ones before them, were wonderful people. Very invested in the community and giving back. But the current generation is a bit of a mixed bag, a brother-sister team that lacks the vision and charisma of their parents. Anita and Vince are good kids. They're kind to me since our families are close. But I've heard grumbling from their employees about all the changes they're making." Gladys pursed her lips. "Have you ever been to The Chocolate Shoppe?"

"Adeena and I used to go all the time in high school. It had a super-cute, old-timey vibe. Like something from the fifties. What were they called? Soda fountains?"

She nodded. "Exactly. In addition to the premium chocolates made on the premises, they also have a counter where you can order old-fashioned sodas, sundaes, milkshakes, things like that. A real blast from the past. But the current owners think the shop is a little *too* stuck in the past. They're trying to modernize the store and turn it into a chain."

"And this is causing problems?"

"A lot of people think doing so will ruin the charm of the original store. But Anita says that the shop has only gotten away with staying the same because there was no other competition. With Choco Noir opening, they can't afford to stay stagnant."

I started to ask another question, when I noticed Gladys was shivering. She'd grabbed her coat before stepping outside, but it was still January in the Midwest, after all.

"Let's go inside before we both freeze. The puppies have had plenty of time to socialize," I said.

I bent over to wrap Cleo in her blanket again before handing her over to Gladys, then scooped up Longganisa and stuck her back in her carrier. We returned to the warmth of the store, where Adeena and Elena were bickering over peach versus apricot preserves.

"I'm going to have to side with Elena here," Gladys said. "The slight tartness of an apricot is the perfect balance for all the sugar necessary to make jam and preserves. Peaches should either be eaten fresh or baked using my peach cobbler recipe. That's it."

I made a note to visit Gladys in the summer during peak peach season before turning to my partners. "Were you able to get everything on the list?"

"Everything except for that fancy vanilla paste you usually get from here," Adeena said.

Gladys apologized. "It's one of our most popular items and we just ran out. I should have more in stock soon."

"I can get it from the baking supply store back home, so not a problem. We should get going though if we want to get there before they close."

We paid for our items and said goodbye to Gladys and Cleo.

"Oh, and if you can increase your inventory of those peach-mango preserves, I'd like to make that part of our monthly order. I know they only do small batches, but I'd love to make the peach mango crumble cookies part of our regular menu since people love them so much."

"I'll see what I can do, honey. You all take care now. And feel free to stop in anytime. You know I'm here to help."

She gave us a knowing smile before waving us off cheerfully.

The three of us waddled up the street to my car, loaded down with the heavy bottles and jars from our usual overeager shopping trip.

"You should've had Jae come with us. Put those muscles to good use," Adeena groaned as she hefted her bags into my trunk.

"He actually offered, but I knew he wanted to visit the hospital with Aria. She hasn't seen her mom yet."

Jae had told me earlier that he and his brother tried to explain to Aria as best as they could that her mommy got hurt and was in the hospital. She was old enough to understand that much but struggled with the concept of her mom not being able to wake up for a while. Mama and Papa Park thought she was too young and that seeing her mom in a coma would scar her, but she insisted on seeing her mom and giving her a kiss.

"She thinks it might be like *Sleeping Beauty* and a kiss will help her wake up." Jae choked up as he told me this when we sat in my car before separating earlier. "What could we say to her? 'Sorry, kid, it doesn't work like that.' We couldn't do it. So I'm going to take her to the hospital for a little bit. And maybe go out for ice cream after."

"I think ice cream sounds like an excellent idea." I held his hand and stroked his arm, offering what little comfort I could. "You're a good uncle, Jae."

He looked at me with sad eyes. "I just wish I could do more."

Didn't we all?

I relayed this conversation to Adeena and Elena, who I knew shared the same sadness and frustration that Jae and I did.

Adeena slung her arm around my shoulders. "We'll catch the people who did this. And when Hana wakes up, we'll throw a big party for her and Aria, and it'll be the greatest party Shady Palms has ever seen. But for now, we take this one step at a time. OK?"

Elena slid her arm around my waist on the other side. "We got this, chica."

I took a deep breath and nodded. They were right.

They had to be.

Chapter Nine

That's everything we learned yesterday. Our next steps are to talk to Shawn Ford and Zoey Hong at the Lancaster Hotel and also visit The Chocolate Shoppe to get an idea of how their business is doing. See if they thought of Choco Noir as a problem or not."

As usual, I gave my report first during the breakfast meeting at Tita Rosie's Kitchen. Everyone helped themselves to grilled fish, fried eggs, scrambled tofu, rice, and tomato salad, with bowls of champurado available for the sweet tooths (aka Adeena). I was glad to see my aunt was serving lighter fare for breakfast this morning—I'd worried that her desire to create comfort food for Detective Park would overshadow her earlier efforts to get him on a more balanced diet. Not that I didn't still love my silog platters, but eating them almost every day did rather unpleasant things to one's stomach. Plus, I always wanted a nap afterward, which made having to switch to work mode immediately after rather difficult.

I'd asked my aunt about her breakfast choices while helping her set the table earlier, and she had said, "When I was helping Jonathan's mom create new, healthy recipes for their dad, I realized that it was another way to show care through food. Before, I would just cook everyone's favorite dishes to make them happy, but the food was always something indulgent. I don't believe there's such a thing as 'bad' food, but I do know certain things should be served in moderation. Indulgence isn't the only way to show you care." Tita Rosie set down the bowl of tomato salad. "Cutting up fruit for someone is love. Brainstorming dishes to get someone like Jonathan, who hates vegetables, to start eating and enjoying them is love. Taking the time to create a balanced meal full of nutrition is love. Keeping the people I care about healthy for as long as possible is important to me."

Considering my job consisted of me making (and tasting) sugary desserts and baked goods, I counted on my aunt to make sure I met all of my other nutritional requirements. Tita Rosie and Elena were the only people in my life who ensured I stayed hydrated (apparently drinking only iced coffee didn't count) and ate something green every day. If Adeena and I were left to our own devices, we'd just stuff ourselves with carbs. And Jae and Detective Park were the type of guys to ignore the lettuce and side dishes at Korean barbecue and focus only on the meat and rice. We all desperately needed those two women to make sure we ate like responsible adults.

"Thanks, Tita Rosie. I don't know what we'd do without you."

She laughed. "It's nice to feel needed. But you know, I'm not going to be around forever. And you're almost thirty years old, diba? Maybe it's time for me to teach you my recipes . . ."

Ignoring the fear that clutched at my heart at the thought of Tita Rosie not being around anymore, I smiled and agreed. "I'd like that. But you know, you'll have to start measuring things so I can at least get a basic idea for amounts when I take notes during our cooking sessions."

"Measuring . . ." Tita Rosie said it slowly and uncomfortably, as if it was a foreign word to her. "We'll see, anak."

Shortly after this conversation, everyone arrived and served themselves before I gave my report.

"What about you all? Anything interesting?"

"I talked to the police, as well as Ben at Safe & Secure Solutions. Both of them say there was no sign of a break-in and that the security system wasn't activated at the time of the crime." Detective Park looked down at his notepad and frowned. "There are several possibilities here. Blake and Hana could've still been inside when the assailant showed up, so they hadn't turned on the security system yet. They could've forgotten to set the alarm before leaving and returned to the store only to interrupt a burglary in progress. They also could've known their attacker and let them in. Unfortunately, Blake and Hana hadn't gotten around to installing a security camera yet, although Ben said it was on their list of upgrades. This is all supposition."

Adeena shuddered. "That's a scary thought. Like, they could've thought it was a customer or someone they were friendly with so they opened the door for them?"

Detective Park looked grim. "A sad but not uncommon circumstance. There are myriad possibilities for why the security system wasn't activated and how the assailant or assailants got in, but those are the most likely ones. I'm going to talk to Ben and the other workers at his security firm to learn how their system works and how easy it would be for someone to bypass it. That should give me a better idea of how they got in since we don't have security camera footage. Choco Noir isn't in a plaza like many other Shady Palms businesses, which means there aren't any security cameras from surrounding buildings. There aren't any stoplights nearby for the police to check out either, so there's limited information to work with."

Ronnie and Izzy had nothing to report.

"The next chamber of commerce meeting isn't until next week," Ronnie said. "I think the Thompson Family board member who has issues with Beth and Valerie's leadership is also on the board of directors for the chamber. I'll have to look it up to be sure, though."

"Oh, unless there's more than one board member who's got beef with Beth and Valerie, I don't think he's our guy." I explained the ugly interaction I witnessed at the Thompson Family Company brunch. "It wouldn't hurt to talk to him, but I don't think you should spend too much time on him either."

Ronnie saluted me. "Got it. Anyway, Izzy and I will make sure to report back after the meeting."

"That means we're up," Ninang Mae said cheerfully. "We learned that there are currently two factions in the county: Team Choco Noir and Team Chocolate Shoppe. Team Chocolate Shoppe is mostly the older crowd, people who complain that Choco Noir is too 'fancy' and a waste of money. Team Choco Noir is the younger and trendier crowd, as well as the ones who are a little more well-to-do."

"There are plenty of people who like both, of course, since they cater to different crowds and occasions," Ninang June added. "But from what we heard, Blake and Hana kept their heads down and focused on their work. They didn't participate in any mudslinging or encourage it from their customers."

Ninang April said, "However, The Chocolate Shoppe wasn't above snide remarks. Their social media is full of posts that are careful not to name any particular store, but it's obvious who they're referring to."

Adeena, Elena, and I all grabbed our phones and each navigated to a different social media page for The Chocolate Shoppe.

Every profile had numerous posts with content boasting variations of the same message: Come to The Chocolate Shoppe if you appreciate great chocolate for a great price! Unlike other stores, we respect tradition AND your wallet!

There were pictures of families sitting around The Chocolate Shoppe and other images that evoked old-fashioned nostalgia, while other posts had photos of fancy truffles with a big red *X* over the pic, with captions like, "Tired of overpriced chocolate with ingredients you can't even pronounce? Then stop by The Chocolate Shoppe, where you can enjoy great American products made the way they've always been: by a real American family."

Gross. It was obvious the kind of consumer they were targeting with images and messages like that, and, based on the number of likes and comments, it seemed like it was working. Still, it's not like they were trashing Choco Noir by name. The posts just seemed like the result of a marketing person who knew their audience and was targeting them aggressively.

But then I saw the comments.

> **shel_bee123:** that's right! Best chocolate ever!!!
>
> **mellymel:** lol why not call out @ChocoNoir by name you cowards
>
> **aim567:** way to snitch tag
>
> **mellymel:** @aim567 oh so you agree that they're trashtalking Choco Noir?
>
> **dvx_ygn:** @mellymel their not even from here
>
> **mellymel:** @dvx_ygn and???

From there, the comment section quickly turned inflammatory (and oddly racist, which was disappointing but not surprising since, you know, social media).

Adeena whistled when I showed her. "That got real ugly, real fast. I wonder who's in charge of their social media."

"Are there similar comments on Choco Noir's social media?" Jae asked. "If so, that would be proof of bad blood between the two stores."

"We can comb through their social media later," I said. "It could take a while, and we still need to finish breakfast and start our days."

"We'll handle it," Ninang June said. "There's a lot of downtime at the laundromat, so it shouldn't be a problem. You just focus on your Shelbyville trips."

I said, "Works for me. Oh, that reminds me. Gladys mentioned that the new owners of The Chocolate Shoppe want to modernize the store, and some people aren't happy about it. Do you know anything about that?"

Ninang Mae laughed. "If you have time to dig farther in the comments, you'll see some people calling The Chocolate Shoppe hypocrites for posting content about how tradition is so important yet they plan on changing everything."

I tried to find the comments she mentioned, but all I saw were people singing The Chocolate Shoppe's praises. "Hmm, I wonder if they deleted it."

"I wouldn't be surprised if they deleted and blocked anyone who left negative comments," Ninang April said. "We'll make sure to screenshot anything we find, just in case."

As breakfast was wrapping up and some of us packed to-go boxes, Tita Rosie ventured a question. "How is Hana doing? Any changes in her condition?"

The Park brothers' expressions went dark.

"Some changes, but still no sign of her regaining consciousness, according to the doctors," Detective Park said. "We have an officer stationed outside her room at all times, but they said no one has stopped by other than hospital personnel and family, so it's been quiet on that front."

Jae said, "I took Aria to visit her last night. She's no longer on the breathing tube, so I'd consider that progress. And I'm grateful that Aria didn't have to see her mom like that. Hana looked like she was sleeping, so hopefully it wasn't too traumatizing for her."

"Are people other than family allowed to visit?" Tita Rosie asked. "I'm not sure if it'll make a difference for Hana, but I could always stop by for a few minutes after work to keep her company."

"You ARE family, and I'll make sure you're on the list of approved visitors," Detective Park said. "I'll put all of you on the list, but don't feel any pressure to visit. I don't know if Hana can sense whether anyone is around or not anyway. If you do want to see her, I suggest no big group visits. We don't want to be disruptive to the other patients."

"The ICU limits visitors to two at a time," Ninang June reminded everyone. "And like Detective Park said, I urge you to be mindful of the other patients in the area. No loud discussions or confrontations or anything like that."

"We know how to act in a hospital, Ninang June. You make it sound like we're going to fistfight anyone who walks by," I said.

"Didn't you get into an argument with Janet Spinelli in the hospital? An argument so loud that the offices surrounding her knew what your business was?" Ninang Mae said.

I flushed. "First of all, that was like two years ago! And we were in the office section, not the area where the patients stay."

"I heard that she might get out early next year," Lola Flor interrupted. "Have you talked to Terrence recently?"

Terrence Howell was one of my oldest friends and Janet's former fiancé. She was the one to end their engagement after being sent to prison, something I knew he was both sad and relieved about.

"It's been a while, actually. He's been doing a lot of travel since his business is doing so well. I know Xander's been making good use of his skills."

Terrence owned his own graphic design firm and was employed by the Brew-ha Cafe, Tita Rosie's Kitchen, the Shady Palms Winery, and a million other businesses in Shady Palms. Our friend Xander Cruz owned a huge hospitality conglomerate in Chicago, where Terrence had been spending the last few months.

Adeena said, "He probably doesn't know about Hana and Blake yet. You should give him a call, Lila. They were his most recent clients, and better that he hear about it from a friend than the *Shady Palms News* or something god-awful like that."

I was not looking forward to that phone call, both because nobody wanted to be the bearer of bad news and also because talking on the phone was the worst. But she was right; he deserved to hear it from me.

"I'll call him tonight. Considering how busy the cafe was yesterday, I want to focus on work during the day and leave investigating until after closing time or during our slow periods."

"Sorry about that. I still have the rest of the week off, so I can help out if you need me again." Jae looked at his brother. "Or I can go with you if you need backup for your part of the investigation."

Detective Park flipped through his notebook again before answering Jae. "I don't think that's necessary for today, but I may take you up on that later this week. Maybe help Lila, Adeena, and Elena out—see if any of the cafe customers will open up to you about anything they've heard."

"Ooh, that's right. If Jae's gonna be hanging out at the cafe, we should utilize his superpower!" Adeena said.

Jae's superpower, as Adeena put it, was both awkward and supremely useful—people loved talking to him, often sharing intensely personal information when chatting with him. I didn't know if he just had the kind of face or vibe that made people think he'd be a good listener, but more than once I've heard random strangers spill their guts to him as if he was a priest and they were confessing their sins. This latent ability had helped more than once in past investigations.

Lola Flor glanced at the clock on the wall. "Hoy, weren't you all leaving? You're going to be late for work."

"Oh shoot, you're right! Thanks for the food, Tita Rosie and Lola Flor!"

We all scattered to our places of work, and the day passed by quickly. It's a good thing Jae volunteered to help today because we were absolutely swamped again. I wondered what was going on since January wasn't a particularly busy month in the past, but I decided not to look a gift horse in the mouth. If business kept up like this, we might be able to afford to hire another part-time worker or two to take the pressure off me, Adeena, and Elena. It would give Leslie more responsibility too, since they could be in charge of the training. Something to discuss with my partners later.

Once the madness of the day was over, and the cafe was clean and put in order, I figured we all deserved a treat. "What do you say we all go out to dinner at Stan's Diner? We can put it on the company card as an employee dinner. You all definitely earned it."

Adeena and Elena agreed right away, but Leslie drooped. "Ugh, I wish I could, but I've got a family thing tonight."

"No worries, you'll come with us next time. Maybe we can start doing a monthly dinner, as team-building and appreciation," I said, thinking out loud. "Based on how busy we've been, I think we should hire a couple of part-timers soon. You could handle the bulk of their training since you've worked in each area and you've been asking for your own project to focus on."

Adeena handled drinks and most of our ordering; Elena took care of the corner where she sold the plants and herbal products she made with her mother as well as negotiating with suppliers; and I was in charge of desserts and most admin duties. We all had our own thing to focus on, but Leslie was forced to be a jack-of-all-trades, filling in wherever we needed them. As the youngest member of our team, they were also in charge of our social media, but in a town as small as Shady Palms, it's not like they needed to spend more than a few minutes a day on it. It would be a good experience for them to be responsible for an area of their own that would require a real investment of their energy and expertise.

Leslie lit up. "That would be great! Let me know once you've written up the job posting, and I'll make sure to share it on our socials and around town."

Leslie left with a new spring in their step, and Jae started to follow them out. "I should head out too, let you ladies enjoy your dinner."

"You're coming too, silly," Adeena said, linking her arm through his.

"I thought it was just for the cafe workers?"

Elena linked her arm on his other side. "And what did you spend all day doing? Let's get out of here, I'm starving."

My best friends marched him out the front door, and he looked back at me questioningly.

I grinned at him. "You heard them. Let's get out of here! Martha's chocolate chess pie is calling me."

"Oh, this might've been a mistake. The human body wasn't made to consume this much fat, sugar, and dairy," I said, leaning back in my booth seat.

Thank goodness I was wearing pants with an elastic waistband, because on top of my Mediterranean meatball meal (A+, Stan absolutely knows his way around some ground lamb), Adeena talked us into ordering every dessert on the menu. And when I say "every dessert," you have to understand that Stan's Diner was not a place that offered only two or three options a day. Stan's Diner was famous for its hearty and cheap meals, prepared by Stan Kosta, and the dessert case that displayed no less than ten desserts every day as well as a daily special, all handmade by his wife, Martha.

Between the four of us, we split twelve (count 'em, TWELVE) different desserts: chocolate chess pie, hummingbird cake, cherry pie, plain cheesecake, carrot cake, key lime pie, coconut cream pie, vanilla cake with sprinkles, baklava, citrus pound cake, banoffee pie, and the day's special: mocha fudge brownie cheesecake. That last dessert was as delicious and decadent and rich as it sounded, and it would be the death of me and my lactose-intolerant stomach.

As we sat around groaning, Stan and Martha Kosta joined us at our booth.

"Looks like we're gonna have to break out the wheelbarrow, Martha. Don't look like these kids will be able to stumble out of here on their own," Stan said with a chuckle.

Martha beamed at us. "Clean plates! I can't believe you not only ordered all the desserts, but ate up every crumb as well. I'm so proud of you."

"Never back down, never surrender," Adeena said. "That's our motto. At least when it comes to sweets. Jae and Lila tried to wave the white flag halfway through, but we wouldn't let them."

"You won't be feeling so proud when one of them hurls and we gotta clean up after 'em," Stan said.

"You're looking a bit green, Lila. Maybe these mints will help," Martha said, placing the hard candy on the table.

My dining companions and I all feebly unwrapped the mints

and placed them on our tongues, the flavor of peppermint soothing our poor tummies.

"Thanks, Martha. How've you been, by the way? I don't think I've seen you since before the winter holidays."

"Oh, the usual. Nothing to write home about, but nothing to complain about either. How about you all? I heard another tragedy struck close to home." She turned her sympathetic gaze to Jae, who sighed.

"You heard correctly. Honestly, my family isn't doing too great right now, so I'm trying to keep busy and do my part."

"You all still busy doing the SPPD's job?" Stan said as he gestured for a server to refill our water glasses.

I forced myself to take a sip of water. "Not because we want to. I'm sure you both know about the burglaries that've been going on lately?"

Stan nodded. "And that they're no closer to catching the culprit than I am to recovering the hairline I had in my twenties. So it's true? This incident is connected to the burglaries?"

"We're not sure yet." Jae fiddled with his napkin. "There's still so much we don't know, and the police have so few leads."

Martha sighed. "What is this town coming to? Well, you know we'll do what we can to help. Pass along anything interesting we hear."

"And if you want to talk to someone who was affected by the burglaries, let us know. My great-niece was one of the victims. She runs a photo studio in town."

"We heard about that!" Adeena exclaimed. "I'm glad she's OK. And I heard insurance is covering everything."

Stan crossed himself. "Thankfully. Anyway, I know she's frustrated by the lack of movement on the case, so I'm sure she'll be happy to talk to you."

"Do you have her business card?" Elena asked. "We should set up a proper time to talk. She's probably still dealing with the aftermath of the burglary, and I wouldn't want us to drop in unannounced."

Stan dug into his pocket and pulled out a beat-up leather wallet. "What do you know, I actually do. Here you go."

Elena accepted the card. "Diane Kosta. I'll make sure to give her a call."

"We appreciate this," I said.

Stan waved his hands. "Don't worry about it. You're good customers and good kids. Besides, ever since you convinced us to start serving your coffee, business has been better than ever."

"It's only right that we help each other," Martha added. "Anyway, let me clear these plates out of your way."

After Stan and Martha had cleared the table, I used the cafe credit card to pay for everyone's meals.

"I don't know about you, but I'm ready to call it an early night," I said as we made our way out to the parking lot. "I'm exhausted, and I still need to call Terrence."

Adeena stretched and let out the most dramatic yawn ever. "Agreed. I'll see you tomorrow at breakfast. Thanks again for your help, Jae."

She and Elena said their good nights and headed to Elena's car while Jae walked me to mine. Instead of riding together, we'd driven separately to Stan's Diner. As much as I loved spending time together, I was glad I wouldn't have to drop him back at his car. I was ready for a hot bath and some snuggles with Longganisa.

"I'm supposed to help my mom with stuff around the house tomorrow, so I might not be at breakfast. If the cafe is slammed, feel free to call me though."

"I will."

With a quick good night kiss, we got into our cars and headed our separate ways. An hour later, I was freshly bathed, skincare routine done, and in my jammies with Longganisa.

"Better get this over with," I said, tapping Terrence's name in my contacts list.

He picked up right away. "Lila? What's wrong?"

I laughed. "I'd ask how you knew something was up, but considering I'm calling, not texting, and this late at night, I guess it was obvious."

I took a deep breath, the brief moment of amusement draining away as I worked up the nerve to deliver the bad news. "I'm just going to get right to it. There was an attack at Choco Noir. Blake died, and Hana is in a coma. I thought you should know since you've been working with them recently."

Silence greeted my words. I knew he'd heard me and was just processing everything, so I stayed quiet until he'd gathered his thoughts.

"That is absolutely awful. I'm so sorry. Are there any leads? How's Jae taking it?"

I sighed. "Several leads, but nothing super concrete. And Jae is . . . keeping busy. Throwing himself into the investigation to make himself feel useful, or maybe to help get his mind off everything. I'm worried about him, but so far staying busy seems to be helping."

We both were quiet for a moment.

"I'll be back in town next week," he finally said. "Let's grab dinner at Big Bishop's BBQ when I return, OK? We've got a lot to catch up on."

"Sounds good. Tell Xander I said hi."

"Will do. Good night, Lila."

I hung up and connected my phone to its charger before snuggling up next to my dog.

"Good night, Longganisa. We've got another long day tomorrow."

Chapter Ten

As Jae mentioned the night before, he wasn't at breakfast the next day. In fact, I didn't see or hear from him until well after lunchtime. I was in the middle of refilling the pastry cases for the afternoon rush when the chiming of the bells above the door had me straighten up to greet our new customers.

"Jae! There you are!" A tiny person peeked out warily from behind his tall form, and I couldn't help but smile. "And you must be Aria."

She looked up at Jae, who smiled down at her before nodding.

"My name is Lila. It's nice to finally meet you, Aria."

Back when Hana first came to Shady Palms to help Blake set up Choco Noir, she left her daughter behind with her parents so that Aria could spend the holidays with her grandparents. Aria didn't move to Shady Palms until after the New Year, so even though I'd gotten to know her mother quite well, this was our first time meeting.

She still clung to Jae's back, so he stooped down and picked her up. "Lila is my girlfriend, Aria. You've heard me talk about her."

Her eyes lit up. "Oh! You're Lila! Nice to meet you, too."

"My dad has a bunch of appointments today, and my mom is with him," Jae explained. "So I promised Aria I'd show her a good time today, isn't that right?"

Aria nodded solemnly. "Uncle Jae promised we'd have lots of yummy food today. Lunch was good, and now it's time for dessert. And he's supposed to take me to the park."

"I took her to your aunt's restaurant. It was her first time trying Filipino food."

"I like rice! And soup. I really liked the soup."

"She had nilaga, based on your aunt's suggestion. Your aunt was even kind enough to take all the meat off the bone to make it easier for Aria to eat."

Nilaga was a simple but delicious soup that consisted of beef bones (usually beef shank), potatoes, carrots, corn, and greens cooked in a light, savory broth. The mild flavors made it very kid-friendly, although handling the bones could be a bit difficult for a young child. It was just like Tita Rosie to take that into account when serving them.

"I love soup, too," Adeena said, peering at us over the counter. "My name's Adeena. Nice to meet you. Would you like something to drink?"

Aria waved at her. "Hi. Could I have a hot chocolate, please?"

"One kiddie hot chocolate coming up. How about you, Jae? The usual?"

"You know it. Aria, what do you want for dessert? You can choose one thing from the case."

She pouted. "Just one?"

"Just one. You know you can't have too much sugar."

Aria took her dessert selection very seriously, veering back and forth among the sweets behind the glass. "I want chocolate! No, wait, that one looks bigger. But that one is purple!"

This went on and on until I suggested, "How about you choose two desserts, but you share them? Two halves make one dessert, right, Uncle Jae?"

"Sure, that makes sense. Which ones should we share, Aria?"

"I want that and that!" she said, pointing to the white chocolate macadamia ube cookie and the red bean brownie.

"Excellent choices," I said, making my way behind the counter to grab her treats. "She doesn't have any allergies, right?"

"No, but thanks for asking. Sometimes I forget that's something I need to worry about."

Adeena handed me their drinks, and I put them on a tray along with the plate bearing their desserts. "Here you go!"

"Thanks, Lila. I'm sure you're busy, so we'll seat ourselves."

I watched Jae lead his niece to an empty table in the dog-friendly section of the cafe and made a note to ask if I could introduce her to Longganisa later. I went back to the kitchen for the last of my bakes, and as I made my way back to the counter, I overheard a few members of the PTA Squad whispering together.

"Who's that kid with Dr. Jae?"

"Oh my stars, do you think she's his child?"

"They do look alike, don't they?"

"I mean, we don't know what he was up to before he moved to Shady Palms . . ."

Mary Ann Randall, leader of the PTA Squad, rolled her eyes

and (without bothering to lower her voice) said, "Honestly, am I the only one here with common sense? Do none of you follow the news? His cousin was attacked and is now in the hospital. That must be her daughter."

"That poor girl, she's so young."

"Did I tell you all about what happened last week at Choco Noir?"

"You said something about a lover's quarrel, but that's it."

"Between the two women?"

"No, with some man. I was at Choco Noir when a guy walked in and the owner started fighting with him. Turns out it was her ex-husband and he'd tracked her down!"

The other three women gasped.

"Do you think he did it?"

"I wouldn't be surprised if he did."

I'd tried to listen inconspicuously for as long as possible, but with something that alarming, I couldn't stay silent any longer. "Excuse me."

The four members of the PTA Squad all jumped.

"Lila! Don't you scare me like that," one of them chided me.

"Sorry, I didn't mean to. I just couldn't help overhearing. You said Blake's ex-husband showed up at the shop recently? Do you remember when? And what he looked like?"

"I don't want to be talking out of turn," she said, looking at the other women at the table nervously.

Mary Ann, who used to be one of my nemeses but had been downgraded to an occasional annoyance, snorted. "Now you worry about that? Go on, tell her what you know. This might be helpful."

The woman still seemed nervous, but since the leader of the

PTA Squad told her to speak, she followed orders. "I was at Choco Noir, looking to buy a present for my mother-in-law's birthday. She'd received their sampler box of chocolates for Christmas and absolutely loved it, so I figured it was a safe choice for a present. I had no idea how many options the store would have though! I must've been there for almost an hour, but the owner was so sweet, answering all of my questions, offering me samples when I couldn't choose which flavors to include in the gift box. I—"

"Could you skip to when that guy showed up? Lila's still on the clock, you know," Mary Ann said.

The woman flushed. "Sorry. I just mentioned all that because I wanted to show you how kind that woman was. Blake, you said? She spent so much time helping me because she could see how stressed I was about the present. Anyway, she was wrapping up the box all pretty for me when this guy walks in. And then she—"

"I'm sorry, but could you describe him? In case I see him around town, it would be good to have a general description," I said.

"Oh, right. Let's see . . . I want to say medium height, sandy brown hair. Maybe brown eyes? He was handsome enough, I guess, but he mostly seemed like an average middle-aged white man."

I made a note of that on my phone. "Sorry to keep interrupting you. So what happened when he walked into the shop?"

"Blake froze. We were discussing the Valentine's Day event she was planning when she just stopped mid-sentence and stared over my shoulder. When I turned around, that guy was there. He was smiling, but she wasn't." She shivered. "And then he said, 'I finally found you.'"

"'I finally found you'?" I repeated. "That's so creepy."

The woman nodded. "I could tell by the look on her face that she did not want to be found. The other woman who worked at the store had been in the back this whole time and finally came out. When she saw that guy, she started yelling at him and chased him out."

"And what happened after that?"

"Blake handed me my purchase and apologized for the disruption, then told me to have a nice day. I could tell she wanted me to leave, so I did. I only knew that man was Blake's ex-husband because I overheard the other woman say so."

I turned that information over in my head. This was more than a week ago, but it's possible he'd stayed in the area after finding Blake. Did he go back to Choco Noir to confront her after hours and it turned ugly? Maybe Hana tried to defend her friend and that's how they both got hurt? Detective Park said it was possible Blake and Hana had let the attacker into the shop because it was someone they knew. But would they have done that for Blake's ex-husband? Based on this woman's testimony, neither Blake nor Hana were happy to see him. And his wording made it seem like she was hiding from him. Still, there's a possibility that he kept coming by the shop and they decided to let him in to talk to him privately, maybe trying to handle the situation before it got too messy and rumors started spreading.

"Did they say his name?"

The woman scrunched up her face, trying to remember. "Peter? Or maybe Patrick? Something like that. Sorry, it was a really tense situation. I don't remember more than that."

I exhaled. "No, thank you for telling me all of this. It was really helpful. The cops might not know that Blake's ex had contact with her shortly before she died, so this could be the break we're looking for."

She smiled, relieved. "I sure hope so. Oh, and please pass my sympathies to Dr. Jae. I'm not sure if he knows this yet, but Father Santiago started a collection to help with his cousin's hospital bills."

Father Santiago was a close family friend and exactly the type of person to do something like that. I tried to swallow past the lump in my throat.

"I'll make sure to let him know. Thanks again for your help."

I made my way over to Jae and Aria's table, where the two appeared to be arguing over something.

"But Uncle Jae, I want to go singing!"

"Singing?" I asked. "I thought you were going to the park next."

Jae's back was to me, and he started at my voice. He glanced up at me and smiled before turning his affectionate gaze back toward his niece. "Aria's dad was from Chicago and used to be active in the musical theatre scene there. He moved to Minnesota to accept a theater arts teaching position at the University of Minnesota and met Hana when she attended one of his shows. He must've passed his love of performing on to his daughter because she's always singing and dancing. Last night, she made us perform *The Phantom of the Opera,* but she wanted to be the Phantom."

I raised an eyebrow. "Which made you . . . Christine?"

"Well, she just had me act the part of Christine. She wanted to sing both parts herself."

"How ambitious. I'd love to see that and so would Adeena and Elena." Thinking of my musical nerd best friends, I said, "Why don't we have a karaoke night? We'll do it at Tita Rosie's Kitchen as usual, but we'll keep it small so Aria doesn't feel uncomfortable around all the strangers."

"That's a great idea! But Aria's bedtime is eight thirty. The restaurant doesn't close that early."

I waved off his concern. "Since it'll just be the five of us, we can do it in the private party room. It'll be a little noisy for the other people in the restaurant, but people book that room for karaoke parties all the time. Our customers are used to it."

"That would be great. Would six o'clock work?"

"I need to double-check with my aunt and grandmother, but it shouldn't be a problem. I'll text you."

Before they left, I asked Aria, "Do you like dogs?"

She looked thoughtful. "I like some dogs. But not if they lick me. Or are too big and scary."

"Would you like to meet my dog? She's small. And she won't lick you if I tell her not to."

Aria nodded, and I went to get Longganisa from my office. I rearranged her red Brew-ha Cafe hoodie and clipped on her leash before leading her to where Aria was waiting.

"Aria, this is Longganisa. Nisa, say hi. No licking!"

Aria cautiously reached out a hand to pet Longganisa, who lowered her head to accept the pets. After a few careful strokes, a smile broke out on Aria's face. "She's so cute! Good dog!"

Jae smiled at the two of them. "If you want, we can bring Longganisa to the park with us. There's a dog park next to the play area."

"That would be great! Is that OK with you, Aria?"

"Does she have toys? We can play together," she said.

"Sure, let me get her stuff and you can go play." I hurried to my office to grab her bag with treats, toys, a blanket, poop bags, and hand wipes, and handed the bag to Jae when I returned. I knelt down to put Longganisa's boots on. "It's pretty cold outside, so make sure to stay warm."

"Don't worry. We're all bundled up, and with the amount of

energy this kid has, she'll have me and Longganisa running all over the park," Jae said with a grin. "Let me know about the karaoke party, but no worries if you can't swing it. We can figure something else out for later."

I watched the three of them leave the cafe, Aria's small hand clutching Longganisa's leash carefully.

"Well, wasn't that disgustingly cute," Adeena said, popping up next to me. "Just one big, happy family, huh?"

I pointed at her. "Don't you even start. Anyway, are you and Elena free later? I still need to talk to my aunt, but I want to throw a small karaoke party for Aria. Apparently, she's a big fan of musicals."

Adeena's eyes widened. "Yes! Corrupting the youth with musical theatre is totally my thing! We're in."

"Corrupting the youth—with musical theatre? Really? Isn't that like, one of the most wholesome things to get involved in?"

"You, my friend, were clearly never part of the drama club or a theater kid. It's too late for you. But taking on a protégé, that should be fun."

"A protégé? Hon, I love you, but being dramatic doesn't mean you're a good actor," Elena said, passing us on her way to the kitchen with a tray full of dirty dishes.

"Just for that, I'm making you watch *Cats* the movie! Prepare yourself for CGI cat buttholes!"

"What? No! Anything but that!"

Chuckling, I left my partners bantering and bickering by the kitchen and went behind the counter to keep Leslie company. Things had slowed down, so they could handle the register by themself, but it was good for me to spend more time with them.

"Oh, Lila! I've been meaning to talk to you. When you said you wanted to hire some part-time workers, were you thinking of using the high school's apprentice program? Or did you want people with previous work experience?"

Leslie's predecessor, Katie, had apprenticed at the cafe as part of the local high school's special program that awarded school credits to kids who wanted to get hands-on job training and/or were looking to work in industries that didn't need traditional schooling. Because of how busy we were, I'd wanted someone a little older and who maybe had previous service or food industry experience. I loved the high school apprentice program, and although it provided wonderful opportunities for the local kids, I worried it might be too stressful for Leslie to have to train someone from the ground up since they would need a lot more time and attention. That was just me projecting though, so I should probably ask their opinion.

I explained my thought process and asked, "So what do you think? I'm happy either way. I want you to think carefully and choose whichever option you believe would be most helpful."

Leslie tilted their head, and I could almost see the mental math going on. "Why not one of each? You said you wanted to hire part-time 'workers,' as in plural. If one of you can handle talking to the school about an apprentice, I can start advertising for a part-time worker who has the qualifications you're looking for. And since the apprentices get school credit, not payment, you'll be saving money as well."

Leslie was uncomfortable with physical affection, so I refrained from wrapping them in a giant hug. "You. Are. A. Genius! I'll talk to Adeena and Elena about this and leave you a memo to help you draft the advertisement."

We would also need to talk about Leslie receiving a raise to match their new responsibilities, but they didn't need to know about that just yet.

"Hiring you was one of the best decisions we ever made. Thanks, Leslie."

They flushed. "No, thank you. I know you only took me on because of my family problems, but I really appreciate everything you've done. This cafe means the world to me. You've built a really special place."

OK, this was getting way too heartfelt and earnest, and I didn't appreciate all these emotions swirling inside me. Luckily, a customer arrived at that moment and Leslie turned to help them after beaming at me one last time.

I took a moment to study the room, taking in the beautiful interior, the exposed brick wall and floating shelves full of plants and herbs and goods for sale, our tables full of satisfied customers enjoying pastries and lingering over a hot drink, and at my best friends and partners on the floor mingling with our regulars. My heart swelled at the sight, and I smiled.

The Brew-ha Cafe really was a special place, wasn't it?

Chapter Eleven

As impressed as I am by this kid's knowledge of musicals, should we be worried that she can sing along to songs from *SIX* and *Mean Girls*? Don't get me wrong, a three-year-old referring to Regina George as a 'fugly cow' will never not be hilarious, but still."

Adeena watched Jae's niece queue up another song, this time from *Sunday in the Park with George*. "Wait, she's a Sondheim fan? Never mind, she's golden."

As someone who loved to sing (and let's be real, as a Filipino), I enjoyed musicals as much as the next person, but I was nowhere near Adeena's level when it came to the theater. The fact that little Aria seemed to match my bestie's energy when it came to show-tunes was as cute as it was concerning.

Yuki, the only mom in our group, waved it off. "As long as there's no cussing, it should be fine. Think of all the songs you used to sing along to as a kid that were absolutely NOT age appropriate, but you had no idea what they were really saying, so it was OK."

I did a mental checklist of the songs I loved when I was a kid: "Candy Shop" by 50 Cent. "S&M" by Rihanna. "Milkshake" by Kelis. Oh, and of course, pretty much anything by Fall Out Boy.

OK, maybe she had a point.

I cringed. "Oof, fair. Well, as long as we're not corrupting the youth, although I know Adeena desperately wants to."

Adeena shrugged. "Everyone knows the real gay agenda is to convince normies that Raúl Esparza's best role wasn't as Rafael Barba on *Law & Order: SVU,* but Bobby in *Company.*"

Tita Rosie and Lola Flor had agreed to let us use the private party room for our impromptu karaoke night but informed us they'd be too busy to provide much service, so they'd laid out a bunch of drinks and snacks in advance: pica-pica, or finger foods, such as chicken barbecue skewers, fish balls, lumpiang togue, and pandesal stuffed with corned beef or cheese, as well as pitchers of water and calamansi honey iced tea.

The iced tea was almost gone, so I got up to retrieve a refill and almost bumped into Lola Flor carrying a tray with more water and tea as well as a single mug full of tsokolate.

"I thought the little girl could use something warm to drink," she said, handing Aria the cup gingerly. "Careful not to burn yourself."

Aria grasped the mug in both hands and took a hesitant sip. "It's hot chocolate! Thank you!"

Lola Flor broke into a rare smile, and I nearly gasped. It was too bad Ronnie couldn't be here because our grandmother actually smiling was like the northern lights showing up over Chicago—an absolutely singular, unlikely-to-be-reproduced experience. Still, his mission at tonight's chamber of commerce meeting with Izzy was more important than even a Lola Flor smile sighting.

"Let me know if you want more. Have fun." Lola Flor smoothed the little girl's hair before tucking the empty tray under her arm and leaving the room, shutting the door behind her.

"That was weird. Right?" My cousin Bernadette was equally shaken by this softer side of Lola Flor. Even though they weren't blood-related, Bernadette had still grown up around my grandmother and knew what she was like.

"Very weird. Not going to complain though." I filled my glass with iced tea before topping off hers. "How are things at the hospital?"

She shrugged. "Same as always. I'm not in the ICU, so I can't keep an eye on Hana, but my friends give me updates."

"Anything worth noting?"

"She's stabilized enough to breathe on her own, but that's about it. So far, no one has tried to visit her room outside of family, so that's good. Detective Park informed the staff that she might have a stalker, so the floor has been keeping an eye on her room."

"Did he provide a description? Adeena, Elena, and I are supposed to stop by the hotel where that guy works on our next day off, but we have no idea what he looks like."

"I believe he gave security a photo, but I'm not sure. Want me to ask?"

I shook my head. "It's fine, I can always ask Detective Park myself. We know the guy's name and are visiting his job on Monday anyway, so it's not like we need a description ahead of time. I was just curious."

"Where is Detective Park, by the way? I thought he always attended these info meetings."

I'd managed to get Bernadette and Yuki to join me, Adeena, Elena, Jae, and Aria for this last-minute karaoke party, but Ronnie and Izzy were handling the chamber of commerce and Detective Park had some outing planned with his friend Ben and the Safe & Secure Solutions team. Sana and Amir weren't here yet, but they both had promised to head over as soon as they could. I was waiting on them to show up before sharing the latest info and hoped Amir had something to share on his end as well.

As if my thoughts had manifested their appearance, the door to the party room swung open and Amir and Sana walked in.

"Sorry we're late!" Sana said, going around the room to give everyone kisses. "I had a consultation that ran over, and Amir was waiting for me to finish so we could ride together."

I led the two of them over to Jae and Aria since they were the only ones who hadn't met Hana's daughter yet.

"Hey Aria! These are my friends Amir and Sana. They're here to sing with us, too."

Aria shook their hands very seriously. "Nice to meet you. What song do you want to sing?"

Amir smiled at her. "Why don't you choose the next song? I'm going to get some food first and will join you later."

Aria looked at Sana. "You're pretty. You can be Christine."

"Thank you?" Sana said as Aria directed her on how to properly perform her favorite song from *The Phantom of the Opera*.

The rest of us watched their performance and cheered once the song was over. Aria bowed and told Sana she should bow as well, so Sana followed suit.

"It's like reliving our childhood," Amir said. "Adeena used to make me perform with her all the time. Bollywood songs, Broadway showtunes, *Glee* mashups . . . and worst of all, our parents encouraged it."

"Did they make you perform at parties?" Sana asked. She'd curtsied to Aria before grabbing a drink and rejoining us.

He groaned. "All the time! I mean, most of the kids were forced to perform something during the parties by their parents, but I wanted to do a simple song on the piano or something like that. Not flashy enough for Adeena or my parents though."

"A song on the piano? Not for our golden boy! How else would our parents show off how perfect you are?" Adeena said, plopping down next to her brother. Her plate was filled with Lola Flor's mocha mamon, which she'd been scarfing down all night. "Choreographed song and dance routine or bust."

"Your family parties were very, very different from mine," Yuki said. She was nibbling on the honey miso mochi Rice Krispies Treats I'd made. "And Lila, these are perfect. We might even be able to make this ourselves. We'd pay you for the recipe and credit you on the menu, of course."

"Works for me," I said. "I'm just glad you can make use of this iteration since it didn't work for the Brew-ha Cafe menu."

"It's simple enough that Naoko should be able to make it. Now that she's in her junior year of high school, she can't help as much as she used to since she's so busy with studying and her art projects. Akio is still holding out hope that she'll take over the restaurant someday, so maybe handling this dessert will appease him for a while."

Yuki's husband, Akio, was the chef at Sushi-ya and rather traditional. Even though Naoko had let her parents know for years that she planned on pursuing a career in art, he preferred to bury his head in the sand and pretend that his little girl was going to follow in his footsteps. Poor Yuki was often stuck as the mediator.

"How's she doing, by the way? Last I heard, she was teaming up with Terrence to create the graphics and merch for the Valentine's Day event that Ronnie and Izzy are planning."

Despite Naoko's age, she was a talented artist and had been designing merchandise for select businesses in town. Many of Longganisa's outfits were also her doing.

Yuki frowned. "She's having a hard time right now. On top of the usual pressures of junior year, she was rather close to Blake and Hana. She'd been working with them on a special project for Choco Noir as well as the Valentine's Day event, and Hana was teaching her chocolate sculpture work. They were even talking about taking her on as an intern, but now . . ."

We were all silent for a moment, our heads tilted down in remembrance.

When a comfortable amount of time passed, I ventured, "If Naoko is looking for an internship, do you think she'd be interested in working at the Brew-ha Cafe? I promised Leslie we'd hire some part-time workers for them to train, and we wanted at least one of them to be a high school intern."

"I'll talk to her. I'll be honest, though: The only reason she was interested in working at Choco Noir was the creative element.

Hana is very artistic, and Naoko has been fascinated with the idea of being a chocolatier since watching *School of Chocolate* on Netflix."

"That show was so good! I wanted to eat everything they made," Adeena said. "I wonder if there'll ever be a show like that for baristas. I'd love to learn more tips and tricks. It's not like I went to school for it, you know? It was all on-the-job training."

Elena clapped her hands together. "Latte art! That could be a fun way to lure Naoko in. After Leslie handles the basic training, Naoko could become Adeena's apprentice and learn how to make drinks and create latte art."

"That's a great idea! If she becomes really good, she might even be able to teach a workshop at the cafe. I know people are becoming more interested in recreating the cafe experience at home," I said. "We could even put together kits to sell. And if she's interested, maybe she could help with decorating desserts, too. I've been wanting to work on presentation when it comes to our special-event desserts, but I just don't have the time."

Yuki smiled. "That's a great idea! I'll try to position it that way. Honestly, I would really appreciate it if you three could look out for her. She won't talk to me about Blake or Hana, but I know it's affecting her. Maybe she'll open up to one of you."

"What're you talking about?" Aria bounced over and held out the microphone toward Yuki and Bernadette. "It's your turn. You two didn't sing yet."

Bernadette cringed. Even though she always came out to our karaoke parties, she was not a huge fan of singing. Dancing was her specialty, which was probably why she tried to get out of singing by saying, "I'm your backup dancer! Why don't you choose a song and teach me the dance?"

"I saw the purple and yellow Wiggles dance to this song!" Aria squealed before running to Jae and instructing him to put on some song I was only familiar with through dance videos on social media. Luckily, Bernadette had seen those videos too, and soon the two were busy grooving.

Jae plopped down next to me and lay his head on my shoulder. "I don't think I've ever had that much energy in my life. And I used to be an athlete."

"You're in luck. When it comes to dancing, Bernadette also has boundless energy, so I'm sure she can keep Aria busy for the rest of the night. Or at least three songs, whichever comes first."

Sana reached over and squeezed Jae's hand. "How are you holding up?"

"Oh, you know." He didn't elaborate. "Anyway, when's the next time you're stopping by my parents' house? My mom was raving about that sorrel tea drink that you brought last time. And the chair yoga has been really helpful for my dad since he doesn't have to bend over too much."

Sana recently started a chair yoga class at the Shady Palms Public Library, and it was a huge hit. Because the class utilized chairs instead of yoga mats, it was perfect for senior citizens and those with health or mobility issues who couldn't enjoy the benefits of a regular yoga class. Mama Park had dragged Papa Park to a class a few weeks ago, and it was so good for him, they hired Sana for private home lessons.

"I'll have to stop by the Caribbean store to stock up on more sorrel! Glad your mom liked the drink. Your dad thought it was too tart, but I'm sure he'll come around eventually. We haven't scheduled our next appointment, but I'll make sure to do that soon."

Jae nodded before turning his attention to Amir. "How about you, Amir? Have you learned anything new about the case?"

"Sorry, but not a lot is happening on my end. I'm representing your family, and there hasn't been any new documentation regarding Hana. I'm not connected to Blake in any way, so I can't get my hands on her autopsy report. Your best bet is to have Detective Park pull some strings, or to talk to Blake's parents whenever they arrive. Unfortunately, I think I'm going to have to take a backseat on the case unless something new crops up and I have to defend one of you."

That made sense. In the past, Amir was most active when one of our group was accused of a crime and he had to defend us. As our counsel, he had access to official paperwork, interviews, and the people who were involved in the case. When there was no one to defend, there wasn't a whole lot for him to do. Still, he had connections the rest of us didn't.

I said, "Don't worry about it. Just make sure to let us know as soon as you hear something about either the burglaries or Hana and Blake. We appreciate your help all the same."

"Oh, I just remembered!" Sana said. "I've been talking to Beth and Valerie about gathering all the female entrepreneurs in town for a special meeting where we can share information, air grievances, brainstorm ways to safeguard our businesses, things like that. Would you be interested in joining us and providing the hot drinks for the meeting? Beth and Valerie want to be fair and support all the new pop-up businesses that've opened recently, which is why they're not asking you and your aunt to cater everything. They're estimating roughly thirty people will be in attendance."

Elena said, "That's a great idea! It's networking and community and a catering order at the same time. What other businesses are participating?"

"Diane Kosta will be there to take photos of the event and also impromptu professional headshots. The Lemonade Stand will take care of the cold beverages, The Gluten-Free Pop-Up will do the snacks, and this new vegan pop-up called Kale Me by Your Name will handle the savories."

"I didn't realize there were so many pop-ups in town. I'm excited to check them out," I said.

"That's a big undertaking," Elena pointed out. "When is this happening?"

"This Sunday. They've been planning a local expo for female entrepreneurs for a while, but after what happened to Blake and Hana, they decided to rein in their plans a little so they could hold the event ASAP. The larger expo has been pushed until next year."

Elena looked thoughtful. "If there isn't any vending, just refreshments and general discussion, the short timeframe shouldn't be too big of a problem since the only people who need time to prepare are the ones involved in the catering. Anyway, you can count us in. Lila, can you make sure our business cards are updated by then?"

"Got it. And Adeena, you're cool with handling the drinks?"

"But of course. This is a great chance for us to talk to all the potential burglary targets at once. And maybe the ones who've already been hit, if they show up."

"Beth and Valerie are pushing for them to be there because they want to show the community turning up to support the victims. That's why we should all be there," Sana added gently.

"That is the most important part, isn't it?" I said, picking up on her subtle nudge. "Showing up for the community. The sleuthing is just an added bonus."

I tended to have tunnel vision when it came to my investigations—in my mind, I needed to do as much as possible as quickly as possible to make sure there wouldn't be any more victims. But when I rushed forward like that, it was easy for me to forget to hold space for not just the victims, but also all the other people who've suffered because of the crimes committed. I made the investigation all about me. And that's not who I wanted to be.

I thought about this the rest of the night. When Detective Park showed up at the end to bring Aria back to his parents' place so Jae and I could have some alone time, I broached the subject with them.

"Hey . . . you guys don't think I'm making the investigation about me, do you? Like, should I take a step back so you two can handle things?"

Jae was in the middle of buttoning up Aria's coat, but his hands stilled as he turned to look at me. "What are you talking about? Do you have any idea how much it helps knowing that you're on the case? That everyone here is doing what they can to help Hana and our family?"

Detective Park agreed with him. "What's this really about?"

I avoided the question, instead crouching down to finish buttoning up Aria's coat. "You're such a good singer, Aria. Did you have a good time tonight?"

Aria's eyes lit up. "Yes! Your voice is so pretty. Can we sing together again?"

"Of course. I'll talk to Jae, and we can plan a special singing date. We can do whatever you want."

"You promise?"

Aria held out her pinky, and I hooked my little finger around hers. "Promise."

Anything to keep this smile on her face.

Chapter Twelve

"Yo, this is the best coffee I've had in my LIFE. And I'm not even into fancy lattes. How is this so good?"

Vinny stared down at the gulab jamun latte that Adeena had set in front of him. He and Hector from Safe & Secure Solutions had stopped by early this morning to do a routine check on our system before we opened, and Adeena was using their presence to help her test her new latte.

Adeena grinned at him. "Flatter me all you want, but we're not upgrading our security package. I appreciate it, though. I've been trying to perfect this drink for a while now but could never get the balance of the spices against the coffee just right."

"Well, I think it's great. I don't think I've ever tried anything with rose, but I can tell there's something flowery about it. Not like in a soapy way though, which is surprising. And I'm liking those spices. What gave you the idea for this drink?"

Adeena had created rose lattes before, as well as rose and cardamom drinks, but even though she'd been working on a drink that echoed the flavors of gulab jamun since the Brew-ha Cafe had opened, she hadn't been able to come up with an iteration she liked enough to put on the menu. Gulab jamun consisted of fried balls of milk solids soaked in a sugar syrup flavored with rosewater, cardamom, and sometimes saffron. Even though the flavors seemed straightforward enough to replicate in a latte, the espresso easily overpowered the rose unless you got the proportions just right. Cardamom and saffron were also strong spices, so she'd been tinkering with the recipe on and off for the past couple of years. With the Valentine's Day event coming up, she figured it was high time she nailed a recipe down.

"I've been focusing on chocolate a lot since that's the food most people associate with the holiday, but I also want to have fun with the fact that roses are a popular gift. Rose is one of my favorite flavors, so I'm hoping to do a whole rose drink lineup."

Now that she mentioned it, I'd also been leaning on chocolate a lot with my desserts. I wondered if I could incorporate rose as well. Maybe white chocolate, rose, and pistachio scones or muffins?

Hector dunked his ube white chocolate scone into his coffee. "These pastries are fantastic as well, Lila. Thanks so much for treating us."

"You two are making sure that our cafe stays safe. Coffee and snacks are the least I could do."

He started to reply but was interrupted by a knock on the glass. We turned toward the door and saw Jae waving at us.

"Oh, perfect! Can one of you let him in? I want to grab the treat I made for him." I rushed to the kitchen to grab the honey butter biscocho I'd prepared that morning. When I came out, Jae had settled in next to Hector and Adeena had already set a sample of her new drink in front of him. "Tita Rosie gave me a bunch of leftover pandesal last night after karaoke, so I was able to test out my new recipe. Let me know what you think."

I watched everyone bite into the slightly crisp honey butter biscocho. To achieve the perfect texture, I had to bake the day-old bread slathered in softened honey butter low and slow to remove the moisture without browning the top too much.

"This plate was in the oven for about an hour and a half while this one was in for two hours. Which do you prefer? And let me know any improvements you think I could make. Like, do you prefer them more or less crunchy? Do you like these thicker pandesal halves, or would it work better with thin sandwich bread? How's the proportion of honey to butter? Things like that."

Jae chomped into the longer-cooked biscocho, and the crunch was audible in the cafe. I waited for him to comment, but he just helped himself to a biscocho from the other plate and sampled that. Finally, he took the longer-cooked one and dipped it into his coffee before grunting in satisfaction.

"I like the ones that are crunchier because they go better with coffee. They're not as hard as biscotti, but they're still firm enough to not fall apart once you dunk them in a hot drink."

Elena said, "I agree. And I think I'd prefer a stronger honey flavor. If you say it has honey in it, I really want to taste it."

I jotted down their comments. "No, yeah, that makes sense. I was a bit timid with the honey because I was worried it'd burn after such a long time in the oven, but I'm sure I can adjust for that."

"You can ignore this," Hector said slowly, "but I think maybe some sesame seeds would work really well with these flavors."

Adeena said, "That's brilliant! The aroma would be absolutely amazing, too. Lila, maybe for the next experiment, you can try it with more honey and have one biscocho with sesame and one without?"

"Ooh, slightly off topic, but that reminds me that I recently picked up a jar of black sesame paste. If the biscocho become popular, I could play around with all kinds of flavors, maybe even some to match our drinks," I said, writing down these ideas as quickly as they came. "Adeena, I think the black sesame paste would make a great latte, too."

"Hmm, the smoky, nutty flavor would work with both coffee and black tea . . ." Adeena muttered under her breath.

I turned to Hector. "Thanks for the suggestion. It opened up all kinds of ideas!"

He smiled at me, his eyes crinkling up in the corners. His eyes weren't as kind as Ben's, but there was something reassuring about them.

Vinny had been enthusiastically stuffing his face with the biscocho from both platters but hadn't offered an opinion yet. He looked younger than me, but I couldn't tell if he was fresh out of high school or in his early twenties, like my cousin Marcus.

"What do you think, Vinny?" I asked.

He was reaching out for yet another biscocho but froze with his hand near the plate. "Oh, um, I think they're great. If you're looking for more flavors, I think a cinnamon sugar one would be so good. My nonna does something similar but using leftover pizza dough fried and covered with cinnamon sugar. It's so good, like a churro, you know?"

Elena grinned at him. "That is absolutely going on the menu! Sorry, Lila, I know you're the baker, but you get no say in this one."

I laughed. "Works for me! I can only make these when my grandmother has leftover pandesal, so I'll put in an order with her later tonight to make sure she always has extra in stock."

"I'm available this time on Sunday," Vinny said with a grin. "Just saying."

As I grinned back at him, I thought, this was what people meant when they described someone as "cheeky."

Hector glanced at his watch and stood up. "Sorry to eat and run, but I'm afraid we have a meeting with Ben at the office soon."

"Don't worry about it," I assured him. "You were a huge help."

"You gave us important insight into our new products, and you also set our minds at ease by checking our security system. We really appreciate you coming out here so early," Elena added.

Adeena cleared away their empty mugs. "Want something for the road? And how does Ben like his coffee? I don't feel right sending you away with nothing for him."

"Your house blend with plenty of cream and sugar for Ben, black for me," Hector said. "We really appreciate this. The drip coffee maker back at the office just doesn't compare."

"I'll have more of that drink I sampled earlier, please. And could you make it iced?" Vinny eyed the last of the biscocho on the plates, but didn't say anything else.

I put them in a takeaway box and slid them toward him. "I expect to see you Sunday morning, bright and early."

"Is this a bribe? If so, it's working."

I rolled my eyes. "It's a thank-you, not a bribe. Make sure to share those with Ben. If I find out you hogged them all to yourself, no more freebies for you."

"Womp womp. You are no fun, Lila." He started to reach for me like he was going to ruffle my hair or something, then seemed to think better of it when Jae slung his arm around my shoulders and glared at him. "Right, no touch, got it. Sorry, I was just playing."

I wasn't sure if he was apologizing to me or Jae, but neither of us responded to him. Instead, I turned my attention to his coworker. "Hector, I'm giving you this box of biscocho for safekeeping. Something tells me Vinny isn't to be trusted."

Hector laughed. "He's a good kid, but your instincts are spot-on in this instance. Vinny, could you grab the coffees since I'm driving?"

Vinny pouted but obediently made his way over to Adeena. She stuck the coffees in a carrier and handed them over. "I made yours extra large, so stop pouting. You're ruining your cute face."

He leaned forward. "Cute, huh?"

"Down, boy," Elena said, squeezing between the two of them. "She's taken."

"And a lesbian," Adeena added helpfully.

Vinny looked between the two of them. "Well, damn. Are none of the cute girls single in this town? And, you know, attracted to men?"

"The Valentine's Day event at Shady Palms Winery is going to have a special singles mixer side," I said. "Why don't you try your luck there? If nothing else, you'll get to have more of our food and drinks."

His eyes lit up. "For real? Maybe I will."

When planning first started for the Valentine's Day event, Blake had been adamant that the event not only cater to couples, but allow those seeking love a chance to enjoy the holiday as well.

"If we had time, I would've loved to do a separate Galentine's Day event as well since platonic friendship is just as important and deserving of celebration as romantic love," she had said. "But because Choco Noir is brand new and Hana and I are the only staff, I don't want to stretch us too thin. Still, if the event space allows for it, I think holding both a singles mixer and special couple's space would allow us to bring in a much larger range of customers than a more traditional event."

Blake, Hana, and Rita, the only single members of the collaboration, were put in charge of the singles mixer while Ronnie, Izzy, Adeena, and Elena handled the couple's side. I was to be the liaison between these groups along with Terrence, who was in charge of the designs for everything. With Blake gone and Hana out of commission for who knows how long, I should probably talk to the group about partnering with Rita to finalize things on the singles' side. Seeing how eager Vinny was for the event made me even more determined for it to go well.

"Vinny, time to go!" Hector called out.

I followed them to the door and turned the sign to OPEN. There were already a few early birds lingering outside, and changing that sign was like flipping a switch for them. They surged in, jostling both Hector and Vinny and narrowly avoiding knocking into the full cup carrier in Vinny's hands as they made their way to the counter.

"Sorry about that," I said. "The customers who come this early are usually on their way to work and in a bit of a rush."

One of the customers must've overheard me because they made their way over to apologize. "I'm so sorry. I really should've let you go through first. You could've been hurt if that hot coffee had spilled on you."

Vinny gaped at the woman, looking at her as if a goddess had descended upon the tiny town of Shady Palms. I couldn't blame him; she was gorgeous—long dark hair that was so straight and shiny, it fell like black silk toward the middle of her back, a perfect glass complexion, and expressive dark brown eyes. She tilted her head, likely waiting for him to respond, so I nudged him.

"Oh! Uh, I'm fine. Thanks. My name's Vinny, what's yours?"

"Charlene Choi. Anyway, sorry again." She smiled before waving slightly and rejoining the line in front of the counter.

Vinny stared for a beat longer before leaning close to me. "Lila, find out if she's single. If so, please please please get her to go to that singles mixer. I will owe you forever if you do."

"Even if I manage all that, you know there's no guarantee that she'll go for you, right?"

He grinned at me, his cockiness suddenly back now that Charlene wasn't short-circuiting his brain. "Yeah, but at least this way I've got a shot. That's all I need."

His cockiness should bother me, but honestly, I admired his confidence. Maybe because he seemed like a sweet guy despite his big mouth. Or maybe it was because Detective Park trusted Ben, and by extension, that meant he trusted all of Ben's employees. Like Hector. He was the one who'd installed our security system and was in charge of routine checkups and maintenance, and every time we interacted, Adeena, Elena, and I were always soothed by his quiet, competent demeanor. As I watched him and Vinny drive off,

I realized he'd be a great addition to the singles mixer for women who preferred a guy who was more on the mature, quiet side. From the time we'd spent together, I could tell he was hardworking and kind, plus he was handsome in a rather unassuming way. I just needed a non-creepy way to check his relationship status and possibly pass on that invite. I wasn't sure why, but I was getting all fired up about this singles mixer.

Maybe that was why I had the courage to snag Charlene on her way out.

"I know you're in a hurry to get to work, but do you have a moment?"

Charlene glanced at her watch and nodded. "It's fine. I own the company, so it's not like I'm going to get written up for being late or anything. How can I help you?"

Another female entrepreneur. Was this woman also a potential target for the burglar? "You own your company? What do you do?"

She fished in her purse and pulled out a business card. "I run an accounting firm. We specialize in tax accounting, but we also do bookkeeping for small local businesses. If you're looking for a new accountant for your cafe, I'd be happy to schedule a meeting with you and your partners."

I glanced at the information on the card she handed me, my thumb unconsciously smoothing over the embossed printing. *Charlene Choi, licensed CPA at Choi & Associates, Ltd.* My childhood friend Joseph (who was Ninang Mae's son) was the cafe's accountant and also handled taxes for my family's restaurant and cousin's winery. I would never switch from him, but there was no need to tell her that just yet.

As if sensing my hesitation, she added, "I can provide a list of references, if you'd like. My firm handles the taxes for many of the businesses in Shady Palms, as well as the chamber of commerce. I'm the treasurer for the CoC."

My ears perked up at that. Maybe this was my chance to get more insider information, and from a board member at that.

I apologized silently to Joseph in my head, assuring him that I wasn't betraying him, before saying, "I'd love to set up an appointment. Let me know your soonest availabilities, and I'll talk it over with my partners."

After settling on a few possible times, she said goodbye and I made my way to my office to finally handle the part-time workers search. I filled in the paperwork to request Naoko as the Brew-ha Cafe's apprentice and wrote up some copy for Leslie to use in the hiring ads, then moved on to the boring admin work that kept the cafe running behind the scenes. By the time I was done, my back was cramping and Longganisa's whining beneath my desk reminded me that we could both use a long walk. There was still some time before the high school office closed, so I gathered the paperwork, made sure Longganisa and I were properly bundled up against the cold, and set out on the almost two-mile walk it would take to get to Shady Palms High.

Chapter Thirteen

"OK, everyone, it's official! Welcome to the Brew-ha Cafe team, Naoko!"

Adeena, Elena, Leslie, and I all cheered and clinked our mugs and glasses together as Naoko beamed at us.

"Thanks for having me! I'm looking forward to working with you." Naoko flushed and rubbed the back of her neck. "To be honest, I wasn't interested in a food service job since I've been working at my family's restaurant most of my life. But my mom pointed out how different your cafe is from our place and that I'd get to flex a different kind of creativity here. Plus, there's a lot I can learn from you all, considering you started your own business when you were pretty young."

"Don't forget the very important fact that we're all awesome and you think we're super cool and all that. We've got rizz." Adeena lowered her voice. "The kids still say that, right? Rizz?"

Leslie patted her on the back. "Whatever you say, boss. Naoko, why don't I show you around really quick? I know you've been here a bunch of times, but each area has different responsibilities so I thought I'd go over that tonight and tomorrow you can shadow us to learn more about them."

"Works for me." Naoko drained her mug of Mexican mocha before following Leslie on their tour around the cafe.

When I had gotten to the high school the other day, I not only was able to file the paperwork right away, but the secretary scanned the form and said, "Oh, that was quick. Mrs. Sato called yesterday to let us know you'd be putting in a request, and that Naoko has accepted and can start ASAP. Let me just have you sign these documents, and here's the information about scheduling and the duties our students need to fulfill to receive school credit."

Naoko had been helping us with our merchandise for almost two years now, and I knew she was a good worker: collaborative, conscientious, and always met her deadlines. But I was still a little apprehensive about taking her on as an actual intern. Yuki was a good friend of mine, and I wanted to make sure her daughter received valuable knowledge and experience in this position. However, I couldn't afford to relax my standards of work just because we were friendly. I also wasn't sure how to broach the subject of Blake and Hana. Naoko seemed like her usual sweet, cheerful self, but even her oversize red glasses couldn't hide the dark circles under her eyes. Unlike me, hers weren't genetic.

I figured maybe that would be an OK place to start, so once Leslie and Naoko rejoined us at the table, I said, "Hey Naoko, is it OK for you to be having caffeine so late? I wouldn't want you to have trouble sleeping. You've got school in the morning."

She waved it off. "It's fine. I don't sleep well anyway, so it's not like this is going to hurt."

Elena frowned. "Have you always had trouble sleeping? Do you want me to make you a cup of my special chill vibes tea? Let me grab you a bag of sleepytime tea as well. It's not magic, but it should help."

"It's not that serious . . ."

"No, I insist. Proper sleep is important for everyone, but especially someone as young as you. You're on the team now, so consider this another perk."

Elena got up to brew the tea. "In fact, let me make a pot for everyone. We could all use a little de-stressing."

"Go work that magic, bruha," I said. "Even when I'm using your tea leaves, it never tastes as good as when you make it for me."

"That's because you're a baker. You rely too much on timers and measurements. There are other things to pay attention to if you want the perfect cup of tea," she said, carrying a tray bearing our largest teapot and five teacups.

She never set a timer, and I refused to believe she was counting out the time in her head, so it was like she just sensed when the tea was ready. After waiting however long that mystical amount of time was, she gracefully lifted the teapot and poured us all steaming cups of tea. We all followed her lead, bringing the cups to our noses and inhaling deeply, letting the curls of steam bathe our faces with warmth, before taking our first sips. Even though the tea contained no sweeteners, the magical blend of chamomile, lavender, and peppermint lent a delicate sweetness to the concoction.

Naoko had looked at the cup suspiciously before drinking, but after her first test sips, she started gulping it down and asked for more. "I thought green tea was the only kind of tea I could drink without milk and sugar, but this is great!"

Elena smiled. "I'm glad you like it, but it's better if you take your time with it if you want the full experience of the tea. Guzzling it down kind of takes away from the relaxing atmosphere. Then again, you're the one drinking it, so you should enjoy it as you wish."

"No, you're right. My mom is always yelling at me for eating and drinking too fast. She's always like, 'It's not a race! Are you even tasting the food?'" Naoko let out an embarrassed laugh. "Maybe one of my goals while working here is to learn how to savor things instead of just gobbling them down."

Elena nodded approvingly. "Not just food and drinks either. Learn how to savor the moment. As an artist, it'd be good for you to learn how to slow down and really absorb whatever's going on. Ruminate on what you see, feel, smell, all of it. The cafe is an excellent place to train your senses."

At this perfect opening, I couldn't help jumping in. "Same goes with your emotions. I know it's easy to just put your head down and work quietly to get your mind off things, but really sitting with your feelings, maybe talking them out with someone, is so important as a creative."

Naoko studied me. "Meaning you want me to talk about Blake and Hana."

Dang, this girl is good.

"Look, I'm fine, OK? Yes, I spent a lot of time with them. Yes, I'm really freakin' upset about what happened. But you don't have to worry about me."

Adeena, Elena, and I shared a look that led us all to the same conclusion: We'd let it go. For now.

Leslie finally spoke up. "You don't have to tell us anything if you don't want. But you also don't have to pretend that you're OK. I only knew Blake and Hana from the times they visited the cafe, and even I'm having a hard time with this."

"Not to be cliché or anything, but it needs to be said." Adeena put her hands on Naoko's shoulders and looked into her eyes. "It's OK to not be OK. We're here for you if you need us."

Naoko burst into tears. "I am not OK. How can any of us be OK after what they did to Blake? And to Hana? It's not fair!"

And she screamed and raged as we held her so she could let it out. We didn't try to comfort her because she was right.

None of us were OK.

It wasn't fair.

And no platitudes could change that.

Chapter Fourteen

I was taking stock of the items that needed refilling in our display cases when the tinkling of the bells above the door had me turn to greet our customer.

"Detective Park! It's been a while since you've stopped in. To what do we owe the pleasure?"

Even though we saw each other every morning at breakfast, he hadn't come by the cafe in a while, relying on my aunt's instant coffee or the Brew-ha Cafe's delivery service when he needed a fix.

"Sorry about that. Your aunt has me watching my sugar intake, and I know I'd be too tempted by your baking if I came in here." An older white couple had followed him in, and he gestured toward them. "This is Mr. and Mrs. Langrehr. They arrived last night."

It took a moment for the last name to click. "Oh! You're Blake's parents? I'm so sorry for your loss. We didn't know each other very long, but she was a great collaboration partner and friend."

Mrs. Langrehr smiled at me. I could tell she wasn't faking it, but it looked like that small movement was a struggle, as if the corners of her lips were weighted down with her sorrow. "Thank you. We hadn't seen our daughter since she moved away, but she was diligent about calling and messaging. She told us about your wonderful cafe, and how you all made her and Hana feel so welcome in this town. I know you're working, but do you have a minute to chat?"

I glanced around the cafe. The morning rush was long over, and the after-work/school crowd wouldn't be coming in for at least another hour. Adeena and Naoko were handling the drinks and register, which left both Elena and Leslie free to assist me in the kitchen.

"I'd love to. Could you give me a minute? I need to talk to my colleagues and make sure everything's covered. Oh, and please order whatever you'd like. It's on the house."

While Detective Park guided them toward the counter, I went over to our merch area where Elena was misting the plants we sold and Leslie was rearranging the shirts, mugs, pet accessories, and other Brew-ha Cafe–branded merchandise.

As I approached them, Leslie piped up, "Hey Lila! What do you think of leaving Naoko in charge of curating our artist area? We kind of let it fall to the wayside after the holiday season."

The Brew-ha Cafe was an ever-evolving work in progress, and our latest project was a wall dedicated to local artists displaying their work for sale. We didn't charge anyone for the display space but received a small commission for any piece that sold. We had implemented it last fall, and it proved popular for holiday shopping. But as Leslie pointed out, we'd been so busy lately that none of us had had time to sort through the artist applications that kept coming in, and the amount of untouched paperwork had reached alarming proportions. Practically a TBR pile–size stack.

"That's a great idea! Elena, would you be able to walk her through the process when you have time?"

Adeena loved knitting, crocheting, and painting and had recently gotten into illustrating, while Elena followed in her mom's footsteps and did mostly ceramic work. The vases holding the plants we sold (which came from the Torres family greenhouse) were all handmade by Elena, as well as some of the plates and cups that were available for purchase. The two of them were the perfect mentors for the voracious Naoko, who dabbled in everything from graphic design to jewelry making to flower arranging. She also made a lot of Longganisa's outfits, for which me and my fashion-conscious dog were very grateful. However, as enthusiastic as Adeena was about her other duties, paperwork wasn't really her strong suit, and we all knew it.

Elena said, "Of course! And Leslie, I love how you're already growing in your new role. If you have any other ideas, don't hesitate to let us know, OK? We're a team."

Leslie beamed. "Work has always been fun, but now I'm even more excited to come in every day."

Considering how much of a wallflower they were when I first met them, always hiding behind their much more popular and outgoing best friend, Sharon (who Leslie was obviously in love with but refused to admit it), seeing how far they'd come in the past year or so made me so proud.

They continued, "Oh, sorry, we can talk about that later. You had something you needed, Lila?"

That brought me back to the moment, and I glanced over at Blake's parents, who were seated with Detective Park in the dog-friendly part of the cafe. Elena and Leslie followed my gaze.

Elena ventured, "Is that . . . ?"

I nodded. "Blake's parents. Her mom asked to speak with me, but I still need to refill the pastry cases. Could one of you handle that for me? The chia parfaits are in the fridge and just need the finishing touches. There are also several kinds of cookie dough that just need to be scooped and baked."

Elena said, "I could do that, I just finished up here. Oven temp and times are in the binder, right?"

I nodded and thanked her.

"I'll walk Longganisa when I'm done with this," Leslie said. "You focus on the investigation. With Naoko here, I can fill in wherever I'm needed if you have to leave."

Leslie's solemn gray eyes and earnest demeanor were so endearing, I was tempted to pull a Jae move and ruffle their hair, but I resisted. Definitely needed to talk to Adeena and Elena about giving them a raise though.

"I appreciate it. I'll keep you updated on what's going on."

The three of us split up to perform our various tasks, and after stopping by the counter for my specialty drink, the Brew-ha #1, I made my way over to Detective Park and Blake's parents.

"Sorry for the wait," I said, seating myself next to Detective Park. "I had a few things to go over with my coworkers."

"No, I appreciate you taking the time in the middle of your workday. Blake told us how popular your cafe is, and I can certainly see why. It's such a warm, inviting space. And everything is so delicious. The woman at the counter kindly put together a sampler platter of your desserts and drinks."

I smiled at Mrs. Langrehr. "That's Adeena, one of the other cafe owners. She's in charge of our drink menu and collaborated with your daughter on special chocolate-based beverages to serve at Choco Noir."

"Oh, we'll have to stop by another time to talk to her then. I'd love to meet everyone who was close to my daughter. Get a better idea of her life here and what she was up to before she . . ."

She choked back tears, and Mr. Langrehr put his hand on top of hers before turning his attention to me. "Detective Park told me that not only were you and your friends the ones closest to Blake before she died, but that you've also handled investigations in the past."

Detective Park said, "I just want to be clear that I'm no longer a detective with the local police force, but a private detective who's involved with this case for personal reasons."

Mr. Langrehr waved that off. "A personal investment means that you actually care and will give this case your all. Detective Nowak was perfectly professional yesterday, but I couldn't help but be disappointed in how little progress there's been. From what I understand, there's a chance our daughter's death is connected to a string of burglaries in the area, and there hasn't been any movement in that case either."

"We still haven't been able to prove a connection, but it's a definite possibility," Detective Park said. "However, I want to make sure we cover all grounds, which requires us to know more about Blake. I'm afraid I'm going to have to ask some very personal questions about your daughter. Is that OK?"

Mrs. Langrehr looked around the room, checking that there was no one near the table who could overhear the discussion. Satisfied, she nodded. "Go ahead. But please take care not to spread any unnecessary information about our daughter."

"Understood, ma'am." Detective Park pulled out his notebook, and I pulled up the Notes app on my phone as well. "Can you think of anyone who would've wanted to hurt your daughter?"

Blake's parents exchanged an uncomfortable look. Finally, her father spoke up. "Blake is divorced. Her ex-husband, Patrick Murphy, was verbally and emotionally abusive, but if what Blake told us is true, he never laid a hand on her. However, he did not consent to the divorce, and it was a pretty ugly legal battle."

"Blake had to get a restraining order because he wouldn't leave her alone!" Mrs. Langrehr said. "Even after the divorce was finalized, he would still randomly show up at the house they once shared. Blake had always wanted to open her own store and was in talks to purchase a building near us, but she eventually decided on leaving town to get away from him."

I leaned forward. "She had a restraining order against him? Do you know if it was still in effect? One of my customers mentioned that Blake's ex-husband stopped by Choco Noir while she was shopping there last week, and that Blake seemed pretty shaken."

"He what?!" Mr. Langrehr roared. "That son of a . . . Restraining order or not, he knows she wants nothing to do with him! What's he doing chasing her across state lines and trying to intimidate her while she's working?"

He stood up. "We have to talk to Detective Nowak. Let him know he needs to track down that piece of trash that murdered my daughter!"

Mrs. Langrehr tugged on her husband's arm. "Wait, Frank! Yes, we need to report him, but I want to hear more. Better we get everything out now than have to keep backtracking."

Once Mr. Langrehr settled back in his seat, she addressed me. "Did the customer say what happened after Patrick showed up?"

I scrolled through my notes. "According to her, Hana was in the back room while Blake helped my customer choose a gift. However, after the commotion, Hana came out of the back and quickly clocked the situation. Told Blake to go in back and that she'd handle the ex. My customer is a bit nosy and tried to hang around, but Hana strongly hinted that it was time for her to leave, so she did. She has no idea what happened after that."

Mrs. Langrehr sighed. "Hana was always such a good friend to Blake. My daughter was very talented and had a great head for business, but she was unfortunately a bit of a pushover when it came to her personal life. Hana did her best to make sure nobody took advantage of Blake, but when it came to Patrick, Blake was unusually stubborn. She saw the light in the end, but it might've been too late after all . . ."

I waited for Mrs. Langrehr to collect herself before asking, "What can you tell us about Blake's ex-husband? And do you have any idea why he'd show up at her job, and how he even knew she was in Shady Palms?"

Mr. Langrehr scratched the scruff on his chin as he thought about it. "He works in sales for a pharmaceutical company and travels a lot for work. He'd leave Blake alone for days, sometimes weeks, at a time, claiming he was on business trips. Sometimes he was, sometimes he wasn't. I have no idea how he knew she was here. I can't see her telling him."

"What about any mutual friends?" Detective Park asked. "Could one of them have accidentally shared her location?"

Mr. Langrehr shook his head. "They were only married for three years, but during that time, he was careful to isolate her. She lost contact with all of her friends except Hana, who continued checking in on her, even when Blake wouldn't answer her messages. Anyone she spent time with during her marriage would've been Patrick's friends, not hers. There'd be no reason for her to share that information with them."

"If he traveled a lot for work, there's a chance that him being in the area is a coincidence," I mused. "But that doesn't explain how he knew Blake was here."

Detective Park said, "When Detective Nowak contacted Mr. Murphy to inform him of Blake's death and ask a few questions, he admitted that he was in the area for work. It could be true, but I highly doubt it's a coincidence. He's supposed to stop by the station for an interview in the coming week. Detective Nowak won't tell me when, but I'm sure I can figure it out and ask a few questions of my own. If you can think of anything that could help guide the conversation with him, please let me know."

The Langrehrs agreed, but Mr. Langrehr's face remained stormy. "You tell him that he better stay away from me and my wife if he knows what's good for him. I don't want to get in the way of a police investigation, but I can't make any promises about what I'll do if he ever dares show his face in front of us."

"I'll pass along the warning," Detective Park assured him. "Is there anyone else you think we should check out as a possible suspect?"

Blake's parents took a moment to think about it but ultimately shook their heads.

"Like I said, Blake cut ties with everyone but Hana," Mr. Langrehr said.

Mrs. Langrehr added, "Even after the divorce, Blake mostly kept to herself. She was too busy planning her move and scouting a place to open her store. Unless she ran afoul of someone here, I can't think of anyone who'd want to hurt her."

"Sorry, I just want to clarify something," I said. "How long ago was the divorce?"

Mr. Langrehr looked at his wife. "I want to say it's already been two or three years? Does that sound right?"

She said, "The divorce was finalized around the time you decided to take early retirement, if I remember correctly."

"So almost two years then," her husband said. "It feels longer. Maybe because it took so long to be official."

Detective Park asked, "And during that time, he continued trying to contact Blake?"

"He just wouldn't accept the divorce. Blake had put up with his cheating and breaking her down for years, so he couldn't believe that she was finally standing up for herself," Mrs. Langrehr said. "The last straw was when he showed up to her previous workplace and tried to get her fired. Her boss knew her situation, and he handled it. However, he told Blake that she needed to file a restraining order against Patrick because he didn't want it happening again."

She sighed. "To think, she fought so hard to get away and achieve her dream, only for this to happen. It breaks my heart. My little girl deserved better than that."

I looked up at the ceiling and drew a deep, shuddering breath to hold back my tears. She was right. Blake deserved so much more. If nothing else, she was going to get justice. I'd make sure of that.

Mrs. Langrehr closed her eyes and inhaled deeply before standing up. "I'm sorry, I think I need to get back to my hotel room. Thank you so much for taking the time to meet with us."

I handed her my business card. "Please contact me if you need anything. Blake was my friend, and she absolutely deserved better. I hope we can help find who did this to her."

Detective Park stood up. "I'll drop you at your hotel. Lila, are you, Adeena, and Elena free after closing? I don't have time for one of our usual dinners, but there are a few things I'd like to go over with the three of you."

"I'll check with them, but I'm pretty sure we're all free. Should I have Jae join us, too?"

He nodded. "I think that would be best."

As I walked them to the door, Elena stopped us to introduce herself and held out a mini carafe of our house blend and a box of pastries. "I'm not sure where you're staying, but it's important to have access to good coffee and snacks. The carafe should keep it warm for at least a few hours, although you can always contact us if you need a fresh delivery."

Mrs. Langrehr accepted the pastries while her husband took the boxed coffee. "Thank you so much. I wasn't sure if I'd have the energy to go out for food later, so this is a huge help."

"If you don't mind telling me where you're staying, we can have dinner delivered to you. My family owns the Filipino restaurant next door, so it's not an issue," I added. "Just let me know if you have any dietary restrictions or food preferences."

Blake's mom reached out to grasp first Elena's hand and then mine. "I'm so glad that my daughter had friends like you here. As for food . . ."

Mr. Langrehr stepped in. "I'm afraid I don't have my daughter's adventurous tastes. I guess you can say I'm a meat-and-potatoes type of guy. If that's a problem, you don't have to worry about us. I'm sure our hotel can suggest something."

Detective Park said, "My girlfriend is the cook at Tita Rosie's Kitchen, and I can assure you, everything she makes is delicious. I'm also a man of simple tastes, and she's attentive to her customers' needs. You can leave it to us."

"That's reassuring," Mr. Langrehr said before glancing at his wife, who had started swaying on her feet. "We really should get going. My wife needs to rest, and I could use a lie-down as well. Thank you all for your hospitality."

"Anytime," Elena said.

I added, "I hope you visit us again before you leave. I'm sure our friend Adeena would like to chat about Blake as well."

"We're here for a week, so we'll definitely take you up on that. Until next time then."

The Langrehrs said their goodbyes and left with Detective Park.

"What do you think he wants to talk about?" I asked Elena as we headed toward the kitchen.

Elena's eyes scanned the room, likely seeing if there was anything she needed to attend to. "It doesn't seem like he has new information, so he probably wants to do a quick check-in and see what our plans are. Which is perfect, since we really do need to nail down our strategy for our trip tomorrow."

We went to our separate domains and finished out the rest of the workday. Leslie walked Naoko through our closing procedure, and the two of them had just finished mopping when Jae and Detective Park arrived.

I hurried to let them in, greeting Jae with a quick kiss. "Careful where you step. Feel free to sit wherever, we're just about done here."

"Great job, you two," Elena said. "We can take it from here. Enjoy your day off tomorrow."

Leslie and Naoko went to my office to grab their stuff, and Longganisa followed them out into the cafe.

"I'm working on a new sweater for Nisa, and I think I can finish it tomorrow," Naoko said, stooping down to pet the little wiener dog. Longganisa had curled up at Jae's feet but lifted herself up to nuzzle Naoko's hand. "I can't wait for you to try it on. You're gonna look SO cute."

After a few more pats, Naoko stood up and waved goodbye and then followed Leslie out the door. Elena locked the door while Adeena prepared drinks for us and I filled a plate with the last of the unsold desserts.

"I know you're watching your sugar intake, so don't feel like you need to eat anything to be polite," I said. "Though if you do want something, I'd suggest something light, like this Milo chia pudding. I used maple syrup instead of sugar to sweeten it."

Detective Park snatched it up surprisingly quickly and dug in. "Chocolate pudding and chocolate mousse are actually two of my biggest weaknesses, so this is great. And the malted chocolate makes it really interesting."

"Chocolate mousse is a bit too fussy to make for the cafe, but I'll keep that in mind. Chia puddings are super easy to make though, so if you want to give it a shot, I'm happy to share the recipe."

"If you think it'll fit into my dad's diet plan, I may take you up on that," Detective Park said. "I get my chocolate pudding addiction from him."

He savored another spoonful before saying, "Let's get down to business, though. I'm meeting with the Safe & Secure Solutions team after this, so I'd only planned on a quick meeting."

Adeena and Elena finished the last of their cleanup and joined us at the table. Once they sat down, he said, "Currently, there is no new conclusive evidence. The Langrehrs' testimony about Blake's ex-husband as well as the witness account from your customer brings him to the top of my suspect list. However, I still need time to investigate what he's been up to. I plan on intercepting him when he comes to talk to Detective Nowak, as well as contact his current workplace to see if he really was in town for work, and if so, what those dates were. I'm also hoping they can shed some light on his mental state before and after the trip. Do you have anything to add? What are your next steps?"

"The cafe's closed tomorrow, so the three of us made an appointment to chat with Zoey Hong at the Lancaster Hotel. She's friends with Ms. Gladys Stokes and works with Shawn Ford, the guy who's been harassing Hana lately," I said.

"What's your game plan once you get there?" Jae asked. "Do you need me to be in the area as backup?"

I glanced at Adeena and Elena to see what they thought. Adeena shrugged, but Elena said, "I think it'd be good for you to come with us to Shelbyville, but it'd be a waste to just have you hovering around the hotel. Why don't you try chatting up Felice at City Hall? She likes you, and she's got eyes and ears everywhere."

Felice was the receptionist at Shelbyville City Hall and had helped us with our previous investigation. She was also friends with Jae's receptionist, Millie Barnes, another member of our information network.

Jae nodded. "That makes sense. I'm sure by now Millie's filled her in on everything. And once we're all done, we can meet up at Wily Cow Emporium for lunch. Will Chuy be there tomorrow?"

Chuy worked as a bartender at our favorite hangout spot in Shelbyville and was also one of Elena's fifty million cousins. On top of making a mean Michelada and stocking some amazing ciders, he'd also helped us with investigations in the past. Even if he hadn't heard anything directly tied to Blake or Hana, he might know something about the burglaries. Rita was also one of his cousins, and since she was affected by all of this, I was sure he'd been busy collecting info for us.

Elena pulled out her phone. "Even if he's off, I can still get him to meet with us. I'll let you know once he gets back to me."

"I think we should also check out The Chocolate Shoppe," Adeena said.

"Right. We've heard rumors that the current owners of The Chocolate Shoppe viewed Choco Noir as competition since they used to have the monopoly on artisanal chocolate," I said. "Gladys said that the new owners are a brother-and-sister team who are trying to modernize the store. It seems pretty far-fetched to think they'd murder someone over something like this, but who knows. We just might find what we need after talking to them."

"We haven't been there since high school, so I wanna see how much it's changed since then," Adeena added. "I'm always looking for inspiration, and Elena's always looking for new ways to collaborate and expand, so we won't have to worry about coming up with a cover story."

I looked up from my notes. "What if they ask why we want to reach out now? The timing might seem a little suspicious, don't you think? Especially if they know we were close to Blake and Hana."

Adeena waved away my worries. "We can just say that Gladys recommended their shop the last time we visited her. Bam, there you go. No need to overthink everything."

No need to overthink everything? Has she met me? But I could see her point. It was possible to overprepare and seem like we'd rehearsed ahead of time, which would draw unnecessary attention to us.

"Makes sense. So we'll handle the hotel stuff on our own while Jae talks to Felice at City Hall. We'll regroup at Wily Cow Emporium for lunch and hopefully chat with Chuy, then grab dessert at The Chocolate Shoppe, where we'll try to talk to Anita and Vince Carter. How's that sound?"

Detective Park said, "That sounds like an extremely full schedule, and things rarely go as smoothly as you'd like. Your general plan is solid, though. I just don't want you to be disappointed if you're not able to meet everyone, or if you do manage to talk to everyone as intended but don't learn anything new. These things take time."

He said this in response to me, but his eyes were on Jae. At first, I couldn't understand why he bothered saying that at all since it's not like I was new to investigating. I knew real cases weren't like a scavenger hunt, where every location held a clue that led you to the next place you needed to go. Lots of leads were dead ends. It was naïve to think that most people and places we visited would have concrete evidence that we could slot into place like a giant puzzle that magically solves the case. But when I glanced over at Jae, I understood what Detective Park was doing.

This was far from Jae's first investigation. He'd helped me in every single one I'd been involved in, in both big and small ways. But his role (at least in his mind) was that of a protector: He got involved in these cases because he wanted to make sure I was safe. Nothing more, nothing less.

But this case was different. If the personal stakes were high for me, as Blake and Hana's friend, they must be astronomical for Jae. He'd been close to Hana his entire life, after all. I already knew I'd have to keep a close eye on Jae to help him through his grief. But I made a note to also make sure he wasn't taking on too much in the investigation. That he wasn't beating himself up over not finding clues, or getting so desperate that he put himself in danger. Detective Park's words weren't just a reminder to Jae—they were a warning to me.

It was my turn to keep Jae safe.

Chapter Fifteen

"I've never been inside the Lancaster Hotel before, but WOW. If we get in good with them, it could mean a whole new era for the Brew-ha Cafe. We might even be able to expand to a bigger space sooner than planned."

Elena was the calm, cool one of our group, so for her to be gazing at our surroundings so excitedly, her head swiveling around to take everything in like a giddy child on a field trip, let me know that getting a contract with the Lancasters would be a major deal. I already knew the Lancaster family was the Shelbyville version of the Thompson family in Shady Palms—the richest, most prominent family in town, their hospitality empire extended throughout the entire county. But their flagship business was the Lancaster Hotel, and Elena was determined that the Brew-ha Cafe put our best foot forward.

Adeena also noted her girlfriend's behavior. "It's like you can smell blood in the water already. I love it when you're like this. You handle all the business talk, and Lila can take care of the investigation stuff. I'll back you both up. Just make sure to signal if you need me to jump in."

Zoey Hong had agreed to a late-morning appointment to discuss working with the Lancaster Hotel. She also let me know when I'd set up the appointment that Gladys had already filled her in on the situation, and she'd promised to answer whatever she could without violating any company rules. Fair enough.

The three of us had taken the scenic route to her office to better understand the scope of the hotel, and once we'd satisfied our curiosity, we headed to a room in the back with a plaque bearing her name and position. Elena knocked on the door and opened it when a voice welcomed us in.

Zoey was an older Taiwanese American woman who looked like she could be anywhere from her early forties to her late fifties. Her asymmetrical black bob had streaks of gray in it, which somehow made her look even more stylish and chic. Her ramrod-straight posture and elegant movements as she stood to greet us gave me the impression that she'd been a trained dancer in another life. She went around her desk to shake our hands, and I was pleased to finally meet someone who was even shorter than I was, even though we were both wearing heels.

Everything about her appearance could be described as "neat," from her minimalist makeup and unpainted but well-shaped nails to her crisp, perfectly fitted skirt suit and polished pumps. I usually found that kind of style suffocating (I'd never be able to hack it at a bank), but on Zoey it just seemed right. There was nothing sterile about her look, and she exuded warmth and intelligence as well as professionalism. I could see why Gladys referred us to her.

Elena introduced herself first, followed by Adeena, and finally me. "Thank you so much for meeting with us, Ms. Hong. I'm sure you must be very busy. Gladys had nothing but wonderful things to say about you."

She smiled, and the crinkles at the corners of her eyes just added to her charm. "Same for the three of you. And please, call me Zoey. Gladys isn't the only one who's recommended your cafe, so I've been wanting to chat with all of you for a while. Would you like to take a seat, or would you prefer a walk and talk?"

I looked at my partners, and Elena gestured for me to take the lead. "Why don't you show us around the hotel so we can get a better idea of what a collaboration would be like? And afterward, there are a few things I'd like us to go over in your office."

She nodded in understanding. "Yes, I think that would be best. There are a few people I'd like to introduce you to."

She motioned for us to follow her out of the office, and after shutting and locking her door, she guided us down the hallway while explaining a little more about her role at the hotel.

"I'm the head of the vendor management office here at the Lancaster Hotel and have been in this position for almost twenty years now." Zoey paused to let a guest pass us and then continued with her tour and spiel. "Well, my title lists me as the head of the office, but there's really only two of us in the department, me and my associate, Shawn Ford. It's our job to find and negotiate contracts with the various vendors and suppliers the hotel uses. As you can imagine, it requires quite a bit of work and hustle, but I love finding the perfect product or service to offer our guests.

"This is our gift room, which is one of the areas I'm in charge of. I do a lot of the ordering for the items we offer, focusing on goods from local businesses. This chocolate sampler box from The Chocolate Shoppe is our most popular souvenir, along with these Lancaster Hotel magnets and mugs, designed by one of our local artists."

Zoey led us over to the edible goods section. "This popcorn mix is a special blend created specifically for the Lancaster Hotel, and the corn is sourced from various farms in Shady Palms. We also have salted caramels created by The Chocolate Shoppe using cream and butter sourced from a dairy farm in Shady Palms. As you can see, the Lancaster Hotel is happy to partner with businesses in Shady Palms as well as in Shelbyville. The owners recognize that there are many wonderful resources in your town and mentioned that they'd like to start carrying more Shady Palms products. Both Gladys and Mayor Reyes mentioned your cafe as a potential contractor. And if you know of other businesses that would benefit from a partnership with us, please let me know."

"My cousin and his girlfriend run the Shady Palms Winery. They have all the regular varietals you'd find at a Midwestern winery, but they specialize in tropical fruit wine, particularly the Filipino coconut wine known as lambanog. I think they'd be a great addition to your gift shop and restaurant."

Zoey's eyes lit up. "Do you have their card? I'd love to schedule a meeting with them. I haven't been to Shady Palms in a while, so I'd love a tour of their winery."

I fished in my purse for my wallet, but I couldn't find any of their business cards. "Sorry, no. But if you look them up on social media, you can find their contact info. Let them know I referred you."

Zoey made a note in the Moleskine planner she was carrying. "Thank you. Do any of you have questions so far?"

Adeena raised her hand. "For the gift shop, are you looking to sell our coffee beans and loose-leaf teas?"

"Exactly. Our guests are big on products that are sourced and produced locally. If you could provide whole beans and ground coffee of your most popular blend, I think it would do well here. According to Gladys, one of you has a greenhouse where you grow your own herbs?"

Elena nodded. "I run that greenhouse with my mom. We sell the plants and herbs, both fresh and dried, and also use them in our bath and body products and in the tea blends that I make with one of my aunts."

"That's right, Gladys did mention that you use her olive oil in your soap. If you could provide samples of your most popular beauty products and teas, as well as your pricing, I can get a better idea of what to budget. Our first priority is the coffee, because that would be most popular with our target audience, but I'm sure I can put together a proposal including all of those items," Zoey said, adding more notes to her planner. "Anything else I should know?"

"My uncle owns an apiary, if you're looking for a source of local honey," Elena said, handing over his business card. "We use his honey at the cafe, and Gladys stocks it at her store as well."

Zoey accepted the card. "You ladies are making my job so much easier by introducing me to all of these wonderful suppliers! I'll have to schedule a visit to the apiary as well. Between Lila's cousin's winery and Elena's uncle's apiary, have you ever thought about joining forces and producing mead? Although I suppose calling it honey wine would make it more marketable."

Elena's eyes widened. "That's brilliant! My cousins and I run a microbrewery on the winery grounds and have used his honey in our cider, but I never thought about asking Ronnie and Izzy to make wine with it."

Zoey beamed. "Glad I could help. I know the fermentation process will take some time, but make sure to share samples with me whenever they're ready. Now, if you don't have any other questions about our souvenir shop, I'd like to show you to our ballroom and various event rooms."

The Lancaster Hotel was a boutique hotel, so it didn't have multiple massive grand ballrooms and meeting rooms like you'd expect in a large chain. But the rental rooms they had available ran the gamut from small and cozy ("For more intimate gatherings," according to Zoey) to mid-size and professional, outfitted with all the technology you'd need to make a work meeting run smoothly. The Lancaster ballroom wasn't as opulent as other hotel ballrooms I'd seen, but it was airy and spacious and contained a warmth and charm missing from the rather sterile chain hotel ones.

"This room is usually used for large-scale events, like weddings, charity fundraisers, and other special occasions. The local high school also hosts its prom here. We've recently invested in a special partition that allows us to vary the room size for groups that are too big for the meeting rooms but don't need or can't afford the full ballroom. This weekend, we're holding a . . ."

Zoey had been sweeping her arm around to indicate the ways the hotel could divide the room but suddenly paused mid-sentence before whirling around to study us. "I know this is last minute, but we're holding a special chocolate-themed afternoon tea this weekend in collaboration with The Chocolate Shoppe. The hotel had to cancel the contract with our previous beverage provider because their quality hasn't been up to snuff lately, and we've been scrambling to find a new supplier. I'd like to ask—would your cafe be available to provide drinks for the afternoon tea? And if it goes well, we could talk about you becoming the main purveyor of the hotel's coffee and tea."

My eyes widened, and I shot a quick glance toward Adeena and Elena, who looked equally surprised by the ask. At most, we had planned on getting bags of our specially blended coffees and teas in the gift shop. Maybe a catering contract or two, if we were lucky. But the main provider for the entire hotel's coffee and tea services? This was a huge opportunity, but we were a small operation. As much as I'd love to jump on this, Adeena was the coffee person and Elena hand-blended all the tea we offered. This wasn't my place.

I nodded at Elena to let her know she should take over the conversation.

"How many guests are expected at this event? And how much variety would you want us to provide? I'm assuming you'd like us to create drinks based around the chocolate theme?"

Zoey nodded. "Yes, I'd like you to collaborate with The Chocolate Shoppe and use their products in your drinks. Or at least as inspiration."

I felt a slight twinge at the idea of collaborating with The Chocolate Shoppe, as if we were being disloyal to Blake and Hana and Choco Noir. But we'd be fools to turn down such a potentially lucrative opportunity.

Besides, I thought, trying to convince myself, this afternoon tea provided the perfect cover for our investigation into the rival store.

A quick glance at my partners let me know we were all on the same page.

Adeena said, "That's perfect. We planned on stopping by there later anyway since Elena's never been and Lila and I haven't been since high school. Do you think they'd be available to talk later today, or should we schedule an appointment?"

Zoey thought it over. "If Anita or Vince is available, it wouldn't hurt to touch base with them now to give you a head start on the specialty drink. But if not, I plan on scheduling a meeting here at the hotel so we can finalize everything and sign the contracts."

"Do you only need one specialty drink for the event? And do you need any baked goods from Lila?" Elena asked.

"We're aiming for a maximum of forty people for this event. Our afternoon teas are quite popular, but this is the first time in years that we're holding a themed one, so we want to keep it rather simple," Zoey explained. "One chocolate-themed coffee drink and one chocolate-themed tea drink. We also want regular coffee, a nonflavored black tea, and a decaf option. The Chocolate Shoppe is handling the food, so we only need you to supply the drinks for this event."

I jotted the information down in my notebook. "So, five drink options total, no need for pastries. Do you need us here to mix and serve the drinks, or do we just need to provide the supplies and recipes?"

"We have staff who handle all the serving, so you can leave that to us. You're free to stick around for the event if you'd like, but our priority will be the ticketed guests."

Adeena grinned. "If there are any delicious chocolate desserts that don't get eaten and need a good home, let us know. I'll be happy to take them off your hands."

Zoey laughed. "I'll keep that in mind. Now, that's all the

business talk I had planned. But I believe you have some questions for me?"

When we nodded, she said, "Let's head back to my office then. We can grab some coffee on the way."

After grabbing mugs of coffee from the self-service beverage area in the hotel's restaurant, we made our way to Zoey's office. We all waited until we were seated around her desk before taking a sip of our coffee, and I instantly gagged.

I glanced at my friends, and Elena quickly trained her face into a neutral expression but Adeena glared down at her cup as if it'd insulted her mother.

Zoey hid a grin as she sipped at her drink, which she'd doctored with a ton of cream and sugar. "Do you see why we're looking for a new supplier? I promise that the coffee wasn't always this bad, but our old supply company got bought out and the new owner is cheaping out on their products."

Adeena shuddered and set down her mug. "At this point, you're better off setting out some decent-quality instant coffee and letting your guests make their own. How did they manage to provide coffee beans that are that weak but still taste burnt? Bleh."

"I'm not a big coffee drinker, but even I can tell this is dire," Elena said.

"Which is why we need to rectify this ASAP. The hotel's reputation has taken a hit after months of subpar beverage service, and upper management is being extra cautious about who the next contract goes to. Here's a copy of the boilerplate contract detailing exactly what would be expected of you, if you were to become one of our suppliers," Zoey said, pulling out a sheaf of papers from a folder on her desk and sliding it over. "Again, this would be dependent on how well the chocolate afternoon tea goes, but I figured it'd be good to give you all the information ahead of time. That way I'll know if I need to audition any other suppliers."

"Thanks," Elena said, accepting the documents. "We'll make sure to look these over carefully, and I'll be in touch if we have any questions. If you still have time, I believe Lila had a few questions of her own that she wanted to ask."

Zoey turned her attention to me, and I launched into my first question. "What can you tell me about your partnership with Choco Noir in Shady Palms?"

Her eyebrows shot up. "Right. Gladys did say you'd ask me about them. Choco Noir wasn't my account. My colleague Shawn Ford first learned about them and approached them to sell chocolate bars and sampler boxes in our gift shop. He would also purchase their chocolate for client gifts as well as personal use."

"Have you ever met the owners of Choco Noir?"

"They've come to the hotel a few times to drop off supplies and discuss new shipments with Shawn. If I see them, I usually take a moment to chat because it's important to build a rapport with our suppliers, even if they're not my clients. Especially since we sometimes have to step in if one of us is out when a client stops by."

"If building rapport is so important, how would you describe Shawn's relationship with the owners of Choco Noir?"

Zoey was quiet for a moment, likely choosing her words carefully. "Shawn and I have rather different styles or methods of building client relationships. He's . . . very friendly. He likes to get personal with his clients, make them feel like he's giving them individual attention. Some love that level of attentiveness; others find it uncomfortable."

I read in between the lines. "So he's hit on clients before?"

"I'm afraid I can't say anything else on the matter."

I glanced over at the other desk in the room and noticed there was no name plaque on it, unlike the one on Zoey's desk. However, Zoey mentioned there were only two people in her department, so it had to belong to Shawn. "Is that his desk? Will he be in later?"

Zoey shook her head but didn't elaborate.

Unlike Zoey's workspace, which was tidy yet bursting at the seams with binders, books, and little tchotchkes, Shawn's side of the office managed to be nearly empty and messy at the same time. Like someone had grabbed all their important things in a hurry and left their junk behind.

"Was he fired?" I asked. OK, we were past the point of politeness now, but come on. I needed her to give me something to work with.

"Mr. Ford is still a current employee of the Lancaster Hotel," Zoey said stiffly. "Now, unless you have questions regarding our collaboration, I think you—"

"Actually, I do have a question about that," Elena jumped in. "This boilerplate contract mentions our responsibilities and lists the amounts for general beverage service, but there's nothing in here about the gift shop. I'd need to know the numbers for that as well before we can sign on for anything."

"Oh, you're right! Sorry about that. Let me just . . ." Zoey searched through the file folder on her desk and frowned. "I could've sworn I had it here. I'm so sorry, this is very unlike me. Give me a moment, and I'll print something out."

She turned to her computer and clicked around for a bit before standing up. "The printer in this room is broken, so I just need to pop down to the main office. Be right back."

Elena got up, too. "I have a few questions about numbers, so I'll walk with you. Adeena and Lila, you can stay here. I know you had some emails you needed to go through, so now would be a good time."

After shooting us a meaningful look, Elena followed Zoey out of the room. Adeena counted to ten, then got up, opened the door, and peeked into the hallway. "Coast is clear. I'll stand watch. You know what to do, right?"

I was up, out of my seat, and at Zoey's computer before she even finished speaking. Neither of us had missed Elena's cues, and I needed to find any info I could on Shawn Ford before they got back (and before I psyched myself out about going through someone's work computer).

Since Zoey had just used it, I didn't need to worry about looking for a password or anything like that, and her email was already open in a browser. A quick search for Shawn Ford's name turned up plenty of gold.

"He's been suspended!" I whisper-screamed at Adeena. "Apparently Hana and Blake filed an official complaint against him, and they weren't the first to do so."

"Does it say what the exact complaint was?"

"Sexual harassment, unprofessional conduct, soliciting 'favors' in return for better contract conditions . . . ugh, what a scumbag."

"Is there anything in there from him? Like his response or whatever?"

I skimmed the email chain. "He refuted the allegations but agreed to take an unpaid suspension and attend HR training courses if 'it would prove his good intentions and earn back trust.' I doubt he's sincere, but he's at least smart enough to not put anything incriminating in writing."

I closed out of the email and set Zoey's PC exactly how she'd left it. I briefly thought about wiping my prints off, but that seemed excessive. Just in case though, I pulled on my gloves as I approached Shawn's desk. My extra caution wasn't really necessary as all the drawers were locked and there was nothing on the surface for me to inspect.

I was about to go through Zoey's desk when Adeena hissed, "They're coming!" and vaulted back into her seat.

I had just enough time to plop back down and whip out my phone to pretend I was checking my emails when Zoey and Elena entered the room.

"I never thought about using bath tea sachets, but that's a wonderful idea! Please add that to the list of items you're offering, and I'll make sure to include it in my proposal," Zoey said.

"Of course. We'll look this over carefully and get back to you ASAP," Elena said, holding up a file folder. "Anyway, thank you so much for your time."

Zoey smiled and shook all of our hands. "It was lovely meeting you all. I'm sure you have a lot of work to do to prepare for the chocolate afternoon tea event, so I appreciate you taking it on with such short notice. Make sure to let Anita and Vince know that I sent you."

The three of us thanked Zoey again for her time and the new opportunity and headed silently to my car.

Once we were inside, I quickly filled Elena in on what I found out. "I was really hoping we'd get a chance to talk to Shawn, maybe snoop through his desk or something. I know the trip wasn't a waste, but it kind of feels like it."

Elena shook her head. "We got an exciting new business opportunity and learned that one of our main suspects has a history of harassment. To the point that he's currently suspended for it. That's not nothing."

Adeena agreed. "Besides, you're the one who's always stressing how slow the process is to us. It's not like this one trip to Shelbyville is going to magically smoke out the killer and tie up all the loose ends by the time we sit down for some ice cream."

At the mention of ice cream, Adeena's stomach let out a comically loud gurgle, and Elena and I burst out laughing.

"On that note, I believe it's time for lunch," Adeena said. "All your doom and gloom is probably 'cause you're hangry. You'll feel better about everything once we get some food in you."

Food sounded like an excellent idea, and it was time to meet up with Jae anyway, so I headed to the Wily Cow Emporium. When we greeted the hostess, she informed us that Jae was already waiting for us at our favorite booth. I slid in next to him, and Adeena plopped down across from me.

"Wonder what the specials are today," she said, grabbing the menu. "Ooh, there's a chipotle salmon burger with spicy sweet potato fries. Done and done."

Elena said, "That does sound good. Make sure to save me a bite? I'm craving something simple, so the spicy tofu burger is calling to me."

Jae, who didn't understand the point of calling something a "burger" if it wasn't made with beef, groaned. "I know I should get something healthy too, but it's so hard to say no to the perfect cheeseburgers they serve here."

"One of my cousins is a nutritionist, and she taught me her favorite rule when I was struggling with eating well when I was away at college: adding, not restricting. If you're craving that burger, then go ahead, but make sure you're also having a salad and veggies on the side," Elena suggested. "You're allowed to enjoy food. Just like, maybe cut down to a regular-size burger instead of a double."

"You're the one always preaching moderation. Isn't that right, Dr. Jae?" Adeena smirked, likely remembering all the times he commented on her sugar consumption.

"Practice what I preach, got it."

Our server arrived and we all put in our orders, then quietly sipped at our waters until nobody was close enough to our table to listen in.

"Unfortunately, Felice didn't really have much to say that we didn't already know." Jae helped himself to the chips and queso the server had dropped off. "She did give me a lead though. She said the previous owners of The Chocolate Shoppe are never at the store because they want the staff and customers to recognize and respect that their kids are the new owners. However, they've become much more social since they retired and recently started taking ballroom dancing classes. If we don't get anything useful from the current owners after this, I can start taking classes there with my mom and try to get friendly with them."

"That is both devious and wholesome," Adeena said. "Which somehow works for you. But why your mom and not Lila? Wouldn't you want her around for the investigation?"

Jae shook his head. "They're more likely to let their guard down if my mom is there. It's less obvious that I have an ulterior motive if people think I'm a mama's boy."

"Which you are," I said with a grin.

"Plus, I've taken dance classes with my mom before. So has my brother since my dad hates dancing as much as my mom loves it. If anyone we know from previous classes sees us there, it becomes that much more believable," he said, ignoring me. "Besides, after all she's going through right now, she could use a break."

I bit my lip, guilty about my urge to tease him. Of course his mom was going through it right now. Hana was her niece. She was currently acting as Aria's guardian, which was an especially tense situation since her sister, Hana's mother, was currently staying at their house and talking about taking Aria back to Minnesota with her.

I squeezed his hand. "You're a good son, Jae."

The two of us gazed into each other's eyes, but before we could really be in the moment, Adeena had to Adeena.

"Yeah, yeah, you're a good son, perfect boyfriend, blah blah blah," Adeena joked. "But are you a good investigator? That is the question."

Jae looked unsure for a moment, but an encouraging glance from me had him sitting up straighter and he returned Adeena's look. "Guess we're going to find out."

Chapter Sixteen

Stepping into The Chocolate Shoppe was like stepping back in time. The black and white checkerboard tile on the floor, the long counter whose sides were covered in pink and mint green tile with matching colored stools, shiny chrome everywhere, and an honest-to-goodness jukebox playing music that sounded like it was from even before my parents' time, so maybe the 1950s or '60s. I half expected someone to come out on roller skates to take our order. The shelves were lined with boxes of chocolates and caramels of all kinds, but the centerpiece of the place was the giant soda fountain in the middle.

They offered sandwiches, old-school drinks like egg creams and lime rickeys, and all kinds of ice cream–based offerings. The ice cream cooler in front had basic flavors like vanilla, chocolate, and strawberry as well as more creative flavors that were rotated out weekly. This week was double fudge coconut brownie, apple pie, pear dark chocolate oat crisp, and white chocolate macadamia nut.

The ice cream could be served plain with a choice of cup or homemade waffle cone; in a sundae or banana split topped with whipped cream, fudge sauce, and cherries; in a float or milkshake; or on top of their award-winning fudge brownies.

A new offering, according to a sign by the register, was affogato style, meaning the ice cream of your choice was topped with a shot of espresso. Adeena's eyes gleamed when she saw the sign—the only thing she loved more than chocolate was coffee, after all (well, and chai, but we're not talking about that), and what a great way to pair them.

The staff on the floor all had name tags pinned to their uniforms, so we knew none of them were Anita or Vince. We decided to treat ourselves to dessert before asking the mostly high school–age staff if we could talk to their bosses. I got a scoop of the double fudge coconut brownie ice cream in a waffle cone (the smell wafting through the shop as the employees made these from scratch made it impossible to resist), Elena requested the cherry lime rickey, Jae asked for an apple pie milkshake, and Adeena, who we had to talk down from trying to order everything on the menu, settled on an egg cream plus a white chocolate macadamia nut affogato. Elena got sick of Adeena's constant sighing and eyes that strayed longingly toward the counter and added a brownie topped with pear dark chocolate oat crisp ice cream for us all to share. The brownie came with a tiny silver pitcher of fudge sauce, and Adeena audibly moaned as Elena poured it over the ice cream and brownie.

"Girl, we are in public. Please keep your lusting to a minimum," I said. Then I took a spoonful of the brownie–fudge sauce–ice cream combo and let out a similar sound. "Never mind, I take that back. That was the proper reaction to this slice of heaven."

Jae wisely left the brownie to me, Adeena, and Elena, and the three of us scraped every bowl, plate, and cup clean.

"I can't believe it's taken us so long to come back here," Adeena said. "This should be part of our weekly rotation."

I hadn't had sweets this simple yet decadent since the last time I was at Margie's Candies in Chicago, and Lord, I missed that place. Adeena was right, we absolutely needed to add this to our regular Shelbyville visits. I licked the last of the fudge sauce from my spoon and sighed. Dessert break over. Time to get our heads back in the game.

Since Jae was in charge of talking to the previous owners, I didn't want him being associated with us in case anyone put two and two together. I had him wander the store, pretending he was buying gifts, while the Brew-has and I handled the current owners. Jae headed to the caramel section while the three of us made our way to a staff member who had their phone out and was snapping photos of the Valentine's Day display.

I glanced at their uniform, but they weren't wearing their name tag. "Excuse me, do you have a minute? Are Anita or Vince Carter around?"

The employee's eyebrows jumped up their forehead. "Is there a problem? If so, I can get a manager. You don't need to—"

"Oh, don't worry! I'm not here to complain. Can you tell them that Zoey Hong from the Lancaster Hotel sent us? We're providing the drinks for the chocolate afternoon tea this weekend," I said, handing them a business card.

A look of relief washed across their face as they glanced at the card before tucking it in their uniform pocket. "Oh, good. I was worried that something was wrong again. Can you give me a sec? I need to post this on our social media."

"Oh, are you the one who updates The Chocolate Shoppe's social media profiles?" If so, maybe they knew about the drama in their comments section. In fact, they were probably the one who started it, considering the not-so-subtle digs at Choco Noir.

"Not that I got a raise or team or anything to go along with the fancy title, but yes. I'm Erin, the social media marketing manager," they said, their eyes looking down at their phone and their fingers flying as they typed out a caption for their post. Once Erin hit submit, they slid their phone in their pocket and gave us their full attention. "Sorry, what did you need again?"

Elena stepped forward. "Wow, The Chocolate Shoppe has a dedicated social media manager? No wonder their recent posts look so professional."

Erin preened. "Thanks! It's what I'm going to school for, so it's nice to get some hands-on experience. I've been working here since high school, but they promoted me to this new position last month."

"Congrats! But if this is a new position, who handled the social media before?" I asked. Erin got promoted to the position right around the time of the comment section debacle, so I wondered if they were the one who got into the fight or if they took over because of that inflammatory interaction.

"Our boss Anita used to handle it. But things happened, and anyway, the winter holidays are our busiest time, so it was decided that social media was taken off of her list of responsibilities so she could focus on other stuff." Erin shrugged. "I was already helping out with the graphics and stuff anyway, so it wasn't a big deal taking over writing the captions and whatnot."

"Anita was the one who decided to step aside and give you the position?" I asked. "That was nice of her."

"Oh no, it was her parents and brother who made the decision. They thought she was making them look bad, but—" Erin stopped and turned wide eyes to me. "Wait, you didn't hear that from me. Please don't mention this to anyone."

"Mention what? I didn't hear anything. Right?" I said, looking at Adeena and Elena.

"Nope, we've both been spacing out and not listening at all. No worries," Adeena said with a wink.

Erin smiled in relief and knocked on the door they'd led us to. When a voice told them to come in, they opened the door and introduced us without stepping in. "Hey boss, Zoey Hong from the Lancaster Hotel sent these people to meet with you. I gotta get back to the floor."

As they turned to leave, they said under their breath, "I forgot my name tag again, and I've already been warned three times. Put in a good word for me, yeah?"

I grinned at them and nodded before entering the office. A man was sitting behind a large desk, looking over a bound document, but he hastily shoved it in a drawer and stood up to greet us once Adeena, Elena, and I were inside.

"Nice to meet you. I'm Vince Carter, the co-owner of The Chocolate Shoppe along with my sister, Anita."

Vince was about average height, maybe just a bit under, and sturdily built. He was dressed in dark jeans with a tucked-in tee and well-cut blazer that somehow perfectly matched his classic all-white Air Force 1s, a look that would work perfectly for Jae.

I filed that away for later and introduced myself. "We met with Zoey this morning and wanted a chance to chat with you and your sister about the event since we just learned about it," I said, providing a quick rundown of who we were and what our roles were.

Vince shook all our hands. "My sister should be back soon. She went to the Olive Oil Emporium because Ms. Gladys has something new she wants us to try."

No sooner had he said that than the door suddenly swung open. "You won't believe what that old bat wants us to . . . Excuse me, who are you?"

A woman I assumed was Anita Carter stood in the doorway, her right hand still on the doorknob while a large paper bag dangled from her left. Adeena was the one standing closest to the door, so she bore the full brunt of the woman's glare.

Vince hurried to smooth it over. "Hey sis! These are the people we'll be working with for the chocolate afternoon tea at the Lancaster. We were just about to start discussing the event."

"Oh, sorry! I'm Anita Carter. My brother and I run The Chocolate Shoppe."

Anita held her hand out, and Adeena gripped it with an oddly intense smile as she introduced herself. "Adeena Awan. Gladys, who is a dear, dear friend, recommended us for this job. I believe you were about to say something about her?"

Anita's eyes flew wide open, and she tried to backpedal. "Oh, no! I wasn't talking about Gladys. I was just about to complain to my brother about this woman from church I ran into on my way back. He knows the one."

She shot her brother a look, and he smoothly backed her up. “Oof, her. Sorry you had to deal with that, but better you than me. She’d probably try to hook me up with her granddaughter again.”

Anita chuckled. “You know it. Anyway, Gladys wanted us to taste these olive oil brownies she made. Said she didn’t want to step on our toes since she knows ours are already famous, but thought it’d be interesting to offer something different.”

“Well, you have been complaining about how you want to change things up. Maybe she’s just trying to be supportive,” Vince said, eyeing the brownies apprehensively.

“Even I’m not fool enough to take our bestseller off the menu. She probably thinks I am though,” Anita muttered.

“These are certainly different. If they’re good, maybe we can make them seasonal or a special or something,” Vince said. “Would you all like to try some? We can’t eat this whole tray by ourselves, and I’d love to have some outside opinions as well. Gladys is a close family friend, so I don’t want us to be biased.”

Adeena perked up. “We’re friends with Gladys too, but I’d never lie about dessert. You can trust us to give our honest feedback.”

He laughed and quickly divided the small pan into eight squares. “Glad to hear it.”

We all helped ourselves to a piece and took a bite. The bittersweet flavor of good chocolate combined with the richness of olive oil and the flakes of sea salt on top overtook my mouth, and for a moment, Adeena and I sounded like we were reenacting that one Meg Ryan scene in *When Harry Met Sally.*

Over the top? A little. But what can I say? Sometimes a good brownie just hits like that.

Anita was a little more discerning with her reaction. "Hmm, these are fudgier than our brownies, which are more on the chewy side. I still prefer ours, but I know we've had customers in the past who've requested fudgy brownies. If we label and promote them correctly, it might work to serve Gladys's brownies alongside ours."

Vince nodded. "We could even offer brownie sampler packs by offering both types of brownies with or without nuts or other mix-ins added. We've always been too scared to touch the brownie recipe, but this could be an opportunity for us to leave our mark."

The two of them were lost in their own world, coming up with idea after idea for how to make their family's store even better. Not gonna lie, when Gladys told me how the new owners were trying to shake things up, I thought they'd be super bougie, looking down on anything too homey or rustic. But watching the two brainstorm together, I could feel how much they loved the shop. The store was their family's legacy, and as the third-generation owners, they must be feeling the pressure not only to carry on their family's traditions, but also do their part to help it thrive. As someone who also had the weight of tradition and family expectations on them for most of my life—Tita Rosie would never pressure me, but I know she wants me to take over the restaurant when she's gone—I felt a connection to them.

Still, just like I shouldn't let Gladys's remark affect how I interact with the Carters, I shouldn't let that imagined connection stop me from looking at them as potential suspects. Just because I sympathize with them doesn't mean they're not capable of committing horrific acts. I've learned that the hard way, time and time again.

"If you want to play around with the flavors, coffee is a perfect pairing with chocolate," Adeena said. "I roast and grind all the coffee beans we serve at the Brew-ha Cafe myself and would love to chat about a collaboration or even our shops becoming suppliers for each other."

Vince glanced at Anita, who looked thoughtful. "Did any of you try our coffee?"

"I had an affogato," Adeena said. "Why?"

Anita laughed. "I was going to ask what you thought of the espresso we used, but your expression tells me everything I need to know."

"Sorry about that. I've been told I have a very loud face," Adeena said. "But coffee is quite literally my life now, and I can tell you that whatever beans you're using ain't it. Whoever pulled that shot probably doesn't know what they're doing either."

Vince grimaced. "We paid so much money for that fancy espresso machine, and it's been nothing but a white elephant. Anita figured that since we already served coffee and had plenty of fixings, we could offer lattes and blended coffee drinks. But nothing we make with that machine tastes good, so our customers have been sticking to the old menu and asking for drip coffee instead. I don't know what to do."

"You got that machine recently then? What kind of training did you provide for your employees?" Elena asked.

"Anita and I watched instructional videos and practiced ourselves before teaching our employees. We could get it to taste OK when it was just us, but we haven't been able to get the flavor consistent."

Anita sighed. "Which is a huge problem, of course, because

when a customer comes in, we want to deliver a quality product and experience every single time. Until we get that consistency down, we might have to take espresso items off the menu."

Elena, the beautiful shark that she is, jumped on this. "Would you be willing to have an expert come in and train you and your employees? It would only take a few hours, and you'll be able to put that espresso machine to work."

The siblings held a silent conversation with their eyes before Anita gestured for Vince to speak. Based on their interactions, I had a feeling Anita was the idea and people person and Vince was the paperwork and general finances one.

"Before making that decision, I'd like to know your general pricing and exactly how many hours we'd need to allot for the training. We'd need to pay not only the trainer, but our employees for their time as well. And I'd also like to visit your cafe and sample your drinks. This isn't shade to you or your business, but if it's at a level that Anita and I can eventually reach on our own through practice, our budget would be better spent elsewhere."

Adeena grinned. "No offense taken. It only makes sense for you to try the product before investing in it, after all. Plus, I love making people put their money where their mouth is, so this should be fun."

Elena and I exchanged amused glances. My bestie was the most competitive person in the world, so Vince's statement would only make Adeena work harder, pretty much guaranteeing us their business. Anita must've sensed a kindred spirit in Adeena because she said, "You're a competitive one, aren't you? I admire that fight, but I'm not as easily impressed as my brother." Before Vince could defend himself, she added, "While I am looking forward to working with you all, our lunch break is almost over and we really do need to eat. We're supposed to meet with Zoey and the hotel event planner on Wednesday. I'm assuming I'll see you there?"

Mondays were the only day that all three of us could make it, but since I was just backup for this event, I said, "Adeena and Elena will be there. Just let us know what time. We have a really small staff, so I'll be at the cafe with our other two employees."

Vince raised his eyebrows. "You only have five people working at your cafe? With a staff that small, either you get no business or no days off. And considering Gladys recommended you, I'm guessing it's the latter."

"The cafe is closed on Mondays, so that's our day off," I explained. "We can't afford a large staff yet. Unlike The Chocolate Shoppe, we haven't been around for generations, building up a loyal following over decades. It's been less than two years since we opened, and I'm proud of what we've built. You'll see once you come visit us."

Anita bristled. "You act like it's a given that we have loyal customers just because we've been around for a while. But those customers wouldn't keep patronizing us if it weren't for the quality products we put out and the blood, sweat, and tears that my family pours into this place. We are the go-to place for things like first dates, birthdays, and graduations. People come to us for gifts for their lover or clients they want to impress. They trust us because everyone knows we have the best chocolates around."

Adeena stepped in front of me. "She wasn't insulting your work ethic. She was just explaining why we have so few employees."

"Then there was no need to mention our store."

"So your family was able to afford a large staff from the beginning? That wasn't something that was built up over the years?"

The two of them were toe to toe, and this back and forth looked like it could go on for a while, but Vince stepped in. "Actually, you're right. The Chocolate Shoppe was purely family run in the early years. It was almost a decade before my grandparents could afford outside help. Though to be fair," he added, "considering they opened one of the first Black-owned shops in the area, things were a little different back then. To put it mildly. So I apologize for my hotheaded little sister here. But we both have a lot of love and a lot of pride when it comes to this shop, just like you do for your cafe. I'm looking forward to working with all of you."

"You're only five minutes older than me," Anita muttered. "But he's right. I didn't mean to get all heated on you. I've just got a lot on my mind. And I still need to eat."

"Hanger always gets the best of me, too," I said, smiling at her. "We'll let you enjoy your lunch in peace. Thanks again for taking the time to meet with us. Hope you'll visit the cafe soon."

Adeena, Elena, and I let ourselves out into the shop.

"Let's get souvenirs for Leslie and Naoko," I said as we met up with Jae. "I should probably get something for my aunt and grandmother, too."

"Souvenirs? It's not like we went to Switzerland; we're just in the next town over," Adeena said. "Though it would be nice for us to get something for Leslie and Naoko since we'll probably be working them extra hard to prepare for the afternoon tea."

Elena leaned closer to her. "It'll look good for us if the Carters know we're spending money in their store. The more beneficial we seem, the easier it'll be to get what we need."

Count on Elena to see the bigger picture.

After purchasing several sampler boxes for us to take back to

Shady Palms, we congregated next to Jae's car for a final briefing before we split up.

"Any thoughts after this initial meeting?" I asked. "I'll just say they're different from how I originally pictured them. They seem cool, but after learning that Anita was the one making those passive-aggressive posts about Choco Noir, I'm not sure what to think."

Adeena nodded. "If nothing else, I think working with them will be good for the cafe. Coming here has already given me all kinds of inspiration for drinks I want to try making. I think they're interesting, but Anita is really defensive when it comes to the shop. There might be motive there, if she feels like she needs to protect it."

"Anita's rude posts aside, I actually think Vince is the one to watch," Elena said. "Did you see him hide those documents when we came in? He probably thought he moved fast enough, but I know a business proposal for expansion when I see one. I looked at a million of them in school and when advising my family. Why bother hiding it? Also, he seems like the calm voice of reason, the quiet guy who handles paperwork, but there's more to him than that. My gut says he's someone who knows how to handle people, and I don't like being handled. Be careful around him."

"You two are the ones meeting with them on Wednesday, so I'll leave it up to you to discern if they're a threat or not," I said. "And if you need backup, for whatever reason, just let me know and I'll head to wherever you are."

Elena smiled her sweet, scary smile. "Don't worry, chica. We got this."

Chapter Seventeen

The opportunity to talk to the Carters again came much sooner than we thought.

"So this is your cafe." Anita Carter stood just inside the doorway with her brother, casting appraising eyes around the shop. "Not bad. I pegged you all as the types to have a light-up sign or some wall art that said something trite like 'Live, Laugh, Latte' or whatever. But this place has real personality."

Elena had briefly thought of doing something like that to encourage customers to take photos in that spot and post them to social media, but Leslie shot that idea down as "too cringe." Score one for the younger generation, I guess. Adeena had pointed out that almost every area of the cafe was perfect for photos anyway, and if we were going to go that route, she wanted to go full cringe with puns like, "I like you a latte" or "Give love a chai" or "Espresso yourself."

Adeena being Adeena, this led to her going down a rabbit hole of coming up with groan-worthy coffee, tea, and pastry puns. And Elena being Elena, she decided that the next set of Brew-ha Cafe merch would be punny greeting cards, stickers, and mugs that the two of them created. Their most recent designs were friendship-themed for Galentine's Day (Bes-teas) and couple-related for Valentine's Day (Hot-teas).

I pointed that out to the Carters. "Our aesthetics were too good to put up something that would draw attention away from our products, but we do like to have fun. That over there is our merch area, which includes plants, herbs, tea, and bath and beauty products that Elena grows and makes. She's replenishing the shelves right now, and I'm sure she'll give you a tour of that area later, but you're here to try our drinks, right?"

Vince nodded. "We'd love to try your espresso straight up and also prepared in a variety of ways to get an idea of your partner's skills and what the training would involve."

"Would you like to try the teas I'm auditioning for the chocolate afternoon tea menu?" Elena asked, joining us by the door. "Since I'm not sure what you're serving, it's hard for me to narrow it down, so I'd love your opinion. I can finish restocking later."

"Why don't we have Naoko do that and I'll assist Leslie at the register?" I suggested. "That way you and Adeena can focus on Anita and Vince."

"Works for me. Just give me a minute so I can give Naoko instructions, and I'll meet you all at the counter." Elena called Naoko over to the merch section and the two started going over the tasks on Elena's clipboard while I led the Carters over to the counter.

"I'm sorry," Anita said. "I knew you had a small staff, and we still showed up without making an appointment first. I was just so curious about your cafe after meeting you all yesterday that I didn't even think about that."

Vince added, "We honestly were just planning on having Adeena prepare us a bunch of drinks while we sat and tried them on our own. We weren't expecting you to cater to us like this."

"It's fine, you came during our slow period. Besides, I've been toying with the idea of offering coffee flights, so this is the perfect opportunity to test it out," Adeena said. "You're here to test my espresso-making skills, so I'm thinking espresso shot, Americano, and latte to start. I plan on bringing my drinks to tomorrow's meeting with Zoey, so there's no need to try everything right this second."

Vince nodded. "Elena said she wanted us to narrow down what to present to Zoey, so we can still help with that while focusing on the espresso, which is what we came for."

While Adeena went to grab the special coffee flight sets she'd ordered, I placed a plate of honey butter biscocho in front of them. "Something simple to enjoy with your coffee. I didn't want to serve you anything too complicated that could interfere with your tasting, but these could help reset your palate. Let me know if you need a refill. I'll be at the register."

Like Adeena said, it was our slow period, so Leslie didn't really need my help at the register, but it was good for me to put my time in up there. Since I was the baker and admin (and self-designated head sleuth), I spent my mornings in the kitchen and most afternoons in my office doing paperwork, running errands for the cafe, or out investigating. I would also be out on the floor refilling the shelves and occasionally greet our customers, but the vast majority of our customer-facing work was left for everyone else to handle.

Even when I was in school and working at my ex-fiancé's family restaurant in Chicago, I was a back-of-the-house person, handling office work and occasionally jumping in to help with prep when needed. The way Adeena, Elena, and I split up the responsibilities had the Brew-ha Cafe running smoothly, but it wouldn't hurt for me to become a little more well-rounded.

We usually liked having two people at the register, one person to handle the line and the other to take care of the orders, but things were slow enough that I asked Leslie to walk Longganisa for me while I worked the register solo. I could walk her myself, but Leslie requested it be one of their duties since they enjoyed being able to take brisk walks in the middle of the day and still get paid for it. As much as I preferred colder weather because it better fit my general aesthetic, I didn't particularly love tromping around outside during a cold, snowy Midwestern winter. This weather was made for staying indoors dressed in thick, cozy knits while consuming soothing drinks and warm desserts, preferably while cuddling with a loved one in front of a roaring fireplace. Not that we could afford one for the Brew-ha Cafe, but I could still dream.

Since there were so few customers, I wandered over to the table where Adeena and Elena were walking the Carters through the various things they'd prepared. The siblings had already made it through the espresso shot and Americano and were now sipping on the latte sample Adeena had prepared.

"I can understand how your first two drinks were so much better than ours since you're clearly a pro who uses quality beans," Anita said. "But this latte is miles above any that I've tried, even compared to some great ones I've had in the city. What's your secret?"

Adeena beamed. "Like you said, it's all about quality products and good technique. My drinks are obviously the best, but even when the other cafe employees prepare the beverages, they're still excellent. That's because I take the time to train them properly and Elena and Lila are so careful about choosing the best local suppliers."

Elena said, "My uncle owns an apiary and has connections with lots of local farmers. We source our butter, cream, and milk from a dairy farmer he's friends with. You can taste the difference."

"They also make the only lactose-free milk that actually works for me," I added. "I usually stick with coconut or soy milk since me and dairy don't mix. But after tons of begging, we got them to make small quantities of lactose-free milk so people like me can still enjoy regular lattes."

"So you form real relationships with your suppliers?" Vince asked. "That's interesting. Our family has stuck with the same bulk suppliers for years, but it wouldn't hurt to broaden our horizons, as long as they're within our budget. We go through tons of dairy ourselves, so I'd love to see what difference it would make for our products. Would you mind sharing the name of your supplier?"

Elena said, "It's the Shady Palms Dairy Haven, and they operate on the outskirts of Shady Palms. Let them know I referred you. Just make sure to set aside plenty of time since they'll want to give you a tour of the facilities and have you sample their various products. Be prepared to ask and answer lots of questions. They only like working with people who align with their farm's mission since they keep their operations fairly small and can only take on so much work."

"I can respect that. Plus, there's a chance they won't meet The

Chocolate Shoppe's needs either, so it's not like there'd be any hard feelings. It's just business," Vince said.

I wanted to respond to that, but Elena had a way better poker face than I did, so I gestured for her to start the investigation.

"That's what everyone says, but that's not always true, is it? You don't reach the level of success that The Chocolate Shoppe has, or the rapid growth that the Brew-ha Cafe has displayed, without being competitive. Hard to not take it personally when you care about winning as much as certain people do." Elena nudged Adeena. "Remember when that new coffee shop opened last year and they tried to steal our customers by making fun of our 'overpriced, froufrou drinks'?"

Adeena's nostrils flared. "I remember our customers literally laughing them out of the shop. They wanna beat me with bargain-basement beans and stale doughnuts? That's not even competition. That's just an embarrassment to coffee."

I laughed. "Girl, you started taking off your earrings the last time they came in here."

"Who told them to come in and disrespect me in my own home? It's not like anything would've happened anyway. Last thing I need is Amir lecturing me for having to bail me out of jail."

"So even you have to deal with local rivalries, huh?" Anita said.

"You have to worry about that stuff, too?" Elena asked. "I would've thought you didn't have those kinds of problems since your store is such an institution."

"We *are* an institution," Anita said forcefully. "And we've earned that right by turning out simple yet quality products for decades. But the younger generation doesn't respect that. They're always looking for something new and exciting. They don't care about the taste; they just want something that'll look good in photos and videos for social media. I hate it, but I'd be foolish to ignore it."

Adeena grimaced. "I can see that. People love jumping on hot new trends, after all. Elena and I are artists, so we're into the aesthetics. It's just another creative outlet for us. But I would never compromise on taste over appearances. Like Paul Hollywood says, I'm not into style over substance."

"I honestly wish I could devote more time to style when it comes to my desserts," I said. "But I'm not a trained pastry chef, and since I do, like, ninety-nine percent of the baking myself, I have to focus on turning out consistently delicious desserts that are easy to mass produce. All the fun fluff has to take a backseat."

Vince surprised me by saying, "I get that. I would love to get more creative in the kitchen, offer more interesting combinations for our chocolate bars and ice creams. Maybe mix up the fillings for our bonbons. But the demand isn't there. Not in Shelbyville. Upping our coffee game is one thing since it's not like we were known for it before, but to mess with proven successes is—"

"Is the only way the shop can grow and catch up with the times," Anita cut in. "You say there's no demand, then why was there a sudden drop in orders when that new chocolate shop opened up?"

He waved his hand. "A fleeting interest in something new. Within the past week, we've not only seen an increase in numbers, but we've actually had more orders than this same time last year."

"Oh wow, that's great," Elena said, cocking her head to the side. "Do you have any idea why there was a sudden bump in sales? I'd love to see if we could replicate that here."

Anita snorted. "I seriously doubt it, unless you decide to—"

"Anita!" Vince cut in. He didn't shout at his sister, barely even raised his voice, but the tone he used and the look he gave her were sharp enough to serve as a warning. He cleared his throat before continuing. "You know we don't share trade secrets, sis."

She let out a small laugh. "Sorry about that. Gotta keep the competitive spirit alive though, right?"

"Now, Elena, I believe you wanted us to try the drinks you want to serve for the chocolate afternoon tea? We haven't finalized the menu yet since the pastries will be handled by the hotel restaurant staff, but our signature brownies will be part of the offerings as well as our chocolate-dipped strawberries and sea salt turtles. Once Zoey confirms what the hotel is serving, we will likely add two more chocolates as supplements for people with dietary restrictions. Do you have any tea blends that would complement our selections?"

With that, Vince dismissed the topic that Elena had so skillfully maneuvered us toward, and none of us could move forward with the questions we most wanted to ask. Unfortunate, but I decided to trust Elena and Adeena to handle the rest of the Carters' visit and went back to the register. It was about the time that business would start to pick up anyway, and Leslie arrived in time to save me from becoming totally swamped. The two of us worked in tandem as a surprisingly well-oiled machine, considering we rarely worked on the same tasks together.

I forgot how quickly time could fly by when you were serving customers, and it wasn't until Naoko tapped me on the shoulder to ask if I wanted her to go on a lunch run since I hadn't eaten yet that I realized how late it was. With my mornings starting so early (the bane of every baker), I was in the habit of doing the majority of my prep work before the sun came up, having breakfast at Tita Rosie's Kitchen, finishing up my desserts to fill our shelves and then doing odd jobs around the cafe until it was time for elevenses, followed by paperwork. That made it easier for me to stagger my lunchtime so that all the Brew-has got to take proper meal breaks.

Now that I took a moment to stop and check my condition, I realized it was almost two o'clock, I hadn't had any water in hours, and the beginning of a headache was starting to pulse in my temples. I needed food NOW.

"Thanks for checking on me, Naoko. I think I'll just head next door and have Tita Rosie feed me since anything else will take too long and I'm about to hit hangry mode."

I felt bad leaving Leslie and Naoko alone, but the Carters had left a while ago, and Adeena and Elena would be returning from their lunch break soon. I'd be right next door in case of emergency, so I pushed down my guilt and headed to my family's restaurant to let my aunt do her favorite thing in the world—feed me until I couldn't move anymore.

I greeted their newest part-time intern, some high schooler related to one of their church friends, and made my way into the kitchen.

"Hey, Tita Rosie, I'm here for lunch! I'll take whatever the daily special is. Where's Lola Flor?"

Usually by this time, the lunch rush was over and my aunt and grandmother would be relaxing in the kitchen. That's why I didn't feel bad about coming over so suddenly to have Tita Rosie feed me. The main part of the restaurant only had a few tables full, and the part-timers were serving them.

"She's in the private room, tending to our guests there. They had some things they wanted to discuss with the restaurant, so your lola decided to handle it."

"Handle what?"

The kitchen door flew open with such force that I would've been knocked out if I'd been standing in front of it, and Tita Rosie and I jumped at Lola Flor's sudden appearance.

"Your fool cousin brought over members of the chamber of commerce. They wanted to know why we weren't more active, and to ask if we were worried about being targets since the restaurant is run by women."

Lola Flor marched to the sink and vigorously washed her hands. While this was standard for anyone who worked in a kitchen, the disdain in her voice and the fervor with which she scrubbed her hands made it seem like she was washing away the interaction she'd just had.

I could only imagine how she reacted to that, but I had to hear it myself. Trying to hide a smile, I asked, "How did you respond?"

She made a *pssh* noise with her lips. "How do you think? I told them that if they weren't helpful when we actually needed them, why would we bother with them now that things are going well?"

Tita Rosie's Kitchen had struggled for years after I went away to college. My aunt didn't want to burden me since she knew living and working in Chicago was my dream, so she tried everything she could to turn the business around on her own. This included asking the chamber of commerce for help. However, as bad as the chamber is now, they were even worse back before Beth and Valerie took over as coheads. My aunt and grandmother received little to no assistance from them, so in a final act of desperation, Tita Rosie begged me to come home after she found out that I had broken off my engagement.

Returning to Shady Palms had been both very easy—after breaking up with Sam, I pretty much lost all my so-called friends and had nothing keeping me there anymore—and also the hardest decision I'd ever made. Coming back home meant saying goodbye to the dreams I had when I first left. Saying goodbye to the person I was at the time. But my family needed me, and as much as I hated to admit it, I needed them as well.

I was able to help save the restaurant after almost losing it during my very first murder investigation, created a sustainable business plan for my aunt and grandmother, convinced them to hire professionals to cover the things they weren't good at instead of trying to do it on their own to save money, and now it was doing better than ever before. Despite how ridiculous my life has become, I wouldn't trade it for anything. It's weird to think about, but my ex-fiancé's betrayal and my family's financial troubles might've been the best things that ever happened to me. They allowed me to open my eyes and see what was really important. That what I thought I wanted from my life wasn't what I truly needed.

"Anyway, it's good that you're here. The real reason Ronnie brought them here was for the investigation. I was going to send one of the servers to get you, but this saves me the trouble. Go join them."

I was dying to see how this was related to the investigation, but my hunger headache was coming on in full force now, and I worried that I wouldn't be bringing my A game to the conversation. Tita Rosie took one look at me and understood.

"Nay, I'm going to bring refills to their table. Lila, can you help me? I was just about to bring them some shrimp sinigang. You can stay and eat with them, see what Ronnie wants."

Shrimp sinigang was my favorite soup in the world, which of course Tita Rosie was aware of. How she knew exactly what I needed after a single glance was like witchcraft. Guess I wasn't the only bruha in the family.

"Of course, Tita. Should I grab these pitchers?"

She nodded and I picked up a pitcher of water and another of calamansi iced tea, then followed her into the private dining room. Seated around the table were Ronnie and Izzy, as well as Charlene Choi, who I'd met at the cafe during a morning rush last week, and a man I recognized but didn't know very well.

"Lila! Your grandmother said she was going to send someone for you, but I didn't expect you to show up so soon," Charlene said, gesturing to the empty seat next to her. "Please, join us."

I set down the drinks and sat in the offered seat. "I actually just stopped by for a late lunch and Lola Flor told me you'd asked for me, so it was perfect timing. I haven't eaten yet, so please excuse me."

I filled a bowl with sinigang and heaped a plate with rice as well as some of the other ulam on the table: chicken afritada, a tomato-based stew that was Ronnie's favorite, and some bistec and sautéed green beans. The others at the table, seeing how hungry I was, let me eat in peace for a few minutes. After I cleared half of my plate and paused to take a sip of my calamansi iced tea, Ronnie took the opportunity to get the conversation started.

"Lila, it seems that you and Charlene have already met, so let me introduce you to Greg Sanders, the owner of Sanders Motors and the vice president of the chamber of commerce. Greg, this is my cousin, Lila Macapagal, one of the owners of the Brew-ha Cafe, which is right next door."

Greg offered his hand, so I set down my utensils and shook it. "Nice to meet you. Thank you for taking the time to patronize my aunt's restaurant. I hope you stop by the Brew-ha Cafe sometime as well."

"The thanks goes to your cousin here," Greg said, clapping a hand on Ronnie's shoulder. "I'd never tried your aunt's cooking before, but he insisted that it was the best meal in town. I'm happy to see he wasn't exaggerating. There's something so homey and comforting about these dishes, even though I've never tried them before."

I picked up my utensils again. "So what did you want to talk about? I'm already a member of the chamber of commerce."

Greg had just shoved a giant spoonful of chicken and rice in his mouth, so Charlene answered. "We wanted to check in with all the women in the group to see how they're doing after this string of burglaries. We particularly wanted to talk to the members who haven't come to the meetings lately and see what we can do to get you to start attending again."

"We've been busy, the cafe is doing well, and the last few times I've gone, the meetings have been rather tense. To put it mildly," I added, before ladling more sinigang into my empty bowl. "I'll still pay my dues and show up if anyone needs me to, but I don't see the point in attending anymore. Especially now with all these burglaries and the chamber is no help."

"Now hold on, you can't blame us for that," Greg said. "If the police haven't caught the guy, what do you expect us to do?"

"We're trying to help as much as we can in our capacity, but to be honest, we're also at our wit's end. We're all exhausted. I'm personally going through it, too . . ." Charlene said. I was all ready to empathize with her, but then she followed with, "I'm undergoing renovations at my house and just, ugh. It's been SO stressful. Having your space be violated and routine disrupted . . . I totally get what those poor women are dealing with."

I slowly turned my head toward Ronnie and caught his eye like, *Did she just say what I think she said?*

Before I could formulate a response, my phone buzzed and a quick glance at the screen showed a text from Jae saying he was at the cafe and needed to talk ASAP. Considering the chamber of commerce was Ronnie's part of the investigation and I'd already finished eating (and Charlene just gave me the ick), I figured it wouldn't be a problem to leave early.

"Sorry, everyone, but I'm needed back at the cafe. Ronnie, I'll catch up with you later?"

He nodded and I said my goodbyes before hurrying next door to meet my surprise visitor.

I was in high demand today.

Chapter Eighteen

The police finally passed along Hana's belongings. I thought we should be together in case we find anything useful among them."

Jae, Detective Park, and I were crammed into my office at the Brew-ha Cafe, staring down at the small box on my desk. There wasn't much inside, but I carefully laid everything out as Detective Park checked the contents against the list he was given.

1. A large zippered tote bag
2. A half-eaten protein bar and two unopened protein bars
3. An open, extra-large bag of organic gummy candies
4. A partially used package of wet wipes
5. A partially full reusable water bottle
6. An empty child's sippy cup
7. A handful of crumpled napkins from a fast-food restaurant

8. A wallet with three credit cards, a Minnesota driver's license, and several folded receipts
9. A cardholder full of Choco Noir business cards
10. A key ring with a heart-shape key chain with the name "Aria" engraved on it and five keys with different-color grips

Detective Park lowered the list. "Notice anything missing?"

I looked over the pile. "Where's her phone?"

Detective Park nodded grimly. "Both Hana's and Blake's phones were missing from the scene. I don't know if the killer or killers took the phones to prevent them from calling for help or if their phones might have incriminating evidence on them."

"Is it possible to trace the phones' locations?" Jae asked.

"Whoever took the phones must have switched them off as soon as they did because the police were only able to trace them to their last known location."

"Choco Noir?" I guessed.

"Choco Noir," Detective Park affirmed.

I stared down at the objects arrayed on my desk, hoping something would jump out at me. Why take the phones but leave behind their bags and wallets? Blake and Hana must've had their phones already out when they were attacked; otherwise, why would the killer waste time digging through purses or pockets when they could've just grabbed the bags and run? Did they have pictures of their attackers? Video? I remembered Detective Park positing that Blake and Hana let the attacker in because it was someone they knew. Was it possible the phones contained texts or a call log that would've caught the police's attention? Was the killer really someone they knew?

My hand drifted toward the set of keys, and I stroked the engraved key chain. Poor Aria. I was about to ask Jae how his niece was doing when something hit me. "Wait a minute. There are five keys here. Do you know what they're for? At least one of these has to be for Choco Noir, right?"

"Yeah, and one is for Blake's apartment above the shop. I remember Blake locked herself out once, and Hana went over to let her in because she had a spare. She spent most of her time in the shop and with Blake, so it makes sense," Jae said, studying the key ring. "You thinking we should head over there?"

"The store isn't a crime scene anymore, right, Detective Park? And it's not trespassing if we're family and have a key," I said.

Detective Park smiled. "We could make that argument, sure. If the SPPD want to cause problems, I can let them know that the Langrehrs gave me leave to help solve their daughter's murder."

I glanced at the clock. "Would it be OK if we wait until after the cafe closes? I still have some things to do, and I know Adeena and Elena will want to come with."

"Actually, I would prefer not to have too many people for this. The more people stomping around, the higher the chance of contaminating the scene. The SPPD have already done their sweep, so we're going to have to be meticulous to make sure we don't miss anything or mess up the scene even more," Detective Park explained. "If you need time, I can always do a cursory search and you and Jae can join me when you're ready."

I understood why he wanted to limit the size of the party (and was flattered he wanted to include me) so I hoped my partners would, too. Still, the thought of Detective Park starting the search without me made my fingers twitch. Maybe the cafe would be OK without me for the rest of the day . . .

"Sure, don't worry about it," Adeena said when I pulled her and Elena aside to ask them for this favor. "Want me to give Amir a heads-up about this in case someone sees you all inside the shop and calls the cops or something?"

"It shouldn't be an issue since it's not like we're breaking and entering, but it's always good to keep a lawyer in the loop," I said. "You sure you don't mind?"

Elena said, "Adeena and I are going to be out most of tomorrow anyway since we have that meeting with the Carters at the Lancaster Hotel, remember? Consider it a trade."

When I still looked reluctant to leave them, she added, "Next time the three of us are out, you'll treat us to a meal. Deal?"

I grinned. "Deal. Just don't go too wild. You know how much I make."

"Yeah yeah. Get out of here."

The Park brothers and I headed straight to Choco Noir. Jae fiddled with Hana's key ring until he figured out which one opened the front door, and he held it open for me. I took a deep breath and stepped inside.

It was still light out, but Choco Noir didn't have massive windows lining the storefront the way the Brew-ha Cafe did, so it was dim inside. I fumbled along the wall, looking for the lights, and switched them on. With a flicker, warm light filled the room, so different from the harsh fluorescent lights or dim mood lighting I was used to at similar stores.

Unfortunately, the sudden wash of light brought the blood spots on the floor into sharp relief, and I instinctively shut my eyes and turned away from them. It didn't matter how many times I'd come across similar scenes, it never got easier. Despite the fact that I'd seen much, much worse, my stomach still roiled at the knowledge that this was the spot that one of my friends lost her life. Where another was attacked so viciously her life hung in the balance.

But if I was going to be any help with this search, I had to pull myself together. Maybe I wouldn't be able to find anything that Detective Park couldn't on his own, but I at least needed to be strong for Jae. In fact, that's probably why Detective Park brought me along in the first place. I just needed to focus on my role of emotional support. I could do this.

With one more deep inhalation, I went to Jae's side and held his hand. "Can I stick with you while we're down here?"

He interlaced his fingers with mine and squeezed. "Please."

"I forgot to warn you that the crime scene wouldn't be cleaned up since that expense would be on the owners of the place," Detective Park apologized. "I'll handle this area. I'll also call a biotech cleanup crew to take care of this once we're done here. Could you two check out the back room and anything else that catches your eye?"

Although the store didn't have a large front window, what was particularly cool about this space was the glass covering most of the back wall that let you peek into the kitchen so you could see the machines (and chocolatiers) at work. Jae and I headed to the kitchen first, followed by the storeroom and then the small office that doubled as an employee breakroom. As fascinating as it was getting a peek behind the scenes, we didn't find anything particularly noteworthy in those areas. Detective Park joined us in the office after he scanned the other areas, and other than mentioning getting a tech guy in to check out the office computer, he had nothing else to share.

The three of us headed upstairs through the separate stairway that led to Blake's apartment. Jae used Hana's key to unlock the door, and we stepped into a spacious two-bedroom apartment.

"Wow, this place is pretty nice," I said. "A little bare since Blake just moved here, but I thought it'd be all rundown like the space above the Brew-ha Cafe."

The deed for the building that housed the Brew-ha Cafe was passed down to me, which meant I not only owned the cafe space but also the floor above it. Adeena, Elena, and I had so many ideas about what we wanted to do with it (our current favorite plans were to turn it into an artist studio for the town or lease it to someone who wanted to open an indie bookstore, something Shady Palms was sorely lacking), but lack of funds meant that floor was still untouched.

"According to Hana, this is what sealed the deal for Blake. The building isn't in a high-foot-traffic area of town, which they originally wanted, but the top floor was recently renovated and ready to move into immediately," Jae explained. "Blake wanted Hana and Aria to move in with her, but Hana preferred a temporary stay at my parents' place until she could afford her own home."

"Hard to beat free rent and childcare," Detective Park said. "I think Hana wanted Aria to experience the security and stability of being around family, too. It was a really big move, after all. Luckily, having them around has done wonders for our dad's health."

"Our mom's, too," Jae added. "I think all the stress from our dad's surgery was getting to her. Having the two of them around has really lightened things up at home. Although now it's . . . Anyway, let's get started. I'll take that first room."

While the Park brothers searched the bedrooms, I handled the kitchen and living room area. The kitchen was always my favorite place in any space, so I headed there first.

The open kitchen was where the apartment's newly renovated status was most apparent. Everything was clean and perfectly placed, but it was obvious that whoever lived here actually cooked—there was a well-loved cast-iron pan sitting on the stove and in the sink were dishes filled with water. Considering they'd been sitting there for more than a week, there was a slightly rotten odor emanating from them, and I made a mental note to ask Detective Park if it was OK to drain the water. A quick look through the cabinets and fridge didn't really turn up any clues, though I did admire how meticulous Blake was about labeling the containers of food she froze for later use.

The kitchen cleared, I made my way to the sparsely furnished living room, which contained a two-seater couch, a child-size rocking chair, a small TV, and a beat-up coffee table piled with envelopes, magazines, and flyers.

I removed the rubber band from a stack of unopened mail and flipped through it. "Overdue bill, overdue bill, Pottery Barn catalog, generic holiday card for clients from Choi & Associates, another bill, dental cleaning reminder from Jae's office, more bills . . ."

Flashbacks to the days when Tita Rosie's Kitchen was in danger of shutting down filled my head as I took in overdue notice after overdue notice. This sight was sadly all too familiar to me. Starting your own business always came with huge expenses, but if Blake had been struggling so much so early on, I worried that Choco Noir would shut down even if Hana woke up.

No, not if. When. I needed to keep reminding myself of that.

I set the mail aside and finished my search of the open area, but considering how empty the place was, it didn't take long. I peeked into the bathroom, where I'd seen Jae head after he was done in the bedroom.

"Anything interesting in here?"

Jae turned away from the open medicine cabinet at my voice. "Other than the staggering amount of skincare products Blake used and an expired Costco-size bottle of aspirin, not really. How about you?"

"Based on the mail I found on her coffee table, Blake was deeply in debt. It might have no relation to the case, but I figure whenever money is concerned, it's worth looking into. Some of those bills looked like they were from debt collectors."

"Good work, Lila."

Detective Park's voice directly behind me made me jump, and I whirled around to face him, my hand clutched to my chest. "Geez, give me a heart attack, why don't you. How can you be so big and so quiet at the same time? I didn't hear you moving around at all."

He shrugged. "I'm a detective. Comes with the territory, I guess. Anyway, the theory about her debt making her a target is a good one. I looked up the cost of the equipment and ingredients that were down in the shop, and my research shows that Blake invested in nothing but premium products. That along with the overdue notices as well as her rather spartan living conditions makes me wonder if she got in over her head opening up her own shop. I'm going to have to do some more digging, maybe call up the places that were sending her these bills. Hopefully it'll lead somewhere."

"So we did good?" I asked.

He patted me on the head. "We did good."

Jae brushed his brother's hand aside. "She's not a child, hyung."

From anyone else, a head pat would've felt super patronizing. But Detective Park wasn't one for physical affection or doling out praise all willy-nilly. So if he was going out of his way to do this, I knew he meant it.

I said as much to Jae, adding, "Let's take today as win. For once, we have some concrete evidence that your brother can follow. This is a good thing."

Jae grumbled a bit before saying, "You're right. We needed a win, and we got one. Thanks for letting us investigate with you."

Detective Park studied his little brother for a moment before venturing a smile. "If I offer to take you both out to dinner, is that still treating you like kids?"

Jae smiled back and play-punched his big brother in the shoulder. "You won't hear me complaining about free food. But it has to be somewhere expensive since we're fancy adults."

"All-you-can-eat Korean barbecue?"

Jae and I grinned at each other. "Let's go!"

Chapter Nineteen

"Longganisa! Look at me! Good girl . . ."

Snap snap.

I shifted my position so that Longganisa's outfit, a frilly white dress patterned with red hearts and accented with a giant red bow on the back, was displayed better. After searching Blake's apartment the other day, Detective Park took over the line of investigation regarding the possible connection to Blake's debt and her death. Which was all well and good, but it left me with no other leads to follow. For a while now I'd been meaning to interview some of the other burglary victims, particularly Diane Kosta, Stan's great-niece, but I could never find the time.

Then earlier this morning I was scrolling through my social media feed and came across a sponsored post from Kosta Photography that let me know Diane not only specialized in pet portraits, but she also was currently running a deal on Valentine's Day–themed pictures of pets with their humans.

Sign. Me. Up.

I'd booked the deluxe package that allowed for up to three costume changes, plus solo pet portraits as well as human and pet pics. Not only was this something I'd always wanted to do, but it was easier to get people to open up once you got them in a good mood and showed them that having you around was beneficial. And what's more beneficial than paying for the most expensive pet portrait package at a business that's been recovering from a traumatizing theft?

Sounded like a win-win if you asked me.

Although maybe I didn't have to choose the *most* expensive package, considering that Stan had already told Diane about me and she was ready to answer all of my questions anyway. Whatever, she kindly threw in a free frame for whichever photo I liked best, which made the extra expense worth it. I planned on hanging the picture next to the oil painting Adeena had made of Longganisa dressed like the queen. True art.

Once the photoshoot was over, Diane let me and Longganisa wander around her studio while she cleaned up. I'd chosen the last slot of the day so we'd have time to chat after. The lock on the front door looked solid, so I wandered to the back to see if there were other ways for the burglar to have gotten in. Sure enough, there was a back door there. I was about to open it up to examine the space behind the building when a hand grabbed my arm to stop me.

"Wait! The alarm is on. You'll set it off if you don't deactivate it before opening the door." Diane dropped my wrist. "Sorry, I didn't mean to scare you."

"No, I'm sorry. I was just being nosy. Well, I'm sure Stan told you all about that."

She laughed. "'Nosy' might be one of the ways he described you, yes. But he also said your nosiness got results, so it's fine. Come on, I'm done cleaning. Care to join me for some tea?"

"Sure." Longganisa was busy sniffing around the back, so I left her there to entertain herself and followed Diane into her small break area. "Is it OK if I let Nisa wander? She's trained, so she won't potty inside or tear up any of your equipment or anything like that."

She smiled. "Most of my clients are pets, remember? If I left anything out for her to get into, that'd be on me."

We washed our hands, and she busied herself heating up water in an electric kettle and pulling out mugs and various boxes of tea bags while I arranged the sweets I'd brought on the plates she provided. Stan told me she had a sweet tooth, so I brought a tin of ube swirl fudge that I was experimenting with. The spirals of white and purple were so effortlessly pretty that just looking at the little cubes of fudge was immensely satisfying. As I debated whether edible glitter was something I should play around with to add a wow factor to some of my desserts, the click of the electric kettle drew me to Diane's side.

"I'm afraid I don't have much of a selection," she apologized. "Just English breakfast, Earl Grey, and chamomile. My only assistant isn't a tea drinker, so I keep it pretty basic."

"No worries. All of these go well with chocolate, so they're perfect. I think I'll be boring and stick with English breakfast anyway. Ube is a subtle flavor, so I wouldn't want a strongly flavored tea to overwhelm it."

Earl Grey was absolutely delicious with both milk and dark

chocolate, but since white chocolate and ube were lighter flavors, it wasn't the best pairing. Though an Earl Grey fudge or hot chocolate might be interesting. Hmm . . .

Diane plucked a piece of fudge from the plate and took a delicate bite. "Mmm! It tastes as good as it looks! I've never tried ube before, but I've seen plenty of desserts with it online. It's such a strong visual, but you're right, the flavors are very subtle. A little earthy, a little sweet, and it pairs perfectly with white chocolate."

She shifted the plate as she studied the fudge from various angles. "If you ever need someone to take professional photos of your food and drinks, please keep me in mind. I specialize in pet photography since that's what's in demand in this town, but I studied food photography in college as well. I'd love to set up a photoshoot to make your products really shine."

"I would love that! I just have to talk it over with my partners to see if it's in our budget," I said, helping myself to a piece of fudge as well. "I had no idea pet photography was in such high demand in Shady Palms."

Diane shrugged. "Pets and family portraits, but nowadays everyone looks at pets as part of the family, so it's all one and the same, right? Anyway, it's cute and fun and pays the bills, so I'm not complaining. I just wish I had more opportunities to diversify my portfolio."

I sank my teeth into the fudge, the sweetness filling my mouth and coating my tongue. Then once the fudge melted, I took a sip of black tea to cleanse my palate with its slight bitterness. Diane's offer to photograph our products made me wonder if we should offer boxed sweets of things like fudge, which had a longer shelf life than most of my other desserts. Maybe we could even offer online shopping and ship it to places that aren't local?

My daydreaming about future Brew-ha Cafe improvements was cut short when Longganisa waddled into the room with a bit of cloth in her mouth.

"Nisa? What've you got there?" I coaxed the object from her and held it up to study it better. "A handkerchief? Diane, is this yours?"

She peered at it. "I think it might belong to one of the security guys who was here recently. I remember seeing him with a handkerchief. I'll ask him next time he's here."

I handed it over to her. Not gonna lie, I was hoping it was a clue of some kind that would break the case wide open, but it was just a green paisley handkerchief or bandana, the type you can buy anywhere. Besides, the cops had already combed through this place from top to bottom after the robbery and so had Diane and Stan when he came to check on her.

We chatted a bit more, but there was nothing else for me to learn so I called it a night.

"Thanks again for your business. Once I've had time to touch up the photos, I'll email them to you so you can choose your favorites and let me know which ones you want printed and which you'll keep digital. After that, you'll get an invoice to pay what's left, and you should receive your photos within three business days. Let me know if you have any questions."

"Sounds good. Do I have to pick them up, or will you ship them?"

"Up to you. Oh, and the invoice email won't be from me, it'll be from Choi & Associates. They handle my bookkeeping stuff. Just wanted to give you a heads-up because I've had clients ignore the emails since they don't bother reading the subject line, they just see the sender and assume it's spam or something."

"Thanks for the heads-up, and for all your time today. I can't wait to see the finished pictures." I picked up Longganisa and waved goodbye to Diane with one of her chubby paws. "I'll keep you posted about the photoshoot for the cafe, but you should definitely stop by sometime."

After she assured me she would, Nisa and I left the photo studio and headed home. "That was fun and all, but I didn't learn much other than she has a security system and there's a back door that leads to the alley. Doubt any of that is useful. What do you think my next steps should be?"

Longganisa let out a big yawn, settled her head on her front paws, and closed her eyes.

"You always have the best ideas, you know that?"

Chapter Twenty

"Blake's ex-husband just gave his statement to Detective Nowak. He's been cleared, but I think he has some info you might find useful. Would you like to meet him?"

My first thought after receiving Detective Park's very thoughtful phone call was, "Well, there goes our main suspect."

Which, I know, not very grateful, considering he didn't have to call me at all or set up these kinds of opportunities, but I couldn't help it. It felt like all we'd done the past few weeks was drive all over the county and talk to a million people, and yet there was no forward movement in the case (other than a stack of overdue notices that still hadn't led us anywhere) or substantial improvement in Hana's condition. I'd gone with Jae to visit her last night, and I listened to him report everything that had been going on and how Aria was doing, but all I could think was that we were no closer to finding the person who had done this to her. Who had taken away her best friend.

But even if Blake's ex-husband had nothing to do with this crime, he could prove to be a good source of information. Or at least, a good outlet to vent my frustration.

"Yeah, set it up. When is he leaving?"

"Early tomorrow morning. I had Rosie book the private room for us for dinner tonight. The restaurant will still be open so she can't join us, but I already talked to Amir and he'll be there. I'll call Jae after this. Is there anyone else who needs to be there?"

I thought for a moment. Adeena and Elena were a given. Ronnie and Izzy were part of the investigation, but they didn't need to be there for every dinner. Maybe the Calendar Crew?

"Would my godmothers being there make things better or worse?"

Detective Park laughed. "Better or worse for who? That's a good idea, though. From my limited interactions with Patrick Murphy, he's a smooth talker and consummate salesman. Having those three around might throw him off his game. I'll tell Rosie to invite them."

"Thanks, Detective Park. Just text me the time once you get everything settled, and I'll let Adeena and Elena know."

We hung up, and I settled back in my office chair to ruminate on what needed to be done before that dinner. Longganisa let out a whimper, so I picked her up and settled her on my lap, slowly stroking her back as I thought. Detective Park said Blake's ex-husband was cleared. He didn't say anything else about that, which means whatever alibi Patrick Murphy provided must've been airtight enough for Detective Park not to question it. So what kind of information could he possibly have that would help with the investigation? Did he see something suspicious that day he surprised Blake at Choco Noir? Is there some secret he knows about Blake that could provide context for what happened to her?

I thought back to my conversation with Blake's parents and realized how little I knew about her, despite our hangouts over the past couple of months. Maybe talking to her scuzzy ex would give me a clearer picture of the woman I barely got a chance to know.

We were only ten minutes into our dinner with Blake's ex-husband, and I already wanted to punch Patrick Murphy in his stupid, smug face. Judging by the looks on Adeena's and Elena's faces, I wasn't the only one.

He'd kicked off the dinner by saying how surprised he was to see so many people had showed up to talk to him since "my Blake has never been very good at making friends."

We had barely helped ourselves to the bounteous feast Tita Rosie had prepared before he lamented Blake's death and said, "If she had just listened to me, she would still be here. She was a sweet girl, but she just never had the right temperament for talking to people. That's why I knew any business she opened was doomed to fail."

Amir had to grab Adeena's arm and shake his head in warning because he knew his sister well enough to anticipate how she'd react to such a disgusting statement. She shook him off and stabbed at her tofu sisig with more antagonism than it deserved.

Elena closed her eyes and took a few deep breaths before focusing her attention on Patrick. "Choco Noir had just opened, and the store was already in high demand as a local supplier as well as for events in the area. Considering she left you years ago and you didn't keep in touch, what makes you think you can talk about her business like that?"

Patrick flushed a violent shade of red. "She didn't leave me, we just—"

"You two were divorced?"

"Well, yes, but—"

"Who initiated it?"

"I don't see how that's any of your business . . ."

"Did you agree to it?"

"Why am I under interrogation? I had nothing to do with what happened to Blake. You," this he directed to Detective Park. "Didn't I prove my innocence earlier? I don't appreciate being treated like a criminal when I've been nothing but cooperative."

"I mean, you did stalk her for a while, so you're not exactly innocent," I muttered.

He slammed his hand on the table. "Have you been talking to her parents? They have no right to talk about my personal business like that!"

"But were they lying?"

"I don't need this," he said, throwing his napkin on the table. "I agreed to have dinner with you all because this detective told me you wanted to find Blake's killer, and I wanted to do my part to help as well. But if you're just going to make me out to be the bad guy, I'm done here."

He stood up and made his way to the door, but Jae beat him to it. "What's the important information you have for us?"

"Like I'd tell you. Now get out of my way."

Patrick tried to maneuver around Jae, but Jae shoved him against a wall. "Whoever killed Blake also hurt my cousin. Hana has a three-year-old daughter who already lost her father and now might have to grow up without her mother, too. You need to tell us what you know."

For a moment, Patrick looked like he wasn't going to back down and I worried that we'd have to break up a fight. But as he continued to stare up at the (much taller and more fit) Jae, the bravado left Patrick's body like air out of a deflating balloon and he sat back down, muttering obscenities under his breath.

"Since you all seem so quick to paint me as the villain and Blake as a saint, you should know that she was in massive debt. She borrowed a lot of money from a loan shark in Minneapolis and then left town."

My eyebrows shot up. "She ran off without paying them back?"

If she borrowed so much money, what was with all those unpaid bills we found in her apartment? Most of the notices were from a collection agency, likely the loan shark Patrick mentioned, but there were others in the pile that I recognized as from suppliers, the mortgage company, etc. Opening a new business and starting a new life cost a ton of money—money Blake didn't seem to have. Was the loan shark pissed that she ran off and decided to make an example of her when he found her? Did we finally find the connection between her debt and her murder?

Patrick scratched the back of his head. "It seems like she was sending them money little by little, but she'd barely scratched the surface on the interest and had been behind on her payments for a while. The only reason I know about this is because she forged my signature as her cosigner and put my address down as her own. The loan shark came after me to pay him back for the last three months of missed payments."

"Did you pay him?"

He let out an ugly laugh. "Not like I had a choice, did I? They knew where I lived, where I worked. People like that don't mess around when it comes to money. They didn't care that I hadn't actually signed the contract. They wanted their money back, and I was the more convenient one to hassle for it."

"Do you think they had anything to do with Blake's death?"

"Doubt it. A dead woman can't pay back her loan."

"But they had you to cover it."

"Exactly. Why bother chasing a woman out of state when they could just harass a sucker like me? They get their money without having to waste their time or dirty their hands."

I studied him. "You must've been real pissed when you found out what she did. Pissed enough to violate your restraining order and chase her all the way here. How did you even find her?"

"Her parents told you about that! Unbelievable," he muttered. "Look, of course I was pissed. First, she leaves me for no reason, then she embarrasses me by asking for a restraining order when I hadn't done anything wrong. Only to find out she ran off with someone else's money that she put in MY name, and suddenly I'm the bad guy."

OK, Blake forging his signature and leaving him as collateral for the loan shark wasn't, like, an awesome move, but the mental backflips this man had to go through to convince himself he was totally innocent regarding his failed marriage was Simone Biles–level impressive.

"You're not the bad guy, huh? Then how did you find out where Blake was? She sure as heck didn't give you her new address."

He held up his hands in a placating manner. "OK, look, this isn't going to sound great, but hear me out. I feel like I was totally justified after that loan shark came to my house and I—"

Detective Park leaned close. "How did you find her, Mr. Murphy?"

"I hired a private detective to find her," he admitted. "And before you look at me like I'm scum, may I remind you that you yourself are a private detective, so don't go acting all holier than thou on me."

"What's their name?" Detective Park asked.

"What?"

"What's their name?" Detective Park repeated, slamming his fist on the table. "They knowingly helped someone track down their ex-spouse who has a restraining order out on them? If you really were Blake's killer, they could be tried as an accomplice or accessory to murder."

"But I didn't kill her! And you know that, so get off my case."

Detective Park scowled but backed off.

"How did they clear him?" I asked Detective Park.

"He won some award at his work conference, so dozens of people confirmed he was not only on stage accepting the award around the time of the attack, but that he spent that whole night partying with everyone at the hotel bar until late. Security footage also shows that he didn't leave the hotel at any time the day Blake and Hana were attacked," Detective Park admitted grudgingly.

"Could you sound a little less disappointed?" Patrick grumbled.

After that, he didn't have anything useful to share, so I left it to my godmothers to pester him with nosy questions the rest of the dinner while I turned over this new info in my head.

Blake was in debt, but Patrick had nothing to do with her death even though he had the most motive, and it was highly unlikely the loan shark and his associates were involved since, like Patrick said, a dead woman can't pay back her dues. There's a possibility they wanted to make an example of her, but for that, they'd have to make it known what they did.

Was Blake's debt another dead end? Well, I could count on Detective Park to follow up on that lead, but what about me?

What could I do?

Chapter Twenty-One

I had been prideful. I realized that now. I knew they were targeting female-owned businesses, but I never really thought they would come for us.

I was wrong.

I stood in front of the smashed-in front window of the Brew-ha Cafe and surveyed the damage. A brick lay amid the shattered glass, and I wondered absently why they had to destroy that panel glass window as well as the glass in our front door. They only needed to break the door to get in. Wouldn't they waste time and increase the risk of getting caught by causing so much noise?

I didn't realize I was trembling until Jae wrapped his arms around me and I snapped out of it. I'd received a call around three in the morning from Safe & Secure Solutions that someone had broken into the cafe. Whoever operated the phones at the security firm assured me they'd call Adeena and Elena as well, so I called

Jae, who said he'd meet me at the cafe, and left a note for Tita Rosie and Lola Flor before slipping out.

The police were waiting when I got there, and so were Detective Park, Jae, and Ben from Safe & Secure Solutions. After the police searched the cafe and confirmed that nobody was inside, I went in with them to see if we were the latest victims of the burglary ring or if this was just vandalism. A quick glance at the front area showed that our cash register was missing. I hurried to my office, where we kept the safe, only to find that missing, too. Thank goodness Elena had made the weekly drop at the bank on Monday as usual, so we only lost a few days' profits. Well, and the safe, which wasn't cheap, but I was clinging to whatever silver linings I could find.

"Oh no . . ."

I turned around and Adeena and Elena were there, accompanied by an officer. Adeena stared into the empty space where our safe used to be, and her face crumpled. I'd been fighting back tears since I first saw that smashed window, and confronted by the grief of my best friends, the feelings of utter wrongness and how our safe space, our happy place, had been violated . . . I broke down and the three of us held each other as we sobbed.

"Sorry to interrupt, but we wanted to give you a quick update." Ben stood awkwardly at the open door of my office along with Detective Park and Jae.

My partners and I separated, wiping away our tears using our sleeves. Ben fumbled in his pockets until he pulled out a well-worn handkerchief.

"Sorry, I've only got the one. It's clean though. Would any of you care to . . . ?"

Adeena and Elena were already using the tissues one of the

officers had offered them, so I accepted it and dabbed at my face so I wouldn't irritate the skin by rubbing too hard. I was a snotty mess though and used the handkerchief to blow my nose before I realized how disgusting that was.

"Oh my gulay, I'm so sorry. I wasn't thinking, I . . . I'll buy you a new one."

Ben laughed. "It's fine. I've got a bunch of these at home. You can keep it. Anyway, I just want you to know that the cafe's alarm sounded at two forty-seven a.m. As per our usual protocol, the police were notified as soon as the alarm went off, and the two-person team assigned to your account were also dispatched. In your case, that was Hector and Vinny."

"Why weren't they here when I arrived?" I asked.

"Hector got here first and reported that he saw someone fleeing the scene. He called it in to the police and the office and went to follow the suspect. Vinny joined him as soon as he could, but whoever Hector saw got away, unfortunately," Ben explained. "I promised Jonathan I'd take good care of you all, and I failed. I'm so sorry, ladies."

"It's not your fault, Ben. The system did exactly what you promised it'd do. And your response time . . ."

I checked my phone to confirm when the security firm called me about the burglary—3:02 a.m. This all happened in the fifteen minutes it took between the alarm going off and the office calling me?

I repeated that question. "Short of you actually living inside the cafe, there's no way anyone could've gotten here any faster. I'm just glad no one got hurt. Did Hector get a good look at the suspect?"

Detective Park gestured for someone outside the room and stepped aside so Hector and Vinny could enter.

Elena surged forward. "Vinny, what happened to your face?!"

His face was scratched up, and a thin cut on his left cheek oozed a small amount of blood. He fixed an easy smile on his face and reached into his back pocket to pull out a dirty handkerchief. "This is nothing, don't worry about—"

Elena grabbed his wrist before he could infect the cut. "Don't! We've got a first aid kit here."

She pointed out the kit hanging next to my desk, and Hector moved toward it. "I've got it."

He sanitized his hands and disinfected the cut on Vinny's face before applying ointment and a bandage. "You good?"

Vinny checked out his reflection in the full-length mirror I kept in the office. "Thanks, man. Hope it doesn't scar up my pretty face. But maybe women will be into that?"

"Enough joking," Ben admonished him. "What happened after you guys got the call? How did you get hurt?"

"I got the call that Hector was chasing after the suspect and joined in so he wouldn't be alone taking them on. When I got to the meeting spot, Hector said the guy ran in the alley and he wanted us to surround it, like a pincer movement, so the guy couldn't get away. I went one way, and Hector went the other. I'm partway down the alley when someone comes up behind me and tases me and I fall forward and hit my head on a dumpster. Next thing I know, Hector is shaking me awake and calling for help."

"Holy crap, that's so much worse than I thought!" Adeena said. "Have you gone to the hospital yet?"

Vinny shook his head, then winced. "I'm good."

"What he means to say," Ben said, his nostrils flaring, "is that he just wanted to give a quick status update on the case and is going to the emergency room immediately afterward. And since he's a smart guy who knows when he needs help and doesn't want to upset his mother even more than she already will be, he's going to ask his beloved boss to accompany him. Isn't that right, Vinny?"

"Sure, boss. Whatever you say," Vinny sulked. "Anyway, I'm sorry we let him get away, ladies. Are you all OK?"

"We just need to finish going through the cafe to document the damage," I said. "Go get checked out, and make sure to get plenty of rest. I'm sorry you got hurt over this."

Adeena and Elena echoed these sentiments, and soon the security guys were gone, leaving me, Adeena, and Elena to do the hard job of going through the Brew-ha Cafe while Detective Park and Jae helped us write down our findings. Luckily, the only damage was to the front window and door, and the only things that seemed to be missing were the cash register and safe. None of our supplies or equipment were missing, and Adeena hugged Mr. Peppy, her espresso machine, in relief.

After answering a few questions and giving our contact details to the officer in charge, the police finally left and we were alone in our wrecked shop.

"We need to call Leslie and Naoko. Let them know what happened. And Helen, too," I said, remembering our part-time delivery person. "Then make signs and social media posts letting people know we're closed until we get everything fixed. We should find something to cover up the door and window for now. And we need to contact our insurance. And a repair person. And—"

Jae pulled me into a hug. "Just breathe, Lila. Breathe. I've got you."

I hadn't realized that as my verbal to-do list grew and grew, my breathing had gotten shallower and shallower and I was in danger of hyperventilating. I hadn't felt the beginnings of a panic attack in over a year, back when I was plagued by them shortly after my first case, but I remembered the ways I'd learned to regulate them. Jae helped me sit down in my office chair as I focused on my breathing.

Adeena took my hands and guided me through the moment. "What are five things you see?"

"I see you. My desk. The open first aid kit. Oh, we need to clean up and put that away. And we need to—"

"No, no, forget about that. Name two more things you see."

Breathe in through my nose, hold. Out through my mouth. "I see Jae and Elena."

"Good. Now name five things you can hear."

She continued like this, and once I'd finished by naming five things I could touch, the panic attack passed and I could breathe normally again. She gave my hands one last squeeze and straightened up.

"Right now, let's focus on the most urgent things. I'll talk to Amir, since he should know how to handle all the insurance stuff and can guide us through getting the repairs done."

Elena put her hand on my shoulder. "I'll call Naoko and Leslie. They'll handle the social media posts about our closure. I'll also contact my cousin Julie. They're in the glass business and can help us with the front window and door, and anything else that might've been damaged."

"I'll talk to the Calendar Crew and church aunties. It won't be the first time they've cleaned up after some vandalism, but I really hope it's the last," I said. "I'll deal with the sign later. Right now, I think we all need to go home and rest. I left a note for my aunt and grandmother, but it's probably better for me to get home before they see it so they won't freak out."

Detective Park stepped up. "Would it be OK if Jae and I stayed over? We can both sleep in the living room. You just went through something really traumatic. Plus, I want to be there when you talk to Rosie so I can calm her down."

I thanked Detective Park for his thoughtfulness. To be honest, I wasn't ready to be alone yet. There was no way Jae and I could sleep in the same bed with my aunt and grandmother around, but just his presence in my home would be enough for me.

"Let's go home, guys. We've got a lot of work to do tomorrow."

Chapter Twenty-Two

"You all have full use of the hotel kitchen. Please let us know if you need help with anything. And again, I'm so sorry to hear about the burglary at the Brew-ha Cafe. If there's anything I can do to assist with the recovery, I'm happy to do it."

Zoey looked up from her planner, where she'd been making notes on the final preparations before the Lancaster Hotel chocolate afternoon tea. She'd called us the day before in a panic after the news of the burglary somehow made it all the way to Shelbyville. She was worried that we'd have to back out of the afternoon tea, but it was obvious that she was genuinely concerned about us as well. Since Adeena and Elena had planned on preparing their drinks on-site anyway, and none of our stock was damaged or stolen, we assured her we'd still be able to participate in the event.

"We really appreciate the offer, Zoey," I said. "We'll make sure to let you know if we think of anything. Now, if I understand correctly, you don't want us to serve the drinks, right? You just want Adeena and Elena to prepare them, and the servers will handle everything else?"

"Yes, once everything's ready upstairs, I'll send the drink servers down to fetch everything. We want our hot drinks to stay hot and ensure that our iced drinks don't get watered down because they were left sitting around," Zoey explained. "Lila, since you're free, could you assist the Carters? They had a delivery arrive late, so they're a little behind."

"No problem."

Speaking of the Carters, Adeena and Elena had caught me up on what they learned about the sibling duo during their meeting at the Lancaster Hotel. Elena had realized the bound document she saw Vince hide when we first met him held expansion plans for The Chocolate Shoppe, so she'd appealed to his ego, saying the Brew-ha Cafe was thinking of opening new locations in the county and asked him for his advice. That's how she learned that both Vince and Anita were in a neighboring town called North Haverbrook when Blake and Hana were attacked—the whole Carter clan was there that entire week for a family reunion, and the siblings had used that time to search for the perfect location for their new shop. Elena had even followed up with the guy Vince recommended, who confirmed that he'd met with the Carter siblings during that time.

Another set of suspects to cross off the list.

Leaving Adeena and Elena to handle their business, I made my way to the area of the kitchen where Anita, Vince, and two of the hotel chefs were constructing the multitiered offerings that would be sent to each table.

"Hey everyone. Zoey sent me to help. What do you need me to do?"

"Oh, Lila, thank goodness. We had a shipment arrive late, so my crew only finished the gluten-free and nut-free chocolates this morning and they were just delivered. Can you fill out the trays that are in the special gluten- and nut-free prep zone?" Anita said, indicating the area. "We owe you one."

While the trays that Anita and the others were working on contained white bread tea sandwiches with smoked salmon and dill and cucumber with butter, as well as mini croissants stuffed with cashew chicken salad, the sandwiches on this tray were made with gluten-free bread and the croissants were stuffed with chickpea salad instead. Regular and gluten-free chocolate chip scones were on offer with clotted cream, although the special dietary trays held a chocolate-caramel spread instead of the chocolate-hazelnut version that went with the regular scones.

One of the hotel pastry chefs was adding immaculate rounds of flourless chocolate cake, the dark chocolate discs topped with flakes of sea salt and cherries that glistened like rubies, while another added a white chocolate mousse that seemed to replace the eclairs on the other trays. Once they stepped away, I filled in the empty gaps with offerings from The Chocolate Shoppe: chocolate-dipped strawberries, milk chocolate filled with a rich sea salt caramel, and dark chocolate enclosing a gluten-free marshmallow and jelly center.

Once we were all done, Zoey gathered The Chocolate Shoppe's and the Brew-ha Cafe's staff and the hotel's servers so that we could explain to them what the food and drinks were, as well as the ingredients in case any of the guests had questions. After the servers asked questions and proved they understood what was on offer, Zoey dismissed them to finish any last-minute checks before the event.

"I reserved a table for you all and made sure to order extras so you could enjoy the afternoon tea as well. Would you like to join us? Or do you need to rush back?"

The Brew-ha Cafe wouldn't be reopening until Tuesday, so Adeena, Elena, and I had nothing but time. Adeena, of course, answered for all of us.

"Heck yeah, we'd like to join! I've been eyeing those silver trays from across the room since we got here."

Vince chuckled. "Ever since we visited your cafe, we've been dying for more of your drinks. Our staff has gotten much better at using the espresso machine since your training, but they still can't compare to you, Adeena."

"Of course they can't," Adeena preened. "But I'm sure in time, one of them will prove to be a worthy foe. Then the student will become the master, and they'll come strike me down on their path to becoming the best barista. The fate that awaits all us master mixologists."

Elena said, "Please ignore the ramblings of my ridiculous partner. What she means is, 'thank you for the compliment, I look forward to working with you all again.' Right, sweetie?"

Adeena shrugged. "Sure. That, too. But let me know if you'd like to send any of your staff for extended training at the cafe. I think it would be cool if we could work out some kind of exchange program."

Anita hid a smile. "As long as I don't have to worry about one of your employees challenging me to a duel to become the best chocolatier in the world, that sounds like a wonderful idea. Let's discuss it in detail over some bougie sandwiches, though. I'm starving."

Zoey led us to the ballroom where the event was being held and had a staff member direct us to our reserved table. "I'll pop by in a moment, but I need to do a check with our event organizer and a quick walk around to see if anything else is needed."

After Zoey excused herself, we settled in at a table set for six. The tiered trays hadn't been set out yet, but servers rolled around drink carts to allow diners to choose their beverages.

We all put in our orders, and the servers filled our cups—delicate porcelain teacups for my rose chocolate puer and Elena's dark chocolate peppermint, and sturdy mugs that were shaped like teacups, but larger and made of a thicker ceramic, for Adeena's ube white hot chocolate, Vince's Mexican mocha, and Anita's spiced hot chocolate.

Adeena picked up her mug and held it up in a toast. "To a successful event! Cheers!"

We didn't clink our cups together for fear of damaging them, but we all cheered with her and took hearty sips in agreement.

Anita hummed in happiness. "This hot chocolate is so delicious! It's as flavorful as the hot chocolate I remember from Paris, but not as rich, which makes it easier to drink. I could see myself drinking this every morning with a fresh croissant, or maybe a churro to dip."

"I wish I were better at pastry-making, but croissants are above my pay grade, sadly," I said. "And I'm not big into deep-frying, but maybe if we invested in a decent deep-fryer, we could start serving doughnuts and churros at the cafe. I've made baked donuts before, but never the fried kind."

"I'm just saying, if we got a soft-serve machine and a deep-fryer, we'd be unstoppable," Adeena said. "Ooh, and maybe one of those nitrogen machines so I can experiment with nitro cold brew and iced tea."

Elena said, "You know the drill. Put it on the list, and present it to Joseph. If he says it's in our budget, we'll do it. If not, it goes on the vision board as something to work toward."

Joseph was Ninang Mae's older son and the Brew-ha Cafe's accountant. As a fellow numbers person, Elena trusted him whenever he said something was or wasn't a sound investment. For pie-in-the-sky dreamers like me and Adeena, she put up a vision board in my office for us to use as inspiration. That soft-serve machine had been up on the board pretty much since we opened. Someday . . .

Vince said, "A vision board? That's an interesting concept. What do you put on there?"

"Anything that inspires us," I said. "Sometimes it's special gadgets, like the soft-serve machine. Elena pinned a grow light setup since she's in charge of the plants and herbs we sell, and she's always trying to keep them at their healthiest. Adeena put up some floor plans she drew of the art studio she wants to open up on our second floor."

Anita said, "Wait, there's a second floor to the cafe?"

"Yeah, but it's unfinished. There were some special circumstances that led to us owning the space where the Brew-ha Cafe is, and we only had enough money to renovate the main cafe. The upstairs area has been untouched and uninhabitable for years. We've debated turning it into a living space, for when one or all of us are ready to move out of our family's homes, or more of a public space in conjunction with the cafe."

We continued with this friendly, businesslike chitchat, with the Carter siblings sharing their own dreams for their family business ("A bustling shop in every town in the tri-county area! Cooking show competitions! A write-up in one of the big national papers!"), when I saw Shawn Ford enter the room. We'd found his staff photo on the hotel website, so I IDed him pretty quickly and jerked my head in his direction when the Carters weren't looking. Adeena and Elena also recognized him and raised their eyebrows at me in a question.

I thought fast. "Oh shoot, I think I left my phone in my purse in Zoey's office. I'm going to run down real quick. Can you two set aside some food for me?"

I directed this question to my friends, who caught on right away.

"Can't promise I won't eat some of your sweets, but sure. We'll keep an eye out for you," Adeena said.

I rushed over to Zoey and gave her the same story. "Sorry, but can I borrow your key? I just remembered I was supposed to call the repair person about a last-minute fix, and I want to make sure I reach them before they leave the shop. I'll bring it right back after I'm done with my call."

She handed it over without question. "Take your time. The event is going wonderfully! Thanks so much for your help."

I took one last look to check that Shawn Ford was still across the room and made my way back to Zoey's office as quickly as I could without drawing attention. Once inside, I locked the door and grabbed my phone out of my purse, which was hanging behind Zoey's desk. The best lies always have a grain of truth in them. I also grabbed my gloves out of my coat pocket and slipped them on.

That done, I made my way over to Shawn's desk. Now that he

was back, his side of the room was impeccably, almost suspiciously, clean. The shelves behind his desk, which were almost empty when I last visited, were full of clearly labeled and alphabetized file folders. His desk was gleaming, with no stray documents or pens scattered on the surface. The only indication that he was back was the plaque on the desk and a lone used coffee mug he probably expected the cleaning staff to take care of for him.

His desktop computer was in sleep mode, so I wiggled the mouse to see if I could get in. Of course not. I needed a password, and Shawn wasn't conveniently sloppy enough to leave it written on a Post-it note or anything like that. I tried the drawers on the desk, and they were all locked as well. I bit my lip and weighed my options.

I could cut my losses and assume there's nothing for me to find here (why would he hide evidence at his job, after all?) or . . . I could practice the lockpicking skills that Adeena, Elena, and I had learned off YouTube and see if I could make it work in a real-life situation. Was that illegal? Probably.

But only if I got caught.

I tiptoed to the door and carefully opened it before peeking my head outside to scope out the hallway. All clear. I checked my phone to see if Adeena or Elena had sent me any alerts or updates. Nada.

Well then. I guess I knew what I had to do.

I quietly shut and locked the door, then pulled my lockpicking kit out of my purse. Side note: It is AMAZING what you can order off the internet.

I got to work on the largest drawer, which was right above where his lap would be if he was seated. Inside that drawer was a hodgepodge of rubber bands, paper clips, uncapped pens, tangled charger cables, half-eaten protein bars (ew, that's how you get ants), and just a general mess of whatever Shawn could shove into the drawer. Guess that immaculate image was just on the outside. Shocker.

Other than that general insight into his character, I couldn't find anything resembling evidence. The next three drawers held more of the same, but in paper form: receipts, scribbled notes about client requests, PTO request forms as well as the papers regarding his suspension, but nothing particularly shady.

I'd just unlocked the last drawer when my phone started buzzing. Adeena.

"Shawn just left the banquet room. Not sure where he's heading, but you better wrap it up NOW."

Her voice was hushed but frantic, and I could imagine her huddling in a corner to make the call.

"Got it. Be up in a sec."

I relocked the drawers I'd already checked out using my lock-picking kit but hesitated at the last one. It seemed like a waste to not at least take a quick peek since it was already open . . .

Praying that my family had enough money to bail me out if I got caught, I yanked open the last drawer. The first thing I saw was a familiar beanie and pair of mittens. Even though I knew I needed to book it out of there ASAP, I had to pull them out to double-check. My stomach churned, and I thought I was going to throw up when I confirmed my suspicions: a brown beanie with bear ears and satin lining plus matching fingerless gloves with a mitten flap.

Adeena had knitted these for Hana. She even made a matching kid-size set for Aria. What was Shawn Ford doing with Hana's belongings?

Screw the time—if I got caught, I got caught. I looked at the rest of the drawer's contents, my nausea growing as I found more and more of Hana's things. A bandana I'd seen her wear while working. The case for a set of contact lenses that I was ninety-nine percent sure belonged to Hana since I knew she'd lost hers a couple of weeks ago and had to start wearing her glasses again.

I lost track of time, unearthing item after item until my phone buzzed again.

"WHERE THE HELL ARE YOU?! Did you get caught? Do we need to rescue you?" Adeena whisper-screamed into the phone.

"I found something. Make an excuse for me, and meet me at the car. I'll grab yours and Elena's stuff from the office. We gotta go."

I hung up and debated taking the evidence with me, but I couldn't tip Shawn off that I'd found his stalker stash. I settled for taking pictures of everything on my phone and rearranging it so he'd never know anyone had gone through the drawer.

I'd just relocked everything and grabbed our belongings from Zoey's side of the office when the door clicked and suddenly swung open.

"Whoa!" Shawn Ford jumped back before recovering his composure and pasting on a big smile. "Sorry about that, I wasn't expecting anyone in here. I'm Shawn."

He stuck out his hand to shake, but I held up my arms, which were overflowing with jackets and purses. "Hi there, I'm Lila. Sorry, my hands are full. I was just about to leave."

"Do you need any help? I can take some of that for—"

"No thanks! Can you give Zoey her key back though? Sorry, my friends are waiting for me. Nice meeting you, Shawn." I put on my friendliest smile so he wouldn't notice how frantic I was (I could literally feel sweat gathering around my hairline and threatening to drip down my face) before nodding to where I'd left Zoey's key on her desk. Then I gave him another quick nod before exiting the room at a totally normal speed.

Adeena and Elena were waiting for me by the front doors rather than the car, which made sense since I had their coats and also they were probably worried they'd have to bail me out. I shoved everything into their arms and hustled to the parking lot.

"Let's get out of here. I've got to talk to Detective Park."

Chapter Twenty-Three

"That sick son of a—"

Detective Park cleared his throat loudly and tilted his head toward my Tita Rosie, who was pouring us cups of salabat. Jae was too busy staring in disgust at the pictures I took in Shawn's office to notice, but I wrapped my hands around my warm mug of ginger tea. My very religious aunt had an aversion to cussing, but I think even she'd be cool with Jae using much stronger language, considering he was looking at the evidence that proved his beloved cousin had a stalker—a stalker who could have potentially hurt Hana and killed her best friend.

"So what's our next move?" I asked. "I know the way I obtained this information isn't exactly legal, but is there a way I can send this to the police anonymously? Will that be enough for them to search Shawn's office?"

"Not on its own. You either need to provide detailed

information connected to your tip that they can verify independently or have them corroborate the tip with other physical evidence," Detective Park explained. "In other words, you need another source that can prove that Shawn Ford was, if not outright stalking, then at least harassing Hana."

I leaned back in my chair, deflated. I'd finally found a clue that could point us toward Blake and Hana's attacker, and we couldn't even use it.

Before I could wallow in pity, Elena spoke up. "Wait, didn't Hana make a formal complaint against him with the Lancaster Hotel? Isn't that why he was suspended?"

I shot up in my seat. "That's right! And I just remembered, the last time I talked to Beth, she mentioned that Hana had come to her for advice on how to handle Shawn since she didn't want to lose the hotel's business. She'd noted it down in her planner. Those have got to be enough, right?"

Detective Park nodded. "Send me the photos. I'll tell the SPPD that I received an anonymous tip about the case and include the information you two just mentioned. Good work."

I thought he was going to give me an earful about the risk I'd taken getting these photos, and instead he actually praised me. I guess since he wasn't with the police anymore, he was willing to let things slide here and there.

He continued. "Just to be clear, I don't condone your actions. What you did was illegal, and if Shawn really is our killer, you put yourself at enormous risk. You got lucky this time, but I don't want it to happen again. Do you understand me?"

Nope, still the same ol' Detective Park.

"I totally understand you," I said.

Whether or not I was going to listen was a completely different matter.

The next day, I found myself at loose ends. The cafe wasn't set to reopen until tomorrow, and Detective Park had taken the evidence to the police department so there was nothing to do on our end until the cops made their move.

Jae moved all his appointments for that morning to the afternoon so he and I could go to the hospital to check on Hana and update her on the case. She still hadn't woken up yet, but I could tell Jae was feeling more optimistic about her situation now that there was a breakthrough in the investigation. After we brought her up to speed, Jae started talking to her about Aria: how she was doing, the new songs she was learning, etc. I wanted to give them some privacy, so I told Jae I was going to pop down to the vending machine to get us something to drink.

As I made my way out of the intensive care unit, I was surprised to see some familiar faces on the pediatric side. Ben, Hector, and Vinny were standing in front of one of the rooms, and Ben had his hand on Hector's shoulder, speaking quietly. I wavered between greeting them and giving them space, when Vinny's eyes met mine and he gestured me over.

"Hey Lila, what're you doing here?" Vinny asked.

"Jae and I are visiting Hana. What about you?"

Ben and Vinny turned toward Hector, who gave me a weary smile. "My daughter has a heart condition. She fainted during her gym class, so they want to keep her under observation overnight."

"I'm really sorry to hear that." Not knowing what else to say, I added, "I was going to the vending machine to get something to drink. Can I get you anything?"

Hector waved me off. "Don't worry about me, I'm fine."

Ben let out a frustrated grunt. "Hector, let us help you. You haven't even eaten today. If you won't take care of yourself, how can you expect to—"

"You know what, Lila? Why don't I join you? I was about to head down to the cafeteria to grab food for us all." Vinny looked at his older colleagues. "You two play nice while we're gone, OK?"

Without waiting for a response, Vinny whirled around and headed in the direction of the hospital cafeteria. I texted Jae to let him know where I was going and silently followed Vinny to the elevator.

He jabbed the button for the cafeteria floor and let out a deep sigh. "Sorry to drag you into this. But those two always get into it over the same thing, and I didn't want to hear it."

"No worries. I wanted to get something for me and Jae anyway." The elevator dinged, and I followed him down the hall to the cafeteria. "The three of you seem to be pretty close."

Vinny beelined to the section that offered Italian food and grabbed a tray. "Ben was good friends with my dad. After Dad passed a few years ago, I went through a 'rough patch,' as my mom likes to call it. Flunked out of high school, and it's not like we had money for college anyway. But Ben looked out for me. Told me that if I got my GED, he'd hire me and teach me everything I needed to know about security systems."

He got three Styrofoam takeout containers of eggplant Parmesan, salad, and bread. "Nowhere near as good as my mom's, but it does the job. Anyway, what was I saying? Oh yeah, Ben made good on his promise, and Hector's been mentoring me since I started. There are other cool people at the company, but those two are like family, you know?"

I ordered the same thing for me and Jae. He wasn't big on eggplant, but I figured he'd be fine as long as it was smothered in sauce and cheese. "That's really great. And I'm sure Hector appreciates you two being there for him."

He scoffed. "Not that he lets us do anything. These hospital bills are no joke, and his wife can only work part-time since she spends most of her day taking care of their daughter. But anytime Ben offers to help, Hector turns him down."

"Too much pride?"

He rolled his eyes. "Yeah, he said he refuses to be a charity case. As if accepting charity is a bad thing. Whatever. I figured out a way to help him without him knowing it."

"Yeah? How so?"

"Eh, don't worry about it. I got my ways." Vinny paid for his order as well as mine and ignored me when I tried to hand him cash. "Come on, we better hurry back. I'm starving."

Something about the mood had shifted and I wasn't sure what or why, but we stood in front of the elevators in awkward silence watching the lit-up numbers slowly making their way down to us. The door directly in front of us dinged open, and I automatically started moving to the side to make way for the person inside, when I realized it was Jae.

He grinned at me and stepped out. "Hey you. You were taking a while, so I figured I might as well meet you and eat down here. More comfortable than balancing the food on our laps in Hana's room."

"I gotta run these up to Ben and Hector before it gets soggy. See you guys around." Vinny gave us a nod and slid into the elevator before the doors closed.

"That was weird," I murmured as Jae and I found an empty table and sat down.

"What was?" Jae opened his Styrofoam container and eyed the food filling the three separate sections. He pursed his lips before shrugging and digging in. "Never thought I'd say this about eggplant or hospital food, but this is pretty good."

I cut into my own helping of eggplant Parmesan and recounted everything Vinny told me. "For some reason, it felt like the vibe got weird at the end, but I don't know why. Maybe it's just me."

It was almost time for Jae to get back to work, so we scarfed down our food, said a quick goodbye to Hana, and then headed to the plaza that housed his clinic and the Brew-ha Cafe. Even though the cafe was closed, there was still a lot of prep to do for our reopening tomorrow, not to mention a pile of paperwork that I'd been avoiding lately. I decided to tackle the admin stuff first since some of the items on my to-do list were rather urgent and those invoices wouldn't send themselves (if only).

I quickly hit an organizational groove, and I had no idea how much time had passed until I checked off the last item on my list and leaned back in my chair to stretch. It was already dark outside my office window, but I still had a bunch of kitchen prep to do. Figuring I deserved a snack before diving into more work, I was about to open my secret chocolate stash drawer when a loud noise from the front of the cafe had me jumping out of my seat. Was someone banging on the cafe door? I peeked my head out of my office and saw a figure standing in front of the door, hands cupped around the sides of their eyes to peer through the glass. It wasn't until the figure straightened up and dropped their hands that I realized who it was.

Shawn Ford.

What the heck was he doing here? Had the cops not talked to him yet? Did he figure out that I was the one who provided that anonymous tip? Why wasn't he arrested?

I'd turned a couple of lights on in the cafe when I first arrived, but the space was still pretty dark, not to mention empty, and the CLOSED sign was very obvious. That should've deterred him, as well as the additional sign Naoko had put up letting people know about our temporary closure and when we'd be back, but he still stood there as if he knew someone was inside. Before I could decide whether to talk to him or pretend I wasn't there, he spotted me and started pounding on the glass door again.

"Hey! Open up! I need to talk to you!"

He was banging on the glass so hard, I worried he was going to break the brand-new, just-fixed door and I'd have to deal with another repair job. The longer I made him wait, the angrier he'd probably get, so I grabbed my phone and keys, hit the silent alarm that the guys at Safe & Secure Solutions had installed for me, and went to confront him.

I'd planned on standing outside to talk to him, but he pushed past me into the cafe. Whatever, the security team was on their way anyway. Just in case, I propped the door open and stood next to the counter, which was near the exit and had several items within arm's reach if I needed to defend myself. Our fancy artisanal syrup bottles may look innocent, but they were made of heavy glass—a fact Detective Park pointed out last year because I kept getting into sticky situations and he wanted to teach me how to scope out any room I was in for potential weapons. That lesson may have saved my life last fall. Here's hoping I wouldn't need to put it into practice again.

I wanted him to make the first move, but he was busy swiveling his head around as if casing the place. Was he the burglar as well as the killer? My hand started inching toward the nearest bottle but stilled when he finally turned his attention to me.

"Are you here alone?"

"What are you doing here, Shawn?"

"You know why I'm here."

I swallowed past the lump in my throat and willed my voice to come out steadily. *Don't give anything away.*

"I'm sorry, but I have no clue. We're closed today, and I still have work to do, so I'm going to have to ask you to leave."

I gestured toward the open door, but he didn't budge. Just narrowed his eyes at me, saying, "I know you were the one who tipped off the police."

"Tipped them off about what?"

He sneered at me. "Did you think I would just brush it off as a coincidence that the day after you were in my office, the cops suddenly show up with a search warrant? I don't know what you think you know, but—"

"You were stalking Hana. Stealing her personal items. Harassing her. That much is obvious. Were you the one that attacked her? Did Blake try to protect her and you killed her in retaliation?"

There was no use in pretending, so what the heck. In for a penny, in for a pound.

"I wasn't stalking her! I loved her, and she loved me."

"Then why did she file a complaint against you? Why did she

take herself off the Lancaster Hotel account so she wouldn't have to deal with you?"

He ran his hands through his hair, rumpling up his perfect do. "She was just confused. We were working it out. I would never hurt her."

"What did the police say?"

"I told them I wasn't going to talk without my lawyer present. I'm supposed to meet them at the station. But I wanted to hear from you first. What did you tell them?"

"Nothing."

"Liar!"

He lunged at me, but before I could grab the nearest bottle or run away, a solid body threw itself in between us, protecting me. Another person tackled Shawn to the ground.

The person who got in between us had their back to me, so it took me a moment to realize who it was. "Hector? Oh thank goodness, I was worried the silent alarm didn't work since no one was showing up."

"We got here as fast as we could," Vinny grunted as he restrained a struggling Shawn on the floor. "The police were supposed to be here by now."

As if on cue, sirens and flashing lights announced the arrival of the SPPD. People from the surrounding businesses spilled out to watch the cops arrest Shawn and lead him to the back of one of their cars. Tita Rosie and Lola Flor pushed through one side of the crowd to get to me, and Jae emerged from the other.

"Anak! Are you OK?"

"Lila! What happened? Are you all right?"

Jae swept me in his arms, and I didn't realize I was trembling until I felt him squeeze me extra tight to calm me down.

"I'm fine. Hector and Vinny saved me." I clung to Jae, forcing myself to take deep breaths as he rubbed my back. I willed my heart rate to go back to normal, but it refused—everything had happened in a split second, and my body was having trouble realizing I was no longer in danger.

"Excuse me, miss. We're going to have to ask you a few questions." The cop car carrying Shawn had left, but one stayed behind. To interview me, I guess.

"She's just had a huge shock," Jae said, not letting go. "She can go make her report at the station after she gets checked out at the hospital."

I pulled away from him but smiled to let him know I appreciated his protectiveness. "I don't need to go to the hospital, but I do need a minute to collect myself. I'll meet you at the station, and you can ask your questions there."

The officer studied me for a moment before agreeing. "Of course, miss. I'll see you in a little bit."

Something warm draped around my shoulders as we watched the cop drive off, and I looked up at Hector as he wrapped a thick blanket around me.

"You're not wearing a coat, and you might be in shock. We keep blankets in our trunk for moments like this. You need to stay warm, but don't drink anything just yet. It could be a choking hazard."

I pulled the blanket tighter, absorbing the warmth and kindness he offered. "Thanks, Hector. For the blanket and for saving me, of course."

He smiled awkwardly. "Just doing our job."

The word "our" reminded me that Vinny was there, too. He lingered behind Hector, not inserting himself into the conversation, which was surprising. I thought he'd be the type to brag about saving me.

"Thanks, Vinny."

He nodded at me. "Glad you're OK, Lila."

"Thank you both so much for saving my niece," Tita Rosie said, taking Vinny's hands in hers. "Are you hungry? Whatever you want, it's on the house."

Hector tried to protest, but Lola Flor literally started shoving him toward the restaurant door, and he gave Vinny a resigned look and shrugged. Vinny laughed and followed them, but Tita Rosie stayed outside with me and Jae.

"Are you coming?"

I shook my head. "I can't eat right now. I still feel kind of sick. Anyway, I need to talk to the police."

Tita Rosie put her hand on my cheek. "Of course, anak. If you're hungry, come join us after. I'll call Jonathan and tell him to meet you at the station."

"Thanks, Tita Rosie."

She went back inside the restaurant, and I leaned against Jae for a moment before straightening up.

"Come on, let's get this over with."

Chapter Twenty-Four

With Shawn Ford now under arrest for Blake and Hana's attack, you'd think I'd finally be in the mood for socializing. You would be wrong.

But I'd promised Beth and Valerie that I'd be at their event, and I knew Elena wanted to network and support her cousin Rita, so here I was at the Shady Palms Community Center, mingling with at least twenty other female entrepreneurs. Of course, the main topic of conversation was Shawn's arrest the other day.

Normally, I'd be annoyed at what felt like callous gossip, but the women gathered here were either victims of the burglaries that had been plaguing Shady Palms the last few months or were worried that they were going to become the next target. It was only natural that they'd want to know more about the arrest. The number-one question on everyone's mind: If Shawn really was Blake and Hana's attacker, did that mean he was involved in the burglaries too, or was that a separate incident?

The burglaries were not my concern (let the Shady Palms Police Department do their job for once), but if it turned out that Shawn wasn't the guy, it wouldn't hurt for me to learn more about the women who'd been targeted. I scanned the room to see if there was someone standing alone or a group conversation I could join naturally. My eyes met Diane Kosta's, and she gestured for me to join her group.

"Hey Lila, good to see you again." She gave me a quick hug and introduced me to the two other women she was talking to. "This is Natalie Nguyen from Natalie's Nails, and Britney Smith from the Grab N Go. Their stores were among the first hit by the burglar."

After introducing myself and pointing out my business partners in the crowd, I said, "Sorry to hear about the burglaries. Hope you were able to recoup your losses."

"Luckily, they only took the cash box and didn't steal or destroy any of our equipment, so insurance was able to cover most of it," Natalie said. "My premiums took a hit because I didn't have a security system installed, though. Never thought I needed it in a town like this, but I finally invested in one after the burglary."

Britney grimaced. "I took over the store from my parents and had no idea our security plan had lapsed. Because it was so old and nobody had maintained it, it hadn't worked in years, but like Natalie, I never really thought about it. I made sure to have a brand-new system installed and am paying extra for monthly maintenance."

So neither business had a security system when the burglar hit? Was it a coincidence? How would the burglar have known? Then again, this was Shady Palms. Maybe no one had been worried enough in our sleepy little town to bother having one installed.

I glanced at Diane. "From what I remember, you have a security system at your studio, right?"

She nodded. "I have a lot of expensive equipment, and the commercial property insurance policy I signed offered lower premiums if I had a security system. I cheaped out and got a DIY system to install myself. According to the cops, the system I had was one of the easiest for a burglar to disable because of wireless jamming or something like that. After all this, Uncle Stan gave me a loan to have a proper system installed so I went with your recommendation of Safe & Secure Solutions."

Britney said, "Oh, I'm with them now, too."

"Me, too!" Natalie echoed. "I'd heard great things about them."

My mind was whirring. It had to be a coincidence that these three burglary victims happened to now be with Safe & Secure Solutions. I mean, in a town this small, where the older generation didn't even bother locking their doors (not my family, of course), it's not like there was a plethora of local security companies to choose from. Right?

I thought about Ben's warmth, not to mention his friendship with Detective Park. Hector's earnest demeanor and quiet kindness. Vinny's friendliness and enthusiasm. I didn't want to think that these men were involved in the burglaries, but considering that they were all professionals with extensive knowledge of security systems, it made a sick kind of sense. And it's not like those three were the only employees at the company. Maybe someone else who worked there was involved. Should I tell Detective Park about this? I had zero proof, and I wouldn't want to do anything to hurt his friendship because I knew he owed Ben a lot. But maybe if I just mentioned my suspicions . . .

"You all look so serious over here! What are you ladies talking about?" Charlene Choi wandered over, clutching a sparkling mocktail in one hand. One of the vendors at the party was a pop-up that specialized in nonalcoholic drinks for special events. I knew the owner was one of the businesses that Elena wanted to collaborate with, so I made a note to check out their offerings later.

Natalie snorted. "Whatchu think? The same thing everyone else is talking about."

"Ah, of course. How are you doing, Lila? It must've been a terrifying experience, but I'm so glad we don't have to worry about these thefts anymore," Charlene said, her forehead briefly creasing in concern before her fingers shot up to smooth away the wrinkles.

"I'm fine, thanks. Luckily, Hector and Vinny came to my rescue just in time."

She tilted her head. "Who?"

"Oh, the guys on my account at Safe & Secure Solutions. They got there before the police showed up and protected me." Something occurred to me. "Oh, wait, you might know them. I think I've seen you talking to them before."

Charlene shrugged. "Maybe? I'm not great with names."

"Not unless you can use them for something," Natalie said, the fakest smile I'd ever seen pasted on her face. "Isn't that right, Charlene?"

Charlene bristled. "What are you trying to say?"

"I thought I said it pretty clearly, but I guess not. Let me try again: You are fake as hell and only keep people around you that you can use. Especially men. You—"

"Is this about your ex-boyfriend? Get over it already. I did you a favor—"

Britney quickly excused herself, and Diane hooked her arm through mine and steered me toward the refreshment table. "I don't know about you, Lila, but I am positively parched. Join me for a drink, yes?"

Part of me was tempted to stay behind and watch Natalie and Charlene volley insults back and forth like a tennis match (the drama!), and the other half was TIRED and just wanted to eat and drink food that someone else paid for and hide in a corner until it was time to go home.

I decided to compromise with the latter half by sticking with Adeena, Elena, and Rita for the rest of the event. Elena could vet the people we actually needed to talk to so I wasn't forced to make small talk with every single person in attendance, and if I ever got tired of chatting, I could count on one of them to fill in the silence. Rita seemed glad for the extra company since she was quiet and introverted by nature, so having someone to be silent with while the more outgoing Adeena and Elena handled things worked well for us.

It worked so well that by the time Beth and Valerie called out that it was time to wrap things up, I could genuinely join everyone else in their praise and enthusiasm for the Thompsons' efforts and their excitement for the future women-entrepreneur expo the two of them were planning. It wasn't until we were all piled in my car and Adeena asked if I'd heard anything interesting that I remembered the possible connection between Safe & Secure Solutions and the burglaries.

"What do you all think?" I asked, wrapping up my recount of the exchange I'd heard. "Is it worth bringing up to Detective Park?"

Adeena said, "It couldn't hurt. He knows them best, so he'll know how to handle it. It might be nothing, or it might be what blows the whole case wide open."

"Better safe than sorry," Rita added. "Ugh, I sounded like my mom when I said that. Don't you dare agree with me."

She directed that last statement to Elena, who held up her hands and said, "I would never."

Jae said the same thing after Shawn's arrest when he installed a special security app on my phone that would track my location and let me call for help if needed. I already had a security alarm on my key chain that Detective Park gave me forever ago, but Jae insisted it wasn't enough. And, sadly, I remember Hana saying it too, shortly before her attack. They were right. If I was wrong and the security guys got upset that I suspected them, well, I would deal with it. But I wasn't going to be a fool (again) and hold back on sharing my suspicions to avoid future conflict.

Once I'd dropped everyone at home and was snuggled in bed with Longganisa, I made the call. "Detective Park? I might have some important information for you . . ."

Chapter Twenty-Five

Detective Park heard me out last night and set up an appointment with Ben to chat with us at the Brew-ha Cafe after work today. Like I thought, he believed in Ben but couldn't ignore the evidence I brought up connecting Safe & Secure Solutions to the burglaries. The hope was that Ben was innocent and would be outraged upon learning that one of his employees was using his company to not only rob the businesses in this town but had possibly killed Blake and hurt Hana. According to Detective Park, Shawn Ford was still insisting on his innocence, so I had no idea what to think.

I felt the tingling in my stomach that meant we were close, oh so close, to figuring out this case. I just had to make it through the workday. Luckily, my fellow Brew-has knew I wasn't in the right headspace to be customer-facing, so they let me stay in the back, blasting my music and preparing tons of ube and Mexican hot chocolate fudge that I planned to freeze until it was time to serve them at the Shady Palms Winery's Valentine's Day party.

I'll show you what shoes to wear!

How to fix your hair!

Everything that really counts to be . . .

I bopped around the kitchen, singing my heart out as I mixed tray upon tray of delicious treats. The playlist looped several times, and the only way I could mark the passage of time was by keeping track of how often I heard a particular song.

I was in the middle of belting out a big dramatic finish when a slight pause in the track allowed me to hear the quiet *click* of a door opening.

The doors from the cafe space to the kitchen are heavy swinging doors that don't make that kind of sound when opening, so I glanced toward the back door, expecting to see one of my coworkers returning from an errand. Instead, Hector stood there, looking sad.

So sad, in fact, that it took me a moment to clock that he had a gun pointed at me.

Before I could react, he came around the table where I was. "Do *not* make a single sound. I just want to talk. But I have an accomplice out on the floor. You try to scream or run away or do anything to draw their attention, I can't promise what will happen out there. Got it?"

The music was so loud, he had to lean in close enough to speak directly into my ear, like he was whispering a secret. A shudder ran through me as I pieced together what was happening. Hector was here, holding me at gunpoint. Which meant he knew that I had figured out the connection between Safe & Secure Solutions and the burglaries and was here to shut me up. There was also someone out in the cafe, likely Vinny, essentially holding my coworkers and any lingering customers hostage. I glanced at the clock on the wall. We weren't due to close for another hour, so the chances of Detective Park and Ben arriving for their meeting just in time to save us was pretty slim.

My eyes drifted to the spot in the kitchen where a silent alarm was installed—there was one under the register, another in my office, and a third one back here under the giant prep table. I was on the wrong side to activate it, but maybe if I could think up a reason to move to that area . . .

Hector's eyes followed mine, and his grip on the gun tightened. "Did you forget that I was the one who installed your alarm? Which means I know how to disable it. You think I would step in here without handling that first?"

Of course he did. He was desperate enough to confront me during work hours, but that didn't mean he was sloppy. He'd planned this showdown as meticulously as all of his other crimes. I drew in a deep breath, racking my brain for the next possible option, when the song that had been playing ended and the playlist looped to the beginning.

Good news! She's dead!

I understood the severity of the moment. Trust me, I fully understood. But right at that moment, the only thing I could think was, *Lord, I'm going to get murdered to the* Wicked *movie soundtrack . . .*

As ridiculous as that thought was, it gave me an idea. I was using my phone to stream the music. On my phone was the special security app that Jae installed. All I had to do was press the button on the screen, and help would be on the way. But if Hector was quick to notice my eyes straying toward the silent alarm, there's no way he'd miss me trying to get to my phone.

"Could I turn off the music so we can talk normally?" I shouted over the song.

His eyes flashed and I winced. Did I make a mistake?

"Keep one hand in the air and just lower the volume slightly. We don't want anyone in the cafe to hear us, do we? And if anyone comes back here, you better play along. No signaling to them."

I kept one hand in the air as I unlocked my phone and lowered the volume. I glanced at him as I did so, willing him to keep his eyes on mine as I jabbed at the special security button that was always on the screen. I had no idea if I actually connected with it or not since I didn't dare break eye contact as I did so.

I set the phone down. "Sure, but it'll be hard to convince them we're having a friendly chat when you've got a gun pointed at me."

He lowered his arm until the gun was hidden behind the high prep table but kept it pointed at me. "Better?"

Before I could respond with a sarcastic remark and get shot for being a smart ass, Adeena let herself into the kitchen.

"Hey, what's up? You never come back here." *Keep it cool, Lila. Keep it cool . . .*

Adeena waved at Hector before answering me. "Something's wrong with Mr. Peppy, so we had to close early. All the customers left, and we're just cleaning up now."

At the angle we were all standing, Adeena wouldn't be able to see the gun, but I hoped she could sense something was wrong because the tension was off the charts.

"All of the customers are gone?" Hector's voice shook slightly, and he cleared his throat. "I mean, my friend was supposed to be waiting for me. You don't have someone just hanging out, finishing their drink or anything like that?"

"Nope, it's just us. I'm afraid you'll have to cut your visit short so we can finish up here, Hector. I need to get a repair person over ASAP."

Hector faltered, the arm holding the gun drifting down. I locked eyes with Adeena and nodded ever so slightly. Before he could even wonder at what was happening, Adeena grabbed a heavy saucepan that was next to her and chucked it at Hector while I dove for my phone. I didn't even have a chance to press the security app button again when Detective Park, Ben, and what seemed like all of the Shady Palms Police Department busted through from both the swinging kitchen doors and the back door, forming a pincer on Hector.

"He's got a gun!" I yelled.

But Hector was no fool. He dropped the gun and put his hands up, surrendering immediately.

Detective Nowak entered the kitchen, dragging a handcuffed and struggling Charlene Choi behind him from the cafe.

"Charlene?!" I said in shock.

"She was his accomplice," Elena explained, following them into the kitchen. "She seemed really shady when she staked out a spot in the cafe and kept glancing back and forth between us and the kitchen. I wanted to know what her deal was, so I pretended we were interested in hiring her company to take over our bookkeeping and had her follow me to the office. Long story short, I got her to slip up when she made some comment about us getting a new safe. It was never publicly revealed what was stolen from us, so I knew she had to be involved. So I texted Adeena that I needed backup."

Adeena added, "I called Detective Park and then faked an accident with the espresso machine so we could send Leslie, Naoko, and our customers home early. It didn't take much for us to overpower her and get her side of the story."

"Which was?"

"She planned the burglaries, and Hector executed them. It was the perfect partnership since her position as an accountant and the treasurer of the chamber of commerce meant she knew how each business was doing financially, who had insurance that would cover them completely in case of theft, all that stuff."

"And since Hector was a security expert, he could scope out each place, see who had good security and who didn't, and figure out how to bypass everything," Adeena said. "It really was the perfect plan, if it wasn't for us meddling kids."

"I just don't understand why. Why, Hector?" Ben had rushed in with everyone else to save me, but he'd stayed in the background during the whole exchange. "You were my right-hand man. I trusted you. I'd planned on passing the business down to you when I retired. How could you do this? How could you hurt those girls?"

"It wasn't me!" Hector burst out, looking truly torn. "I mean, yes, I was the one committing the burglaries. I was the one who betrayed your trust. But I swear I never put my hands on Blake or Hana. It just . . . everything went so horribly wrong so fast."

"Shut your mouth! Don't you dare pin this all on me!" Charlene yelled, struggling against the officer holding her. "This never would've happened if you hadn't listened to Blake's sob story and let her blackmail us. She's the one who set everything up. It's only right she be the one to pay for ruining everything."

Jae said, "Wait, Blake was part of the burglary ring? Then why did you kill her? Why did you hurt my cousin?"

Hector turned to Jae but couldn't seem to look him in the eye. He dropped his gaze to the floor. "Blake was in heavy debt, and the loan shark she borrowed from was coming to collect. She somehow pieced together what Charlene and I were doing and said she wanted in. She would use the insurance money and a little extra from us to pay him off. It was supposed to be a one-time thing. She got the money she needed, and she'd keep her mouth shut about what we were doing."

"Did . . . did Hana know about it?" Jae asked.

Hector shook his head. "Blake insisted we keep Hana out of this. I think she wanted to make sure Hana wouldn't go down for the robbery if we got caught."

"Worked for me since the fewer people who knew what we were up to, the better," Charlene said. "But then she messed up. Apparently, Hana got an idea for some new chocolate whatever she wanted to experiment with and headed back to Choco Noir to work on it the day Hector was supposed to rob the place. She called Blake on the way there to let her know since it was late and didn't want Blake to get worried if she heard someone messing around in the shop. Blake freaked out and called me to help Hector while she stalled Hana."

"But it was too late," Hector said. "Blake wasn't at the shop when Hana called because she was supposed to be at a neighborhood bar where someone could alibi her for the time of the burglary. After all, she lives above the shop, and it would be suspicious if she didn't hear anything."

I asked, "Why didn't you just leave and do the fake robbery another day?"

Charlene snarled. "I told you, Blake ruined everything. Hector was already at the shop, and she told him that he had to finish the job. She needed that money ASAP, and she figured that if she couldn't hide the truth from her partner, she might as well confess and convince her to keep quiet."

"Knowing my cousin, she wouldn't have gone along with that plan," Jae said. "Is that where it fell apart?"

Hector nodded. "Hana got there just before Blake and caught me and Charlene inside the shop. She was running out to call the cops when Blake arrived and dragged her back in, said she'd explain everything."

He took a shuddering breath. "Hana freaked out, said she couldn't believe Blake would do this to her, that she couldn't go to jail and leave her daughter behind. Blake and I thought we could convince Hana to stay quiet, pretend she didn't see anything, but Charlene didn't trust her."

"Of course I didn't. Nothing went down like it was supposed to, and it was all Blake's fault. She didn't have to get hurt either. She's the one who threw herself in front of Hana to protect her. She didn't have to die."

"No one was supposed to get hurt!" Tears streamed down Hector's face. "I just needed money to pay for my daughter's hospital bills and medication. You're the one who kept escalating everything, and now look at us."

"That's why? Hector, that's what started all of this? Why didn't you ask me for help?" Ben looked utterly heartbroken. "Vinny and I set up a collection fund for you at the office since you were too proud to say anything. We could've—"

"I'm sorry, Ben. But you have no idea how bad these bills are. I feel like I've been drowning for the past few years, and I couldn't take it anymore. My little girl needed me to provide and so I did." Hector lifted his watery eyes to Detective Nowak. "My family didn't know anything about what I was doing. My wife thinks I got a promotion at work. I'll cooperate with whatever you need, but please leave them out of this. They don't need to see me like this. And Ben . . ."

Ben clapped a hand on Hector's shoulder and squeezed. "I'll take care of them. You don't have to worry about it."

"Thank you. And I'm sorry. Everyone, I'm so, so sorry . . ."

Hector repeated that over and over as the police led him and Charlene away.

I made my way to Jae's side and wrapped my arms around him. "We did it, Jae. It's over. It's all over."

He squeezed me back, not even bothering to hide the tears coursing down his face. "Let's go tell Hana."

Chapter Twenty-Six

I know it was a last-minute idea, but I think including a third area where family and friends can celebrate their own special kind of love for one another was a wonderful addition to your Valentine's Day event, anak."

Tita Rosie proudly surveyed the packed area where many families with young children were having a great time making Valentine's Day–themed cards in the art section with Adeena and Elena. Or doing flower origami with Naoko. Or making simple screen-printed T-shirts with Terrence.

The buffet table was being handled by a few staff members of the Shady Palms Winery as well as the Calendar Crew and our friends Nettie and George Bishop from Big Bishop's BBQ. Because the majority of Ronnie and Izzy's employees were working in the other two rooms, catering to the couples lounge and singles mixer, my cousin reached out to our little community to see if we could help out at his event.

Jae was playing his guitar to accompany his mother singing happy love songs to a circle of enraptured children. Even Papa Park was having a great time, sitting with Aria in his lap and quietly singing along.

As sweet as that image was, what made me happiest was seeing Hana leading a simple truffle-making demonstration for kids. She came out of her coma shortly after those harrowing events at the cafe, and after a week of tests and observation, she was released with a clean bill of health. However, lying in a hospital bed for almost a month with no physical activity meant that she tired quickly and lost a bit of the muscle strength necessary for her profession. Even though Blake's parents gave Hana full ownership of Choco Noir as well as the apartment above the shop, Hana decided to stay with Jae's parents until she was back to full capacity.

Shortly after she woke up, Jae, Detective Park, Mama Park, and I had brought Aria to see her mother at the hospital.

"Choco Noir is waiting for me, and I can't wait to get back to work. But right now, I need to focus on what's best for me and Aria." Hana stroked her daughter's head. "The thought that I might not be around to see her grow up, to be there when she really needs me . . . I need to make up for the time we lost. And to let her know how much her father and I love her and will always be with her, even if she can't see us."

We also decided it was time to let Hana know all that had transpired while she was in the hospital. Her memory of that fateful night at Choco Noir was a little spotty, but she clearly remembered

Blake trying to convince her to go along with the insurance scam and how Charlene attacked her when she refused. Detective Park told us that when questioned about her motive for the burglary ring, Charlene just said, "Do you have any idea how expensive home renovations are?" Jae and I kept that selfish tidbit to ourselves but explained everything else in detail.

"It's a dangerous thought, I know, but . . . I wonder how different everything would've turned out if I had just played along. If I wasn't so stubborn and hotheaded in the moment and just waited to talk to Blake privately. But I felt so betrayed, and I responded without thinking, and I . . ." Hana broke into sobs, her frail body heaving with the force of them. "Even after all that, she still tried to protect me. She was always looking out for me, and now I . . ."

Mama Park held her as she cried, and after a few moments, Aria reached up to wipe her mother's tears away. That seemed to bring Hana back to herself.

"Thank you, baby. Your imo halmeoni says you were such a good girl while I was asleep! I'm so proud of you. I really missed you though. Why don't you tell me what you've been doing?"

Aria lit up. "OK! I go out on a walk every day with Gino Pacino and Grandpa Jack. We sometimes play with Lila and Longganisa, and it's so much fun."

Another gift the Langrehrs left Hana was Blake's six-year-old shih tzu mix, Gino Pacino. The dog had been living with Blake's parents while Blake was busy with the move and opening up Choco Noir, but she was supposed to pick up Gino in the spring. The Langrehrs knew how much Aria loved the dog, and with Hana's permission, they decided that Aria should be Gino Pacino's new human.

Gino and Longganisa became fast friends, and I loved having a new way to bond with Jae's niece.

Aria continued. "We've also been doing chair yoga with Miss Sana. And imo halmeoni is teaching me a new song."

"Shh! That's a secret, Aria." Mama Park put a finger to her lips and winked at her great-niece. "Your mom will have to wait and see what we're preparing for the big Valentine's Day event next week."

"I can't believe how much time has passed. I guess there's no way we can provide the chocolates for the event." Hana gave me a pained smile. "Was your cousin able to find a replacement vendor? Blake and I were really looking forward to it, so I hope it turns out great."

"The Chocolate Shoppe in Shelbyville is helping us out," I said. "A lot happened recently, but now they see you as worthy competition, not an enemy. Anita and Vince asked me to let you know that if you need any help getting back on your feet, they'd be happy to send you some of their employees to work temporarily at Choco Noir until you find staff of your own."

Her eyes widened. "Wow, a lot really did happen. I'll make sure to reach out to them once I'm ready. But for right now, all my attention is on my daughter and my recovery."

"Of course. We're all here for you." I reached out to give her hand a squeeze. "Does anyone need anything? I'm going to the cafeteria to grab something to drink."

Hana didn't want anything, but Mama Park and Aria requested apple juice and Detective Park wanted a black coffee. Jae insisted on coming with me to the cafeteria, even though I was doing this to give the family some private time to themselves.

When I pointed this out, he grabbed my hand and interlaced his fingers with mine. "Lila, I don't know how you don't get it yet, but you ARE family. So if you're going to be kind enough to grab drinks and snacks for my relatives, of course I'm going to go with you to help carry them. You'd do the same if the roles were reversed, wouldn't you?"

I leaned my head against his shoulder. "We are family, aren't we?"

He smiled down at me. "And someday, my dream is for us to truly become a family. But until then, I hope you'll stay by my side, supporting me like this."

I stood up on my tiptoes and gave him a kiss, hospital PDA be damned. "Always."

Seeing Jae's gentle smile as he played the guitar at the Shady Palms Winery reminded me of that promise we made at the hospital, and a flush crept across my face. That was practically a proposal, wasn't it?

"Everyone, we've got a very special program planned!" Ronnie stood on the small stage near the area where Jae and Mama Park were performing. "Dr. Jae Park, his mother, and his niece are performing an original song that they wrote together. The song is dedicated to Hana Lee, the owner of Choco Noir. She's just been through an extremely difficult ordeal, and her family wants to express their love and support for her. Let's give it up for this evening's main star, Ms. Aria Lee!"

The room erupted in applause, and everyone settled into seats around the stage to watch the performance. Adeena and Elena sat next to me and Hana, and I could see Tita Rosie with Detective Park and Lola Flor. Sana and Amir as well as Bernadette and

Xander wandered over from the kids' dance zone, where Sana and Bernadette had been leading sessions. Yuki's husband, Akio, made a rare appearance, joining his family in the craft section. The Calendar Crew had grabbed Terrence and dragged him over to the buffet area, where he stood watch with them, a full plate in his hands that Nettie had forced on him.

Jae strummed his guitar while Aria sang a sweet, simple song about the many kinds of love and families that exist in the world, and how they have the power to get you through the tough times. And that even when someone's gone, that love still persists.

I held Hana's hand as tears streamed down her face, and I imagined all of us in the audience were remembering those we've lost and feeling the ache of love that time and grief can never erase. I had no idea how a child could pack so much emotion into such a short song, but I was soon weeping along with Hana (and most of the audience). What a strange Valentine's Day celebration. And yet, it felt utterly right.

After the song, everyone erupted into applause and went to congratulate Jae and Aria or stopped to chat with Hana. The room filled with laughter, and as the event drew to a close, I took one last look around the room, full of the people I cared about.

This was what we worked so hard for. This was what I wanted to protect.

When I first moved back to Shady Palms more than two years ago, who knew how much my life would change? That the small step of working to rejuvenate Tita Rosie's Kitchen while recovering from a broken heart would lead to such a wild ride? Despite all the pain and tragedy, I couldn't help but be grateful for it all. How could I not be?

Adeena and Elena grabbed my hands and dragged me over to join Jae in the middle of the singing circle, and as I sang and laughed and danced with the people I loved best, I wished with all my heart that this peace would never end.

Acknowledgments

Well, here we are. The final book in the Tita Rosie's Kitchen Mystery series. As with all creative endeavors, there have been major highs and intense lows. But I wouldn't trade it for anything. I am so, so lucky to be able to do what I love and to have received the kind of support I barely dared dream of.

As always, thanks to my superstar agent, Jill Marsal, for championing my work. To my acquiring editor, Michelle Vega, who first saw the potential in me and my series and who had the brilliant idea to bring on rising star editor Angela Kim. They help me shape my stories into the best versions of themselves, and I'm immeasurably grateful for their expertise and patience. Sorry for making you deal with my immensely s***** garbage-fire first drafts.

Thanks to my Berkley/Penguin Random House team, including my publicist, Ariana Abad; my marketing team, Anika Bates and Tyler Simon; my absolute GOAT cover designer, Vi-An Nguyen; interior designer, Kristin del Rosario; production editor, Lindsey Tulloch; managing editorial team: Christine Legon, Sammy Rice, Heather Haase, Emma Tamayo, and Brittney West; copyeditor,

Christy Wagner; as well as my outside publicist, Ann-Marie Nieves, and the rest of the Get Red PR team.

Shout-out to the Berkletes, who help keep me sane and provide a safe space in the weird world of publishing. Special love to the Jaded Old Hags (IYKYK).

Much love to Lori Rader-Day and Kellye Garrett, two amazing writers who've guided me down my mystery writing path and who give so much of themselves to the community. If you've never read their books before, go get them NOW. They're fantastic people who also happen to be fantastic authors.

To the organizations/groups that have helped me become the writer I am today: Sisters in Crime, Crime Writers of Color, Banyan: Asian American Writers Collective, Mystery Writers of America Midwest, my Chicagoland kidlit writers, and many more. I appreciate you all.

To the people who bid on my charity auctions to name characters and pets in the series: Thank you for supporting wonderful causes and helping remove the burden of coming up with names. (Names are hard, y'all!) Blake Langrehr from the St. Louis County Library, thank you for so enthusiastically offering up your name to be the victim in this story. I'm glad you weren't joking because it's too late for me to change it now.

Major thanks to my IRL Brew-ha crew, the Winners Circle (Kim, Jumi, Linna, and Robbie), the Hayeses (that's right, Aria, I named a character after you! Now I'm the new favorite), and Ivan aka Snookums. You all are the main reason I ever leave the house, so thank you for making me touch grass and all that good stuff.

To my biggest supporters, my family. Love you all. And James, someday I might dedicate another book to you without revoking "funniest person" status, but today is not that day. Gumiho, you are the bestest and deserve all the butt scratches. Max Power, you were the goodest boy, and I miss you every day.

Speaking of support, I would be remiss to not shout out my wonderful Pamilya tier Ko-fi subscribers: Max and Abby Hayes, Moxie and Brisket Doktor, Sarah Best, Miles and Benji Madriaga McHale, Faye Bernoulli Silag, Kimberly M. Johnson, Maria Remedios Boyd, the Villarente Hipol Family, Christine Bradfield, Tim and Kristen Sorbera, Katie Davidson, Kimberly Peters, Christine K. Asuncion, the Boucher and Randle families, Eliose Celine Labampa, Matthew Galloway, Mikita Kie, Sam Bertocchi, Jonny Duran-Rodriguez, and Allison Player and family.

And finally, to my readers. The words "thank you" feel inadequate to describe all that you've done for me and all that you mean to me, but those are the words strongest in my heart. Thank you, thank you, thank you. ❤❤❤

Recipes

Tita Rosie's Dinuguan

Dinuguan, also known as "chocolate meat," is a tasty and comforting savory stew that can be a rather hard sell to people unaccustomed to eating offal. However, thanks to the strong aromatics and how perfectly it pairs with white rice (puto—a steamed Filipino rice cake—is a common accompaniment), you can't even tell that blood is one of the ingredients. It's my middle brother's favorite Filipino dish, and this recipe comes from the friend of one of his coworkers, Ann Sta. Agneda. Thanks, Ann!

Ingredients:

2 tablespoons chopped ginger

2 tablespoons chopped garlic

1 bay leaf

1 teaspoon black peppercorns

1 medium onion, chopped

2 pounds pork shoulder, boiled and cubed (small)

Salt and freshly ground black pepper, to taste

⅓ cup white vinegar

1 tablespoon sugar

1 (about 10-ounce) tub beef or pork blood

4 banana peppers

½ cup chopped green onion (optional)

DIRECTIONS:

1. In a medium pot or large saucepan over medium-high heat, sauté the ginger until slightly brown. Add the garlic, bay leaf, peppercorns, and onion, and cook until fragrant and the onion is softened.

2. Add the pork, and season with salt and pepper. Add water to the level of the meat (about 3 cups), and simmer until the pork is tender. If you can easily pierce the meat with a fork or knife, it should be ready.

3. Add the white vinegar and sugar, and simmer for 10 minutes. Add more salt and pepper to taste.

4. Add the blood, gently stirring as you add it to prevent clumps.

5. Add the banana peppers whole.

6. Reduce the heat to low, and simmer for 10 minutes.

7. Remove from the heat. Remove and discard the bay leaf, top with the green onion, and serve.

Lola Flor's Mocha Mamon

Mamon are individual Filipino chiffon cakes that are light and fluffy, simple yet delicious, and a lovely addition to breakfast and meryenda. They're often topped with butter and sugar and come in a variety of flavors and toppings, with mocha being one of the most popular. Despite the name, these aren't really "mocha" since they traditionally don't include any chocolate. For a true mocha flavor, you could probably sub out part of the instant coffee for cocoa powder, but this recipe is based on the mocha mamon I grew up with.

YIELD: 16 CUPCAKE-SIZE MAMON

Ingredients:

Dry Ingredients:

*1 cup cake flour**

⅓ cup sugar

½ teaspoon baking powder

½ teaspoon salt

Wet Ingredients:

6 egg yolks

*¼ cup vegetable oil***

1 tablespoon instant coffee dissolved in
¼ cup water

Meringue Ingredients:
6 egg whites
¼ teaspoon cream of tartar
½ cup sugar

Toppings (optional):
Butter
Sugar

DIRECTIONS:

1. Preheat the oven to 350°F. Grease or line 16 cupcake tins or mamon molds.

2. Combine the flour, sugar, baking powder, and salt in a large bowl, and sift three times. Set aside.

3. In a separate large bowl, combine the egg yolks, oil, and instant coffee water, using a whisk or hand mixer, until well blended.

4. Slowly add the dry ingredients to the wet ingredients, continuously mixing as you add. Once all the dry ingredients have been added to the wet, continue mixing for a couple of minutes, scraping the bottom and sides of the bowl as needed, until everything is well combined. Set aside.

5. Add the egg whites and cream of tartar to the bowl of a stand mixer fitted with a wire whisk attachment (or use a large clean, dry

bowl and a clean, dry hand mixer). Beat on high until the egg whites double in volume.

6. With the mixer still on high, slowly add the sugar. Continue mixing on high until the meringue reaches medium peaks—they don't deflate immediately, but they don't stand perfectly straight when you pull the whisk out.

7. Using a rubber spatula, carefully add and fold in about a third of the meringue to the egg yolk mixture. Continue adding and gently folding the meringue into the egg yolk mixture in two or three batches until all of the meringue is added and the batter is evenly mixed. (A few streaks of meringue here and there are fine.) Do this carefully because you want to maintain the air you whipped into the meringue to prevent it from collapsing while it bakes.

8. Using a ⅓ cup dry measuring cup, scoop the batter into the prepared tins or molds.

9. Bake in the preheated oven for 15 to 20 minutes, until a thin knife inserted in the middle comes out clean.

10. Remove from the oven, let cool slightly, and remove the mamon from the tins. Serve warm, topped with butter and sugar (if using).

* *If you don't have cake flour (I never do), use this easy substitute: Measure out 1 cup all-purpose flour, remove 2 tablespoons, and add 2 tablespoons cornstarch. Whisk or sift together the ingredients, and you've got cake flour!*

** *Mamon are chiffon cakes, which utilize oil to get their light, airy texture. (Think angel food cakes.) If you want, you can substitute in an* *equal amount of melted butter for the oil. It will be delicious, but it will change the texture and make it a sponge cake rather than chiffon.*

Lila's (and Jae's) Honey Butter Rice Krispies Treats

Lovers of Korean honey butter snacks and/or salty-sweet combinations, this is for you! Fast, easy, and delicious, this tasty collab between our lovebirds Lila and Jae makes the perfect treat for parties, potlucks, gifting, and more. Cooking the butter until it's browned and the honey until it's almost burnt adds so much depth to the dish, but if you're in a rush or don't want to worry about "how burnt is TOO burnt?" then quickly melting the butter and honey together works just fine.

YIELD: ONE 9 × 13-INCH PAN OR ONE TIGHTLY PACKED 8 × 8-INCH PAN

Ingredients:

*1 stick (4 ounces) salted butter**

¼ to ⅓ cup honey

1 (10- to 12-ounce) bag of marshmallows

*1 teaspoon white miso (also known as shiro miso; optional)***

6 cups puffed rice cereal

½ to ¾ cup mini mochi (optional)

*Flake salt (optional)***

DIRECTIONS:

1. In a medium saucepan over medium-high heat, melt the butter and cook until it's brown and gives off a light, nutty smell.

2. Add the honey, and cook until it's very dark brown and smells almost (but not quite!) burnt.

3. Add the marshmallows and miso (if using), and stir with a spatula until the marshmallows are mostly melted.

4. Add half of the puffed rice cereal, and mix until mostly combined.

5. Add the rest of the cereal and the mini mochi (if using), and mix until the mini mochi are evenly distributed and the puffed rice cereal is thoroughly combined with the marshmallow mixture.

6. Pour into a greased 9 × 13-inch tray, and use the spatula to spread into a smooth, even layer.

7. Allow to cool completely before cutting into bars and serving.

* *If you're using unsalted butter, add a pinch of salt, too.*

** *If you're not using the miso, I suggest sprinkling flake salt on top of the treats after spreading them out in the tray. The saltiness of the miso balances out the sweetness of the honey and marshmallows.*

Hana Lee's Mexican Hot Chocolate Fudge

Easier to make than the chocolate bar Hana sells at Choco Noir—but no less delicious—this is a great recipe for those who appreciate a bit of spice. Everyone has a different spice tolerance, plus the strength of your spices varies according to the brand and the freshness, so if you're worried about the heat level, I'd say start with the smallest amount and then taste and adjust accordingly. You can even make this fudge vegan by using nondairy chocolate chips and sweetened condensed coconut milk!

Ingredients:

1 (approximately 12-ounce) bag semisweet chocolate chips

1 (14-ounce) can sweetened condensed milk

1 teaspoon ground cinnamon

¼ to 1 teaspoon cayenne pepper, or to taste

1 teaspoon vanilla extract (optional)

Toppings (optional):

½ teaspoon ground cinnamon

¼ to ½ teaspoon cayenne pepper

DIRECTIONS:

1. Place the chocolate chips and condensed milk in a large, microwave-proof bowl.

2. Heat in the microwave in 30-second intervals, mixing with a spatula between each interval, until the chocolate chips are fully melted. (It usually takes about 3 times for me.)

3. Add the cinnamon, cayenne, and vanilla (if using), and mix quickly and thoroughly so that the spices distribute evenly before the fudge starts to set.

4. Pour into a greased (and lined, if you want) 8 × 8-inch pan, and sprinkle with the cinnamon and cayenne toppings (if using).

5. Allow to cool completely and set fully before cutting into small squares (it's rich, so you don't need a lot) and serving.

Keep reading to see where it all began with

Arsenic and Adobo

the first in the Tita Rosie's Kitchen Mystery series

My name is Lila Macapagal and my life has become a rom-com cliché.

Not many romantic comedies feature an Asian-American lead (or dead bodies, but more on that later), but all the hallmarks are there.

Girl from an improbably named small town in the Midwest moves to the big city to make a name for herself and find love? Check.

Girl achieves these things only for the world to come crashing down when she walks in on her fiancé getting down and dirty with their next-door neighbors (yes, plural)? Double check.

Girl then moves back home in disgrace and finds work reinvigorating her aunt's failing business? Well now we're up to a hat trick of clichés.

And to put the cherry on top, in the trope of all tropes, I even reconnected with my high school sweetheart after moving back to town and discovered the true meaning of Christmas.

OK, that last part is a joke, but I really did run into my high school sweetheart. Derek Winter, my first love.

Too bad he'd aged into a ridiculous jerk with a puffed-up sense of importance and weird vendetta against my family. Pretty much tried to shut down my aunt's restaurant on a weekly basis. Odd behavior from the guy who'd wanted to marry me right after graduating from high school, but what can I say? I had exceptionally bad taste when I was younger. You're dumb when you're fifteen and hopped up on hormones.

Heck, I'm twenty-five and still make bad decisions based on those same dumb hormones.

Hence I was working at my Tita Rosie's restaurant rather than running my own cafe, which is what I'd been going to school for before I found out Sam was a cheating scumbag. That was right around the time my aunt sent me a distress signal, and here we are. So instead of grinding my own coffee beans or brewing the delightful loose-leaf teas I'd sourced for my dream cafe in Chicago, I now spent every morning preparing mugs of Kopiko 3 in 1 in my hometown of Shady Palms, Illinois, over two hours outside the city.

And yes, the town really was named Shady Palms. Rumor has it some rich dude from the Caribbean got homesick after moving to the area and tried transplanting a bunch of palm trees along the main street. Surprise, surprise, they didn't take, so he replaced them with tacky plastic replicas. Both the fake palms and the name stuck.

Anyway, the morning clientele at my tita's restaurant always included a bevy of gossiping aunties, none as loud or nosy as the group of fiftysomething-year-old women I privately referred to as "the Calendar Crew." Their names were April, Mae, and June—they weren't related, but all three of them were completely interchangeable, down to their bad perms, love of floral patterns, and need to provide running commentary on my life.

It was their due—after all, they were my godmothers (yes, plural). They bore the important title of "Ninang" and were my late mother's best friends. They loved and cared about me.

In their own infuriating way.

I brought over their morning plate of pandesal and they descended like a pack of locusts upon the dish of lightly sweetened Filipino bread, spreading the warm rolls with butter and dipping them in their coffee or drizzling them with condensed milk. And like locusts, once they were done devouring one thing, they moved as a pack on to their next victim: me.

"Lila, why's everything you wear always dark? You look like a bruha."

"And your hair's always in that ponytail and hat. Not sexy."

"Ay nako, what is this? You get bigger every time I see you!"

This last statement, accompanied by a firm pinch of my arm fat, was from Ninang April, who always had to have the final say. April always was the cruelest month.

I was used to these digs against my appearance—it was how older Asians showed affection. While I was no beauty queen (well, except for that one time, but that's a story for another day), my brown skin glowed and my long, black hair was thick and shiny from straightening it every morning. My pride and joy. Too bad I had to keep it under a baseball cap for work.

I could ignore my godmothers' first two comments—while being told you looked like a witch would bother most people, I considered it a compliment. I loved natural remedies, dark color palettes, and made bewitchingly delicious baked goods, so I'd learned to lean into the bruha image. Everyone needed a personal brand.

As for the baseball cap, it's not like I wore it as a fashion accessory. I worked in food service, and my family were sticklers for hygiene. It was either a cap or a hairnet, which, thanks but no thanks.

My weight gain, however, was a sore topic. Bad enough that I'd been eating my feelings and couldn't fit into my old clothes anymore; I didn't need them and their fatphobic comments rubbing it in. Then again, I hadn't been home in almost three years. The recovering Catholic in me recognized that these barbs were just the beginning of the penance they would make me pay for being away so long.

I waved my hand dismissively. "Ay Ninang April, I'm just adjusting to being back home. You know everybody eats well when Tita Rosie is around."

The Calendar Crew all nodded as they helped themselves to the coconut jam and kesong puti, or salty white cheese, that I'd added to the table.

"Why do you think we come here all the time? The decor?" Ninang Mae asked, gesturing around at the scuffed tables, mismatched silverware, and appliances from the 80s. "Nobody cooks better than your Tita Rosie."

A loud "Ha!" was the response to Ninang Mae's comment. We all turned toward the source of this rudeness, and my stomach clenched as I locked eyes with the only man I hated as much as my ex-fiancé: Derek Winter.

Derek sipped at a travel cup of coffee and tapped his foot in a cartoonish show of impatience. "Hey, could I get a table already?"

My godmothers all clicked their tongues in unison and began whispering furiously in Tagalog as I approached him. "I thought I made it very clear you weren't welcome here."

His eyes crinkled in amusement—something I used to find so attractive. His charms were wasted on me now.

"Now, Lila, is that any way to treat a customer?" the man behind him asked.

My eyes snapped to the newcomer—I hadn't realized Derek was dining with a guest. He'd always eaten alone before. Supposedly, dining solo made it easier for him to focus on the food so he could write his "reviews." I figured he just didn't have any friends.

And even more surprising than the idea of someone willingly spending time with Derek was his companion. What was Derek doing with our landlord?

"Mr. Long? What are you doing here?"

"What, a man can't have brunch with his son?" He clapped Derek on the shoulder, who flinched. "I've owned this plaza for a while now, but I've never tried your aunt's cooking. You missed another payment, so after seeing some of Derek's reviews, I figured I'd come see what the problem was. See if I could offer any assistance."

I narrowed my eyes at Derek. "The problem," huh? And since when were these two related? You'd think he would've told me his mom had remarried when we first saw each other again, but I guess this was just another of his little omissions.

I knew Mr. Long was just his stepfather, but still, looking back and forth between the two, I couldn't picture someone less likely to have sired him. Mr. Long was thin, wiry, and balding, with pale gray eyes and the red flush of the constant drinker. Derek, unfortunately, was still absolutely gorgeous, with wavy, sandy brown hair that matched his eyes perfectly, as well as the stocky build of a football player gone slightly to seed. The only thing they had in common, appearance-wise, was they were both White. Derek's hair had thinned quite a bit over the last few months though, so maybe the baldness would unite them.

Derek met my glare with a smirk and gestured toward his favorite table near the window. Honestly, how was it even possible to have a favorite table at a restaurant you allegedly despised?

"Of course, make yourselves comfortable." I smiled sweetly and added, "But no outside food or drinks allowed."

Derek rolled his eyes and started toward the door, but Mr. Long intercepted him. "Here, son, why don't you finish your drink and I'll put the thermos in the car? I gotta call your mom real quick, so go ahead and order for me. I don't know what any of this food is anyway."

I waited till Derek gulped down his drink and handed over the travel cup before hurrying to the kitchen to talk to my aunt and grandmother. Those two coming here together—especially after our latest warning about being behind on rent again—could only mean one thing for us.

Trouble.

Photo by Jamilla Yipp Photography

Mia P. Manansala is an award-winning writer and book coach from Chicago who loves books, baking, and badass women. She uses humor (and murder) to explore aspects of the Filipino diaspora, queerness, and her millennial love for pop culture. A lover of all things geeky, Mia spends her days procrastibaking, playing RPGs and otome games, reading cozy mysteries and diverse romances, and cuddling her dog, Gumiho.

VISIT MIA P. MANANSALA ONLINE

MiaPManansala.com

MPMtheWriter

MPMtheWriter

MPMtheWriter